"Morgana," "there's nothing to be afraid of."

"Don't be silly, of course there is. Not for you, perhaps, but certainly for me. Let us at least be honest about that."

She was right, of course, and they both knew it. She had far more at risk than he.

Much later, the marquess would realize that it was at this precise moment he banished any thought that he could enjoy a pleasant little fling with Miss Morgana Penrhys.

"I'm sorry," he said gently. "But I cannot remake the world."

Maura Seger began writing stories as a child and hasn't stopped since. A full-time writer, Maura experienced her very own romance in her courtship and marriage to her husband Michael, with whom she lives in Connecticut, along with their two children.

LIGHT ON
THE MOUNTAIN

Maura Seger

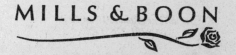

MILLS & BOON

First published in Great Britain 1997
Harlequin Mills & Boon Limited,
Eton House, 18-24 Paradise Road, Richmond, Surrey TW9 1SR

© Maura Seger 1992

ISBN 0 263 80011 3

Set in Times Roman 10 on 12 pt.
04-9701-72663 C1

Printed and bound in Great Britain
by BPC Paperbacks Limited, Aylesbury

Chapter One

Wales, spring, 1857

Between the mist-draped hills and the crashing sea stretched the narrow, rocky road bracketed by slender yew trees. It wound past the cliffs and around the hills, here rising, there falling, until it came to Gynfelin. The village was a pretty place of whitewashed cottages clustered around a church and commons. The kind of place artists paused to paint on their summer sojourns. When they moved on, carting their canvases, they remembered Gynfelin fondly.

But then they didn't see it in early spring while the land was still barren and the leaden sky was weeping rain. Morgana Penrhys would wager that no one had ever painted Gynfelin looking like that. Well, not actually wager. Schoolteachers didn't do that sort of thing if they wanted to keep their jobs.

She sighed and tightened her hold on her sodden cloak. Damn the weather, damn the endless road, and above all damn Thomas Trelawney, drunken fool that he was and a poor father to boot. Nothing could have gotten her out on such a day for such a trek except the discovery that her prize student was about to be taken out of school.

Owen Trelawney was only twelve years old, a slightly built, gentle boy who listened far more than he spoke. But he had a keener mind than most people two and three times his age, and a hunger for learning that matched Morgana's own. Given the smallest chance, he would be able to build a life far beyond the constraints of Gynfelin. The smallest chance, that was all, but his father would deny him even that.

All of which put Morgana in a fine enough temper to flush her cheeks despite the icy rain. She was a tall, slender woman of twenty-five with eyes the color of a storm-tossed sea and fiery hair that curled tightly in the dampness. Besides being soaking wet, her cloak was plain and serviceable, as was the sensible wool dress beneath it and the equally sensible boots sloshing through mud up to her ankles. Sensible described her perfectly, so far as Morgana was concerned. She would have been surprised to know how many people disagreed.

Through the lashing waves of rain, she could just make out the Trelawney cottage. It was a poor tumbledown affair that could have been very different had Thomas extended himself the slightest bit. Owen's mother had tried; the remnants of her rosebushes still struggled to survive. But she'd been dead these five years past, leaving Owen to his father's tender mercies.

Damn Trelawney and the whole stupid system with him. The country bled itself dry of its children and then complained when the future was no better than the past. Not this child, though. Not if she could possibly help it.

There was no answer to her knock. Although it was late in the afternoon, Trelawney might well be asleep, since he kept the usual irregular hours of drunkards and brawlers. But if that was the case, he was in for a rude awakening.

She knocked again, and when there was still no answer she cracked open the door a bit. Inside was not as bad as she'd feared. The cottage was poorly furnished but neat and orderly. The floor was freshly swept, a fire readied and the table covered with a worn but well-patched cloth. All that was Owen's doing, not his father's. Beyond the main room was an alcove where Trelawney had his bed. It was unoccupied.

Morgana withdrew. Trelawney had to be somewhere around. She'd already checked the village pub only to be told he'd left. He had no friends in Gynfelin and he wasn't known to frequent anywhere else, so he must be nearby.

She turned, intent on finding him, when a door slammed. Morgana glanced toward the small shed beside the house. Trelawney was stooped over to clear the low portal and didn't see her at first. His clothes and hair were rumpled, and he was several days past a shave. He carried a large earthen jug with a stopper protruding from it.

Home brew, Morgana thought with disgust. The lethally potent and illegal poteen had been brewed in the hills of Wales since time immemorial. Most of the still keepers at least had the sense to be discreet about what they were doing, but not Thomas Trelawney. Why should he be when he thought he could bully and intimidate anyone who got in his way?

But not Morgana Penrhys, as he was about to learn. She took a deep breath and stepped forward.

"I'd like a word with you, Mr. Trelawney."

He jerked, startled by her sudden appearance. It took him a moment to peer past the previous night's drunk and realize who she was.

"Oh, ye would, would ye?" he snarled. His thick black brows drew together. Beneath them, small eyes gleamed. "Yer wastin' yer time. I've nothin' to say to ye."

Morgana's chin went up. Her finely drawn nostrils twitched at the smell of him, but she wasn't about to let that or anything else dissuade her.

"I have something to say to you, Mr. Trelawney. I found out today that you're taking Owen out of school."

His soft mouth, blurred around the edges, twisted in a sneer. "The snivelin' little fool been complainin' to ye, has he? Thinks he's too good for an honest day's work. Time he learned otherwise. Make a man of him."

"A man like you?" Morgana demanded. The temper her father had always warned her against was rising in her. She struggled to control it but without great success. Angrily, she said, "I don't see you worrying about honest work, Mr. Trelawney, or much work of any sort for that matter. But you're willing to send your son into the mines—'' she almost choked on the word ''—just to be sure you'll have the price of a pint whenever you want it.''

''Why, ye...''

He took a step forward, brandishing his fist, but Morgana refused to give way. She faced him determinedly. ''Your son is intelligent, he can make something of himself. Why won't you give him the chance?''

''What chance did I ever have?'' Trelawney demanded. ''I been spat on since the day I was born. Owen's had it damn good compared to that. It's time he paid.''

Morgana knew nothing of Trelawney's background but she was willing to believe it had been harsh. So it was for many people. She could sympathize with him but she couldn't accept his wallowing in self-pity. He was a grown man, for Lord's sake. He ought to be able to put aside his own resentments to do what was best for his son.

But Trelawney had never put aside anything for anyone, and he wasn't about to start now.

''Git out of me way, Miss High-an'-mighty,'' he snarled as he advanced up the path. ''Owen's me son, I say what he does, and that's an end to it.''

Not so far as Morgana was concerned. Though he was close enough for her to see the red glint in his eyes, she still refused to retreat.

''Owen's a human being, Mr. Trelawney, he has rights of his own.''

Had she suddenly begun to speak in Latin or Greek Trelawney would not have looked more surprised.

That and angered. The constant repetition of his name preceded with the unaccustomed "Mister" had finally sunk in. He knew when he was being mocked. Or at least he thought he did. Actually, no mockery was intended. Morgana would never stoop to so feeble a tactic.

She had contempt for Trelawney, plain and simple. To her way of thinking, if he disappeared off the planet in the next instant, there'd be no harm done. But Trelawney wasn't about to disappear, and since she wasn't either, perhaps what happened next was inevitable. He was, after all, a violent man. One moment they were both standing in front of the cottage, he clutching the jug and she staring straight at him. The next moment he'd dropped the jug and advanced on her with both fists raised.

"I'll be master in me own house, I will," Trelawney said. "And no snot-nosed schoolteacher'll say otherwise."

Despite her youth, Morgana was not a sheltered, naive woman. But she had never before been exposed to violence. She was therefore unprepared when what had been a surly threat turned suddenly into harsh, inescapable action.

The blow hit her heavily across the cheek and sent the breath rushing from her. Pain shot through her even as whirling blackness swallowed the day. She hardly felt herself falling, nor did she hear the anguished scream that was not her own.

Owen Trelawney had stopped on the way home from school to do a few chores for the Widow Cardon. He had lingered over them, less anxious than ever to return to the bare cottage and his father's sullen wrath. But eventually one foot in front of the other had brought him there just in time to see Morgana fall.

Owen was not an aggressive boy. His size and circumstances weighed against that. He had long since learned the harsh lessons of survival through endurance. But in a single blinding instant all those lessons were forgotten.

Miss Penrhys was the bright light in his life, the only person who truly knew and believed in him. The only one who told him he could be somebody. With the greatest regret and shame he had told her of his father's decision, then done his best to pretend it was fine with him. But she hadn't believed him and she'd come, as he should have known she would, to fight for what he hadn't been able to fight for himself.

And now she was hurt.

Owen launched himself at his father. He put his hands around Trelawney's neck and held on for dear life. His father roared like an enraged bull and jerked to shake him off. But Owen clung, fueled by rage made greater by all the years it had been repressed. Trelawney bellowed again and made to ram his son against the cottage wall. At the same instant, Owen saw the hoe propped against the building. He loosened a hand and reached out, grasping it. At the end of the hoe was a steel blade. Owen raised it.

"Owen, no!" Morgana cried weakly as she came around. God help the boy, she'd never intended anything like this. To raise his hand to his father as he was doing, to seek to...

Light on the Mountain

She screamed as Trelawney slammed into the wall. The hoe fell from Owen's hand. Dazed by pain and shock, he loosened his grip on his father.

Trelawney picked up the hoe. He grasped it in both hands, blade down, and swung it toward the small, exposed head of his son.

A shot rang out. It rent the air like a clap of thunder loosed by a vengeful god. Hard on it came the sound of hooves galloping. Morgana staggered to her feet. The rain had eased enough for her to see farther than before, but there was no need. The great black apparition was almost upon her, less than an arm's length away.

She would have screamed again, this woman who had never in her life been given to such displays, but she had no breath left.

Distended nostrils blew steam, making her think for an instant of the dragons that had populated Wales in a long-ago time. Except this was no dragon with its sweating flanks and flinging mane. This was a horse of such size and magnificence as to take her breath away, had she any left to be taken.

On the horse sat a man enveloped in black with black rage stamped on features that looked chiseled from hardest stone.

''Get up,'' he said, and the voice was like the thunder as it came rolling across the hills bringing the great storms born over the sea.

He did not mean her. His gaze was on Trelawney. It shimmered in the mist-drenched air, seeming to reach out to haul the moaning, trembling man upright.

A serpent, black as the man's cloak, shot out. Ah, no, not a serpent, her fear was running away with her. It was a riding crop, like a thousand she had seen, but this one used to very different effect.

The hilt of the crop lodged itself beneath Trelawney's spongy chin and pressed into his throat. "You scum," the man said, no longer in that voice of thunder, but quite ordinarily, which somehow made it all the more terrifying.

Trelawney was no fool. He knew he stood on the precipice of disaster and tried his best to draw back. "Please, yer lordship," he begged, "'tis all a misunderstanding. This woman..."

"Be silent," the man said. Trelawney opened his mouth again, saw the nearness of his death lingering on the air before him, and shut it.

"Who are you?" the man asked Morgana, speaking more gently. She struggled to respond, hoping she wouldn't sound like the poor terrified thing she felt. The man was the most remarkable being she had ever seen, huge of stature and bearing, with features a Greek god would have gladly claimed. Thick black hair framed his broad face, with a lock or two curling over his forehead. Eyes the color of tempered steel met hers, compelling her to respond.

"Morgana Penrhys," she said faintly, then said it again more strongly. That was better, she was coming back to herself now. Swiftly, she smoothed her hands along her skirt to stop their trembling. "I teach school in Gynfelin. This boy—" she looked at Owen "—is one of my pupils. I came to try to convince his father not to send him to the mines."

"She had no right, yer lordship," Trelawney burst out. He curled his shoulders and ducked his head, making himself look as wheedling and humble as he could. "Surely a man's home is his castle, however poor it may be, and surely I've the right to decide what's best for my boy?"

The man looked from Trelawney to Owen, who had staggered to his feet and stood, head down, trying desperately to conceal the shamed tears that stained his ashen cheeks. A single glance raked the boy's threadbare clothes and stick-thin body. "It looks as though your judgment leaves much to be desired," the man said quietly, returning his gaze to Trelawney.

Morgana put an arm around Owen's shoulders and straightened her own. "I thank you for your help," she said, "whoever you may be."

The man smiled faintly. A devil's smile, her mother would have called it. And yet it was singularly appealing.

"Forgive me," he said with grave solemnity. "I am the Marquess of Montfort."

Several things happened then. Trelawney moaned and turned a color that suggested whatever he'd had to eat that day wouldn't be staying in his stomach much longer. Owen's eyes widened to the size of saucers, and he turned even paler than he had been. Morgana, who prided herself on remaining calm in any situation, did just that. Never mind that her legs beneath the concealing cloak and skirt were trembling like young willows in the winter wind.

The Marquess of Montfort was an impressive title in its own right, but in Gynfelin it carried a special significance. Very simply, the Marquess of Montfort owned Gynfelin. Every field and cottage, every tree and bush, the church, the school, the commons, the road, the air. Well, perhaps not the air, although Morgana wasn't sure about that. Like almost everyone else in Wales, she had lived her whole life under the shadow of the landlords, those otherworldly beings whose directives from London and other foreign places could spell doom for the hapless souls who were their tenants.

Never mind that it was the nineteenth century, well into the age when industry would span the globe and reason would conquer all. In this corner of the world, the Marquess of Montfort might as well have been a king or a feudal lord.

Worse yet, he was very much an unknown quantity. Until a short time before, no one in Gynfelin had so much as laid eyes on him. He had been born and raised well away from the Welsh manor and had never set foot in it until a fortnight before. His coming sent tremors through the village. It was widely feared that he came only to extort even more from tenants who were already hard-pressed to keep body and soul together. Speculation about him was rife, but only those who served in the great house had had any contact with him, and they held their tongues for fear of losing their positions.

Now that was changed. Three ordinary citizens of Gynfelin had just met their lord and met him with a vengeance. Of the three, Trelawney responded fastest. Gone was the brutish, bullying man, replaced by a sniveling, ingratiating serf who pulled at his forelock and moaned of his loyalty, all the while shooting fierce glares at the woman and boy who had gotten him into so dangerous a spot.

"It's shamed I am, my lord," he said, "to have you troubled in such a way. I'll take care of the matter myself and ye'll not be bothered again, this I swear."

"Anxious to smooth it all over, are you?" the marquess inquired mildly.

"Of course, yer lordship. As a faithful crofter of yerself for all these many years, never missing a payment on me rent . . ."

"Actually, you're several years in arrears," the marquess said, still perfectly pleasantly. As Trelawney blanched, his lordship went on. "I haven't paid much attention to that sort of thing in the past, but I can see it's time I did. However, first things first."

He turned to Owen. Looking directly at the boy, he said, "No man can be held blamed or praised for his parentage, only for what he makes of his own life. What do you want to do with yours?"

Owen took a deep, shaky breath. Morgana murmured a silent prayer. Never mind that any such sentiment regarding parentage was remarkable coming from an aristocrat. That could be figured out later. For the moment, please God, let Owen say the right thing.

"I want to learn," the boy said with such steadiness that Morgana was swept by pride.

"Learn what?" the marquess asked, not making it one whit easier.

Owen looked puzzled for a moment. He had never thought of narrowing it down. "Whatever I can," he answered simply. "Everything."

The marquess laughed, not a cruel sound but a pleased one, as though he liked what he had stumbled across.

"You won't do that in the mines," he said, "and you won't do it here." He thought a moment before he said, "Best come along, then."

"Sir?" Owen murmured.

"To the manor. We'll see what can be done with you there."

Matter-of-factly, he dismounted and walked over to Morgana. They stood, scarcely a foot apart, looking at one another. "You, too," the marquess said.

She opened her mouth to protest, most certainly she did. The problem was that no sound came out. It did not—could not—when his hands closed around her slender waist and without so much as a by-your-leave lifted her onto the saddle in his place.

"Hold on," he advised gently as he took the reins.

Trelawney gawked at the apparition before him: the great lord walking in the mud with the boy beside him and the bruised schoolteacher seated on the proud stallion, holding onto the pommel for dear life.

He was still gawking as they walked down the road and vanished into the mist.

Chapter Two

Beneath the church in Gynfelin was an ancient stone catacomb built centuries before, when an abbey had stood on the site. In the catacomb was a large iron box bound by lengths of leather frayed and cracked by time. The mark of time was appropriate, for it was time itself that, in a way, was captured inside the box. It was the resting place for the parish records of Gynfelin. There was sporadic talk about moving so rare a historical source elsewhere, but so far nothing had come of it. The archives of Gynfelin parish remained where they had always been, to the secret delight of the Right Reverend Jonathan Armbruster, who believed quite firmly in tradition. And, not incidentally, liked having the archives near to hand for his own study.

In all the centuries of their existence, no one had ever studied the records as thoroughly as the Reverend Armbruster. He knew them as well as he knew Holy Writ. The names within them were as real to him as the names of people presently living within Gynfelin. But then many of the names were the same, handed down from one generation to the next seemingly without end.

Toward the very beginning of the records where the ink was particularly pale and the vellum so fragile it could turn to powder in the hand, one name stood out above all others: Montfort. It was a Norman name redolent of mighty fortresses and men who kept them so. The name—and the men who bore it—had crossed the Channel with William the Conqueror. Within a generation, they were settled throughout the whole of England. Some of them came also to Wales and some of those to Gynfelin, the holding awarded by a grateful monarch for services well rendered.

Their first manor was a rude stone tower designed purely to hold off enemies. Then came a keep, somewhat more generously designed, but still a function of war. Over the years, as the Montforts in particular and the English in general tightened their hold on Wales, the keep gave way to a Tudor mansion with wattle and timber walls and a red-tiled roof. That yielded, in turn, to a gracious Georgian structure that to the good reverend's eye captured the best of British taste and refinement.

Morgana saw it rather differently. Perched on the stallion's broad back, weighed down by the sodden mass of her clothing, with her cheek throbbing and the rest of her chilled to the bone, she stared at the vast house rising before her.

Of course, she had seen it before. It was impossible to go much beyond the village on the main road without seeing Gynfelin Manor, if only in the distance. On sunny days, the light of its gleaming white exterior was nothing short of dazzling. In the mist, it looked like a glorious vessel skimming the earth. Always it was beautiful, impressive and more than a little intimidating.

Up close it was even more so.

A gravel drive bordered by ancient oaks led to the columned portico. Already, despite the rain and the gathering dusk, servants were out, alerted by the appearance of their lord's mount and anxious to receive him.

Or perhaps merely curious about who he was bringing home with him.

Nothing was revealed in the stern faces of the groom and butler who awaited them. The groom quickly took the stallion's reins, but not before giving Morgana a startled glance. An instant later her feet were on the ground, not through any effort of her own. The marquess had simply plucked her from the saddle as effectively as he had deposited her there to begin with. The return of his slight smile suggested that he knew she wouldn't have been able to get herself down for all the tea in China, or all the rain in Wales, which at the moment was probably more.

"Sir," the butler murmured. The word carried a wealth of meaning, at least to Morgana's prickling ears. She could feel the weight of the older man's glance as, unlike the groom, he scrutinized her thoroughly.

"All in good time, Sebastian," the marquess said. He seemed to find nothing unusual in such behavior by a servant. On the contrary, he appeared amused by it.

Taking Morgana's arm, he said, "Inside."

Barely had he spoken than the heavens let loose again, ending the brief respite from the rain. Thunder cracked behind them as they stepped into the entry hall.

Morgana did her best to restrain a gasp and almost succeeded. It came out more like a hiccup. "Oh, my," she murmured.

"A bit much, isn't it?" the marquess said pleasantly. "My grandfather had it built. No one knows why, since he never lived here."

Outrage replaced shock. Surrounded by towering walls of marble and gilt extending up two stories to a domed roof across which gods and goddesses gamboled, Morgana felt as though she had stepped into another world. Not that the rules of the old one didn't still apply.

"He built all this, spent all this money, and never even lived here?" she demanded. Squeaked, actually, for rain and exhaustion had caught up with her. In another moment she'd plop herself down in the midst of the black-and-white mosaic floor and stay there until her heart stopped hammering against her ribs and her legs turned into something firmer than the jellyfish that washed up along the beach after storms.

"He was daft," the marquess said, still quite pleasantly. He gestured to the butler. "This is Miss Morgana Penrhys, the village schoolteacher. She will require dry clothes and tea. And this young man is Owen Trelawney. He would undoubtedly appreciate the same. He'll be staying on."

If Sebastian found anything at all odd about this, he resisted saying so. But then he looked like a man who could resist just about anything. Whoever had thought of making him a butler? Morgana wondered. Almost as tall as the marquess himself but with the muscular squatness of a wrestler, he looked as though he'd be far more at home in a barracks or on a battlefield.

Certainly he knew how to take orders even when he so clearly thought them bizarre.

"As you say, sir," he murmured. A flick of the wrist was sufficient to summon a footman who promptly led Owen away. The boy looked anxiously over his shoulder at Morgana. She gave him a reassuring smile as though all this was the most natural thing in the world.

In fact, she was finding it anything but. In her childhood, Morgana had discovered the ancient legends of the Tylwyth Teg, the Fair Ones of Welsh lore. According to the haunting stories, it was possible to visit the magical land of the Fair Ones. All that was necessary was to place one's foot atop the foot of a fairy. In an instant, the enchanted world would be revealed.

Granted, the Marquess of Montfort made as unlikely a fairy prince as anyone could meet, but he had succeeded in removing her to a world vastly beyond any she had ever known.

Only now he had turned her over to a troll. The sheer unkindness of that thought shamed Morgana, yet the housekeeper who appeared at Sebastian's side did bear an uncanny resemblance to a creature accustomed to leaping out from under a bridge to terrorize unsuspecting travelers.

Mrs. Dickinson was her name. She was very stout with iron-gray hair, a square face, several chins and a mouth as smooth and unwrinkled as a child's, undoubtedly because she never smiled. Nor did she frown. She merely looked at Morgana with steely eyes and sniffed.

Sebastian must have given some sort of instructions and the marquess must have thought them suitable enough, but Morgana was taken in hand before she could recall them. Mrs. Dickinson bustled her up the wide curving stairs, down a vast hallway and into a room that to Morgana's dazed eye could have been the abode of a princess.

"Who lives here?" she asked, glancing around at the canopied bed with its embroidered hangings, the delicate Aubusson rug, the fireplace with its marble mantel and brass screen shaped to look like a swan. Paintings she would have loved to linger over hung on each of the walls. High windows yielded views of the surrounding lawns just visible in the gathering dusk.

Now, Mrs. Dickinson did frown. "This is a guest room, miss. The girl is bringing hot water for you, and I'll see to clothes myself. Tea will be in the library when you're ready."

Morgana murmured her thanks. She was uncharacteristically subdued. Her cheek still throbbed, and she touched it without being aware.

The housekeeper's frown deepened. "That will need tending to." Having made that observation, she made no effort to act on it but merely stood, hands clasped stiffly in front of her, staring at Morgana.

"The warm water will set it right," Morgana said, although she wasn't sure of that. An ointment would have helped, but she couldn't bring herself to ask for it, or for anything else. She breathed a sigh of relief when a serving girl entered with a jug of steaming water.

The girl skittered across the room, avoiding Mrs. Dickinson's eye, and poured the water into a basin. A little of it splashed on the floor.

"Fool," the housekeeper spat out. Before Morgana's horrified gaze, she raised her hand to strike the girl.

Morgana's own hand closed tight around the housekeeper's wrist. "Don't," she said. The single word, so simple, reverberated in the room.

"You dare—" Mrs. Dickinson began.

"Hit her and I'll march right down those stairs and tell your master what you've done," Morgana said, very quietly but with unmistakable intent. "I've seen what he thinks of bullies. You'll be packing your bags before the hour is up."

In fact, she had no idea whether that was true, but the marquess had shown himself to be an unexpectedly decent man. He had stood up against Trelawney when many another would have ridden away, and he had brought her and Owen here to his own home. Surely he wouldn't show such care for strangers and let his own servants be abused.

Mrs. Dickinson's face turned an unhealthy shade of red. For a moment, she looked as though she would strike both Morgana and the serving girl. But she thought better of it. Grudgingly, she withdrew.

When she was gone, the girl put her head in her hands. Her thin shoulders shook soundlessly. "Oh, miss," she whispered, "I thank you for standing up for me, but she'll be just unbearable now, she will. She'll find some way to lose me my post, and I can't afford that. My family needs my wages. What am I to do?"

Morgana sighed. Even at the advanced age of twenty-five, she was always being surprised by life's complexity. Or perhaps she was merely clumsy in her approach to it. She had tried to help Owen, only to precipitate a terrible confrontation with his father that had surely cost the boy the only home, however bad, he'd ever known. And now she had placed the serving girl in an untenable position. All because of her good intentions. Or perhaps, she thought despairingly, there was more to it than that. Perhaps it was vanity to think she could make the world better, and had the right to interfere in people's lives to do it.

"I'm sorry," she said.

"Oh, no, miss. You've no reason to say that. I am grateful, truly I am. That old harridan—" she laughed nervously at her own daring "—has no right to treat people the way she does. The look on her face when you stopped her, that was priceless, miss. I'll remember it all my life."

And possibly remember exactly what that *priceless* look had cost her, Morgana thought grimly. Her back stiffened with purpose.

"I don't think Mrs. Dickinson will remember the fresh clothes for me," she said, "but my own really aren't too bad. If I could just dab and brush them..."

"Of course, miss," the girl said quickly. "But I'll do it. We'll have you right in no time."

They shared a quick smile before getting down to work.

David Harrell, Marquess of Montfort, stood with his back to the room. A fire burned cheerfully, its light reflecting off the polished leather spines of the books arranged in orderly ranks in the floor-to-ceiling shelves that lined the library. Many of them he had read before coming to Gynfelin, but there were hundreds more to keep him occupied. When he had read all of them, he would order more, and when those were read....

He shrugged his broad shoulders. The curtains were still open, and he could see his reflection in the window glass. He was not a vain man, to the regret of various valets who had come and gone over the years and whose services he had with relief finally dispensed with once and for all. His appearance concerned him so little that he customarily went for days without seeing any part of himself except what was reflected in his small shaving mirror. But seeing himself in the window glass as he did now, he was struck by how ordinary he looked.

No one would have agreed with him, of course. He was, at the very least, an extremely impressive man in both size and manner. But to himself, he was as he had always been, and that surprised him. He would have thought that the events of the past few years would have made themselves more outwardly visible. Not that it mattered. He was as he was, and he accepted that. The hard line of his mouth softened at the thought. Men who had been with him in battle would have scoffed at the notion, but that simple self-acceptance was his greatest victory.

Would that the boy Owen could know the same. Which brought his mind around again to the extraordinary scene by the cottage. Extraordinary, not because of the father's brutality toward his son—that was all too common—but because of the young woman who had dared to oppose it.

Extraordinary.

Far in the back of his mind, he realized that it had been a very long time—possibly never—since he had used that particular word to describe a woman. That he should do so now for a fiery-tempered Welsh schoolteacher was nothing short of...

Extraordinary.

He sighed. Order and simplicity were all very well— he had come to Gynfelin seeking exactly that—but repetition was merely dull.

Happily, he had little time to ponder that before being interrupted by a soft knock at the library door.

"Come," he said.

The door opened. Sebastian stood there, looking very butlerish. Morgana was beside him.

"Miss Penrhys, sir."

"Ah, good. Do come in." Well aware that he was sounding a tad avuncular, the marquess strove to get a grip on himself. It wasn't easy. He had forgotten how beautiful she was.

Schoolteacher? His masters at Eton and later at Cambridge had been universally male, and not terribly attractive specimens of their sex to boot. Miss Penrhys was the contrary in every respect.

Beautiful, vital, courageous, exactly as he remembered.... Exactly. Hadn't he said something about fresh clothes? And why was that awful bruise on her cheek still untreated?

David frowned. Sebastian, formerly Sergeant Major Sebastian Levander of His Majesty's Fifth Fusiliers, felt the muscles of his stomach tighten. He had faced down marauding infidels with greater composure than he faced the wrath of the Marquess of Montfort. But then the marquess was far more dangerous. Sebastian knew that better than most. He owed his life to the brutally efficient warrior lightly disguised as a British nobleman.

Knowing none of this, Morgana still found herself possessed of the hearty wish that the floor would open up beneath her feet and obligingly swallow her.

It didn't. She was left standing exactly where she was, just inside the library door, with the marquess staring at her and Sebastian shifting nervously from side to side.

"You will recall, sir," he said, "that I mentioned Mrs. Dickinson to you night before last."

"Apparently, you were mild in your assessment."

Sebastian inclined his head gravely, took two steps backward and shut the door, leaving them alone. Morgana resisted the impulse to lurch after him.

David looked at her for what seemed like a very long time, but probably wasn't more than a moment or two. At length, he said, "I apologize, Miss Penrhys.

My household is not yet as well ordered as I require."
Unspoken was the assertion that it soon would be.

Morgana cleared her throat. "That's perfectly all
right." Seizing the moment, she added, "Actually one
of your maids—" she mentioned the girl's name
"—was most helpful."

The marquess nodded. "I'll remember that. Now
about the tea I promised . . ."

It was set out on a silver serving tray beside a settee
that faced the fireplace. The marquess indicated that
she should sit. "Will you pour?" he inquired pleasantly.

Why did he have to be so infernally polite? Couldn't
he see that she was exhausted, overwhelmed and utterly out of her depth? She'd be lucky if she didn't
slosh the tea over both of them and anything else that
got in the way.

"Of course," she said. Her hand was rock steady as
she lifted the heavy pot, but she took no comfort from
that. She couldn't while her heart was hammering
away in so disconcerting a fashion.

"Cream," she inquired, "sugar?"

The marquess preferred his tea plain, which suited
Morgana perfectly well. She took a quick sip of her
own, felt the warming liquid spread through her and
allowed herself to be emboldened.

"It was very kind of you to help Owen as you did."

The marquess looked surprised. "Kind?" he repeated as though the word was unfamiliar to him. He
set his cup down and crossed one long leg over the
other. Morgana did her best to ignore how snugly his
breeches fit and how exceedingly well-formed his legs

were. He must do a great deal of riding to have thigh muscles like that.

Her eyes, which her father had likened to the sea a mile or so beyond the coast where the land fell away abruptly into impenetrable depths, darkened perceptibly. What on earth was happening to her? She had never noticed such things about any man, and this was hardly the moment to begin.

"The boy is a tenant of mine," David said. "I would hardly stand by and allow him to be abused."

It was on the tip of Morgana's tongue to say that it was already abuse to allow a child such as Owen—or any child, for that matter—to grow up in a rattrap cottage with the barest education and no hope for a future that didn't lie deep underground in the hellhole of the mines. But for once in her life, she managed to hold her temper.

Quietly, she said, "Whatever the reason, what you did was kind." Let him try to deny it if he must, although she couldn't help but wonder why he should. Most people enjoyed being credited with compassion. The marquess, however, seemed to hold such a character trait in low regard.

"However," she added swiftly, "you certainly won't lose by what you did. Owen is extremely intelligent, and I'm sure he's more than capable of discharging any responsibility you choose to give him."

The marquess gave her a long, level look such as she was already accustomed to receiving from him. Not that custom made the experience any easier. It was all she could do not to quail before that steely gaze.

He stood abruptly and walked over to a sideboard near the high French windows leading to the garden. He looked amused, although she couldn't begin to fathom why. "You apparently value directness," he said. "Therefore, you will undoubtedly appreciate my reluctance to pretend to enjoy tea when I would really prefer whiskey." Disingenuously, he asked, "Will you join me?"

Morgana folded her hands in her lap, the better to stop their trembling, and lifted her chin. Meeting his coolly mocking gaze, she said with equal coolness, "Thank you, that would be very nice."

He raised an eyebrow, quite eloquently she thought, but otherwise said nothing. She accepted the cut crystal tumbler with a grave nod.

The marquess watched her as she took a sip. The whiskey was a double malt and very smooth. It went down easily, and warmed her far better than the tea ever could have done.

"Actually," she said, "there is something not quite right about drinking whiskey after dealing with Thomas Trelawney, since it's the whiskey that caused the problem in the first place. But I suppose I can work that out later." She took another sip.

"I suppose you can," the marquess said softly. He was busy observing the color rising in her cheeks, which bore an uncanny resemblance to a damask rose. Her lips were full and looked impossibly soft. She had quite an adorable chin, firm yet feminine, and her throat tapered in a most beguiling way.

Without warning, he reached out and touched her injured cheek. The gesture surprised him as much as it did her. She started as though something very hot had brushed her skin.

"My lord," she murmured.

She had tried to restore some order to her hair, but without great success. Wisps of it drifted around her face, and one long, silken curl fell across her breasts. The marquess was very tempted to pick it up, twine it around his fingers and pull her gently but inexorably to him.

That he did not was testament to the strength of will bred into uncounted generations of Montforts. That he seriously considered doing so would have made those same generations of ruthless warlords cheer.

"Miss Penrhys," he said.

"Yes," she murmured.

"I think I am going to take an interest in the schooling of Gynfelin's young."

"Oh . . . well, that is very—"

"Miss Penrhys?"

"Yes?"

"There is something I think we should be very clear on. I am never kind, not ever. I do what serves my own interest. Do you understand me?"

"No," Morgana said with her customary honesty. Because she had always thought knowing when to leave well enough alone was a highly overrated skill, she added, "But I expect I'm going to."

Which left the marquess taken aback, a sensation he could not remember ever experiencing before. He was used to many things in women—desire, avarice, deference, even, occasionally, fear. He was not used to candor, and he was at a loss as to how to deal with it.

Gynfelin was proving a good deal more diverting than he had expected. The thought made him laugh.

On the other side of the library door, Sebastian heard the sound and started. He could not remember the last time he had heard the marquess laugh, but he did know what to do about it. Briskly, he went off to inform cook there would be two for dinner.

Chapter Three

"Tell me about yourself," the marquess said. He sat back in the great wing chair, his long legs stretched out before him and the whiskey close at hand. His manner was that of a man anticipating pleasant entertainment—and taking it as his due.

Morgana kept her expression perfectly bland, but inside she seethed. The nerve of the man! He helped Owen because the boy was one of his tenants, say rather his possession. He went out of his way to deny being kind. And he was—what was the word?—provocative, yes, that was it, deliberately so. He looked at her as no man had ever done, sending tremors down her back and causing a queer tightening in her middle. Why, after just a few minutes alone in his company she was flustered, a most extraordinary occurrence for so self-possessed and competent a young woman.

She wouldn't put up with it a moment longer. Never mind who he was. Firmly, she set her glass down and faced him squarely.

"I am Morgana Penrhys, as you already know. I have been teacher here for three years. Before that, I taught in Cardiff. Your steward hired me, but it is you who pays my wages. Officially, I am your employee. That being the case, and although I thank you greatly for your help and hospitality, it is not proper for us to be together like this."

She stood up, ignoring the stab of pain in her injured cheek, gave him a small curtsy and turned toward the door.

The marquess made no attempt to stop her. Indeed, he hardly seemed to blink. Quite mildly, as though it was really of no importance, he asked, "Officially?"

Morgana stopped. His tone did not mislead her. He was amused, but under that was lethal steel. His lordship was not a man to taunt. Anyone with any sense wouldn't try.

Morgana knew herself well, certainly better than most people her age. She was many things—honest, fair, determined and, while she thought herself sensible, she also considered sensibility to be, at times, a highly overrated virtue. *"L'audace,"* the tyrant Napoleon had said, *"toujours l'audace."* With such audacity, he had almost ruled the world. Morgana saw no reason not to try a bit of it herself.

She turned, head high, and smiled slightly. Never mind that she still looked the closest thing to a beggar woman confronting a prince. She had right on her side. "Yes, officially. Oh, don't mistake me, without your money there would be no school here at all so for that I'm grateful. But my true responsibility is to the children of Gynfelin. They need me."

The marquess stared at her. In his lifetime, he had come across many fascinating, bizarre and sometimes terrifying sights. But he had never encountered anything quite like Morgana Penrhys. Did she have any idea at all of what she invited?

There she stood, disheveled, delightfully flushed and furious, daring him. Make no mistake, that was exactly what she was about, whether she knew it or not. The question was, was she as innocent as reason suggested she must be? Or was the hint of ancient fury swirling in her sea-green eyes more than a trick of nature?

The dreadful clothes she wore did not manage to conceal the slender beauty of her figure. He had always preferred fleshier women but his taste must be changing. Her face was perfection, save for the blow she'd taken. He frowned at the memory of that. Her hair, despite her efforts to control it, looked like a wild thing born of ancient fire. It slipped the bounds she tried to impose and tumbled in glorious curls around her shoulders.

He raised a hand languidly, not easy when the hand in question was all hard bone and sinewy strength. The fingers were long and blunt, the palm callused. No soft-skinned aristocrat this, but a warrior accustomed to instant and unquestioning obedience. Without a flicker of expression, he said, "Sit down."

A stab of fear shot through Morgana. Her usual firm, no-nonsense approach wasn't doing her much good of late. It hadn't worked with Trelawney, and it wasn't working now. Unfortunately, she had very little else to fall back on.

"I cannot," she said. Sometimes honesty was the best policy, indeed the only one.

An eyebrow quirked in the burnished face. Distantly, she noted that the brow and its twin were like dark wings, and of a beauty a woman would have given much to possess.

"What did you say?"

Her mouth was very dry. The throbbing in her cheek had returned with a vengeance. "I cannot. As I said, it is not proper."

"My dear Miss Penrhys, are you seriously suggesting I have designs on your person?"

She flushed so hotly that her skin burned. Long ago her father had pointed out that only members of the middle class worried about being gentlemen. The aristocracy, who had invented the term and to whom it was generally applied, never gave it a second thought. They lived by their own rules devised for their own benefit. Clearly, her father had been right. The marquess was living proof of that.

"I am not suggesting anything," she said stiffly. "I am merely stating what we both already know full well, it is not generally considered proper for an unmarried woman of my years to be alone in the company of a man not of an age to be her grandfather, especially not when she is dependent on that man for her employment. You can afford to ignore propriety, I cannot."

The marquess heard her out patiently. Why should he not when she was proving the best diversion he had come across in a considerable length of time? Not only was she articulate, but her argument was well-reasoned, accurate and succinct. All of which troubled him not one whit. He simply chose to ignore it.

He stood up and took a step toward her, noting as he did that she did not draw back even though she clearly wanted to. Staying power as well; he liked that.

"I am master here," he said simply. "That means you do as I say. There is no reason to make it any more complicated than that."

When she continued to look at him, wide-eyed and disbelieving, as though confronted by an apparition from a bygone world, he added, "You will sit down. Since the whiskey does not seem to have eased the discomfort in your face sufficiently, I will see what can be done about that. It will be dark soon, and the weather is foul. Therefore, you will spend the night. If it makes you feel any better, that maid you mentioned can sleep in your room, or failing that, one of my hounds can lie across the door."

He smiled at the notion, the maiden in the tower guarded by the hound of hell. Except that his dogs were not at all hounds of hell, but singularly affectionate and compliant. Rather like the women he had always enjoyed, at least up until now.

He strolled over to the bellpull and tugged it once, anything more being superfluous. He expected his summons to be heard and answered without need of repetition.

"As you are staying, you will take dinner with me. I want to learn about Gynfelin, and you seem as good a source as any."

Before she could reply, presuming that she was prepared to do so, there was a knock at the door.

"Come," the marquess said.

Sebastian stepped into the room, the speed of his appearance suggesting he had not been far away.

"My lord?"

"Miss Penrhys will be joining me for dinner and she will stay the night. The maid, Lenore, will see to her needs. Also, find my medical case and bring it here."

The butler inclined his head gravely, but not in time to conceal the tiniest hint of a smile. "As you wish, my lord."

"See now?" the marquess said when they were alone again. "That's the proper response. Do you think you could manage it?"

"Not if the fires of perdition were licking at my heels," Morgana said. Perhaps it was the whiskey that had loosened her tongue or the strange, dizzying sensations spiraling through her whenever she looked at him. Or mayhap it was the phase of the moon hiding out there somewhere beyond the sodden clouds. Whatever it was, she spoke bluntly, if unwisely.

The marquess gave her a startled glance—indeed, it verged on stunned. He threw back his dark head and laughed. "By God, woman, you amaze me. You are either very brave or immensely foolish." He paused a moment, his gaze raking her. Heat washed along the path of his scrutiny, over her breasts, her slender waist, the curve of her hips, her long tapered legs. She felt unbearably exposed, stripped naked, helpless. Her legs trembled, she was going to fall, she was...

"No," he said softly as he took her arm and guided her toward the chair. "Not either. Fey is better, that old Gaelic term for the blessedly crazed. But it has another meaning, as well, doesn't it? A meaning you should be well acquainted with. Your namesake, the original Morgana, was called 'la Fey.' What did it mean then, little schoolteacher?''

Morgana felt the chair behind her and sat down automatically. His face seemed very close. She stared into eyes gray as the storm-tossed sky beyond the snugly curtained windows. Her mouth moved slowly, the words seeming to come from far away. ''There are those who believe it meant 'doomed' but that is a mistranslation. The old word means 'faith.' Morgana of the faith. She was a priestess, but those who came after called her witch and condemned her for it.''

''And how is it,'' he asked softly, ''you know that? Good Christian woman that you surely are, you should have been sheltered from such pagan thoughts.''

Morgana bristled. It was good for her, helping to restore her equanimity and offering distraction from the fateful emotions he set off within her. Never mind about them. She loved an argument.

''My father was of much broader mind. He believed a person should be educated according to his or her ability and nothing else. Finding me bright enough, he taught me everything he could.''

''Did he now? Did it ever occur to him he was ruining you for a woman's proper role in life?''

''No, it did not! He thought he was preparing me to be of use in a way that actually mattered, and he was right.''

The marquess grinned. He was enjoying this. "Are you suggesting being a wife and mother is of no consequence?"

"Of course not. I suspect it's the most difficult job on earth. Children have no end of legitimate needs, which must be met, and men... Well, the less said of them, the better."

"Indeed? You seem to have a high enough opinion of your father."

"He was my teacher and my friend, but my mother raised me as well as my six brothers and sisters. She fed and clothed us on a pittance, sat by our bedsides when we were ill and managed to convince us we were fortunate simply to have one another."

"I see," the marquess said slowly although, in fact, he did not. Making do on a pittance was totally foreign to him, nothing in his life having ever required him to even consider it. Money was simply there, whenever he wished and virtually in whatever quantity he required. But a mother sitting by the bedside was a different matter altogether. He was always mildly startled to be reminded of his mother, that remote stranger who, having attended to the necessary unpleasantness of birthing him, promptly absented herself from his life.

He was saved from any further reply by the timely entrance of Sebastian, who brought with him a small and very battered leather case. The butler set it on the table next to his lordship, inquired if he could be of any further assistance and, having been told he could not, departed.

"What is that?" Morgana inquired suspiciously.

"What does it look like?"

"You are not a physician."

"Most assuredly. I have a fully functional brain and an interest in something other than money."

"Nasty. There are good doctors, you know."

"I saw none of them in the Crimea. A few decent nurses, that Nightingale person, you know. But generally we had to make do on our own. I learned quite a bit."

Morgana looked at him in surprise. The Crimea? That hellhole of death and disease masquerading as war? Horror darted through her. Softly, she said, "I'm sorry."

"For what? That I learned something?"

"No, that it happened the way it did."

A shadow darted behind his eyes. He snapped the case open and looked at her sternly. "Be silent."

His fingers, when they touched her, were surprisingly gentle. She flinched not from pain so much as from the shock of the contact. He drew back at once. "That hurts?"

"No," she murmured, not daring to wonder what he would make of the denial.

"Trelawney is a pig," he said matter-of-factly as he began to brush on a soothing, pungent ointment. Almost at once the throbbing in her cheek eased.

"He is a drunkard," Morgana said, "and a bully. If you hadn't come along when you did, he would have killed Owen."

"So I observed." He shook his head. "His own son."

"Perhaps." No sooner was the word out than she wished she could grab it back. Too late, the marquess was looking at her with undisguised interest.

"Oh?"

"Forget that. I had no right."

"Nonsense, good gossip needs no excusing. Get on with it."

"It's just that Owen bears no resemblance to Trelawney. His mother died before I came here, but I've seen a charcoal drawing of her. She was a pretty woman with beautiful eyes, but again, there's no resemblance."

"Perhaps he is a throwback to an earlier generation."

"That must be it."

"But you imagine otherwise."

"No...that is, he is so intelligent and he loves music, indeed he has a particular gift for it. In an earlier age, he would have been trained as a bard. Now the best I can hope for is that he might become a teacher someday or perhaps even a lawyer."

"A lawyer?" The marquess raised his brows in mock horror. "Heaven forbid. Surely we can do better by him than that. At any rate, put your mind at ease. The boy is safe now."

Morgana's eyes widened, the thick lashes brushing his hand as he finished applying the ointment. Put her mind at ease? Oh, certainly, she'd just been about to do that. Never mind the effect his touch and nearness had on her. Never mind the storm crashing immediately beyond the windows that had its echo within her. Never mind the hard-scrabble, despairing world of

Gynfelin, whose beautiful children seemed to exist only to be trampled underfoot. The marquess waved his hand and all such concerns were supposed to vanish.

Sweet heaven, if only it could be so. If only the world—her world—weren't so brutally different.

"I appreciate your kindness to him," she said gravely.

The marquess put the top back on the vial of ointment and returned it to its place in the leather case. "You're very pale," he said, almost accusingly.

"It has been a difficult day."

"Yes, I suppose it has. Do you usually become so involved in the lives of your students?"

"Not quite so much. Fortunately, most of them don't have fathers as vicious as Trelawney."

"Nor are as gifted as Owen?"

"No, but they all have gifts of one kind or another. I shudder to think of them being sentenced to work in the mines."

"Sentenced? That's an odd way to put it. Surely they receive gainful employment and a decent wage. That is hardly to be sneered at."

Morgana's eyes flashed. Such ignorance was inexcusable. Granted, he owned no mines himself so far as she knew, but surely he had eyes and ears as well as that brain he had mentioned only a short time before. It was time he used them.

"It is not gainful," she insisted, "and the wage is far from decent. What would you pay men—or women or children for that matter—to risk their lives day after day under the worst imaginable conditions?

They receive barely a pittance and when their health is broken, as inevitably happens, they are discarded like so much rubbish. Is that how you think honest Britishers should live in this day and age?''

David looked at her thoughtfully. The paleness was gone. Her cheeks were flushed once again, her eyes bright with disdain. He wasn't used to arousing that emotion in women; quite the contrary. It was a new and unsettling experience.

''You are a reformer,'' he said as though it had only then dawned on him, as indeed it had. He had met members of that species from time to time, but they were invariably male, or, if female, hardly distinguishably so. Morgana was an exception. He smiled slightly, aware that he had set her teeth on edge. For good measure, he added, ''And a bluestocking.''

''Call me what you will. I offer no apology for caring about the fate of the children who are my responsibility. What is wrong needs to be proclaimed as such and changed.''

''Indeed? Then I should think you would welcome the opportunity to have dinner with me. You will have a captive audience.''

She turned her head away and said stiffly, ''I would never seek to abuse your hospitality in such a way. As I said, it would be best for me to leave.''

''We already settled that.''

''No,'' Morgana said firmly, ''you did.''

The marquess smiled, as though approving her perceptiveness. ''I did, didn't I? No more chatter about it then. How does your cheek feel?''

"Better," she admitted. As graciously as she could manage, she added, "Thank you."

The marquess restrained himself. He did not say what he thought, namely that her gratitude irked him. She lived on his land, she was in his employ, therefore she was under his protection. That Trelawney should have gone so far as to overlook that even temporarily suggested reforms were indeed required, if not of the sort Miss Morgana Penrhys envisioned. Apparently, the hand of Montfort rule had lain too lightly on fair Gynfelin. It was time for that to change.

But first there was the most pleasant prospect of dinner. Sebastian returned a short time later to announce that the meal was served. The marquess stood aside for Morgana to precede him. In her sensible if threadbare dress, with her bruised cheek and disheveled hair, she was well aware that she looked anything but the proper lady. But she was a Penrhys, member of one of Wales's oldest families, and pride had come to her with her mother's milk. Head high, shoulders straight, she walked into the great dining hall of Montfort as if she had been born to be there.

Yet for all that she could not quite restrain a gasp when confronted by so dazzling a display of wealth. The table was immense, capable of seating sixty with ease. Each place was set with the finest china, service of gold and sparkling crystal. Chandeliers and multi-tiered candelabra glowed with the flickering flames of dozens of beeswax candles. Some of the aristocracy and a few of the more ambitious middle class had begun to use gas lamps, but at Montfort the old ways were kept, no matter how expensive or inconvenient they might be.

Sebastian appeared as though magically behind a chair to the right of the head of the table.

"Do you always dine in such state?" Morgana inquired as she took her seat. She was thinking of the terrible, almost obscene waste and yet also of the beauty, for surely she had never seen anything lovelier in her life, unless it was the hills beyond Gynfelin when spring turned them into a riot of waving daffodils.

"Not usually," the marquess replied as he took his place at the head of the table. "There is a smaller family dining room." He glanced at the butler. "Perhaps Sebastian has temporarily misplaced it."

"There is a spot of dampness on the outer wall, sir," the butler murmured. "It will be repaired tomorrow. Until then, I thought you would prefer this."

The marquess smiled. He did not doubt that there was a spot of dampness nor that it would be swiftly seen to. That it rendered the more intimate dining room unusable was another matter altogether. Sebastian was doing what he had always done since that long-ago time when he assumed responsibility for the young and virtually untamed marquess-to-be, namely, reminding him of who and what he was. The palatial dining hall decorated with ancient shields and family banners drove home the point nicely. Between him and the threadbare schoolteacher was a gap no man should attempt to breach, not if he had the slightest claim to honor.

He sighed and took a sip of the excellent wine, eyeing Morgana over the rim of his glass. She was looking pale again. And why not, for he had put her in a difficult position. It wasn't like him to feel repentant, not at all, so obviously that wasn't what prompted him to begin a long and gentle discussion of the neighborhood. It lasted clear through dinner and in its very ordinariness left her much relieved.

As for the marquess, suffice to say it was one of his better performances. He remembered the hound as he was bidding her good-night and wondered briefly if he shouldn't send one to guard her after all. She was altogether too enticing, this fiery-haired reformer named for the long-dead priestess. What had her father been thinking of? Or had the scholarly Penrhys been responsible? Mayhap it had been the steadfast mother, sitting by the bedside, thinking unknown thoughts.

There would be time to ponder that. Miss Penrhys might be under his roof for only a single night, but she could not remain at Gynfelin without being close beneath his hand. His interest in her, so odd and unexpected, would likely vanish of its own accord. Or it would not. For the moment, he was content to wait and see which way the fair Welsh wind blew.

Disarmed by his gentle attentiveness, better fed than she had ever been and made drowsy by the wine, Morgana hardly remembered reaching her chamber. Lenore was there to help her out of her dress and ease her into a fine night rail. She sank into the down-filled mattress, beneath the silken sheets, and sighed luxuriously. Far in the distance, she heard the maid close the door and the soft padding of the girl's feet going down the hall. The great house settled itself around her, and soon she slept.

Chapter Four

The marquess was gone the following morning.
Sebastian informed Morgana of this as he served her
breakfast. He had bowed to her insistence that she
would be perfectly comfortable taking her meal in the
kitchen. The thought of being relegated to the vast
dining hall alone dismayed her. All that splendor was
bad enough in the marquess's company; in his absence it would be intolerable.

"Is something wrong, miss?" Sebastian inquired.

Morgana shook her head hastily. "No, not at all,
everything is fine." Never mind that she'd caught
herself thinking about the marquess yet again, for only
the twelfth—or was it the twentieth—time since
awakening scarcely an hour before. Never mind that
she'd been on the verge of missing him. Most of all,
never mind that she couldn't seem to stop herself from
feeling safe and protected in his presence when every
ounce of sense she possessed told her she was anything but. Best to think of something else altogether.

The kitchen was a large, cheerful area, too big and
rambling to be called merely a room, situated at the

back of the manor house. The massive stone walls and slate floor suggested it was part of the original structure. One entire wall was taken up by a massive fireplace where a cheerful blaze dispelled the dampness lingering from the previous day's rain. Several hooks and a spit could be seen against the fire-blackened stone, showing how the cooking had been done until fairly recently. That task was now performed on the large, wrought-iron stove set nearby, gleaming in its metallic perfection, with elaborately decorated fire doors guarding its twin ovens and half a dozen burners on top that could be lifted off to inspect the crisp little blaze glowing within.

The food that came from that modern marvel more than lived up to its promise. "This is lovely," Morgana said, glancing at her plate, "but I'm afraid I've put you to a great deal of trouble."

"Nonsense," Sebastian said. "It is no trouble at all. Don't you agree, Mrs. Mulroon?"

"Most assuredly, Mr. Levander," the cook said. Guardian of the stove and proprietress of the kitchen, she was a tall, austere presence engulfed in crackling white linen even to the cap framing her narrow face much like a nun's cowl. Yet when she smiled, as she did now, her features were transformed. She became more believably the source of such fundamental comfort and care. "'Tis a pleasure to cook for you, miss. Mrs. Fergus, the egg woman, has a son at your school. She speaks very well of you."

Wynne Fergus lived just outside of Gynfelin. She kept herself and her four children by raising hens and selling or trading the eggs. Of the children, only the eldest was old enough for school, but the rest were to follow. Wynne Fergus was very clear on that. She had a brother working in the mines. There had been two, but one had died in a cave-in the previous year. All Wynne Fergus's energies were devoted to keeping her children from the same fate.

Morgana smiled. ''Willy's a very energetic little boy,'' she said diplomatically.

Mrs. Mulroon chuckled under her breath. ''His mother puts it a bit differently.'' She went back to her cooking as Sebastian asked if Morgana would like anything else.

She assured him she could not possibly. After the dinner she'd eaten the night before, she feared she wouldn't be able to do justice to what was before her. Yet the mere sight of thin pink slices of ham, fresh-baked brown bread spread with honey and two of Wynne Fergus's eggs lightly crisped around the edges was enough to make her stomach growl.

Ruefully, she thought how very easy it would be to become accustomed to such things. Not merely the food itself but the notion of it appearing almost magically without the slightest effort being expended on the part of the person who would enjoy it. What would it be like to have every need, not to say every desire, seen to in the same way? To never be cold or hungry or fearful? To never look at a beautiful child— and which of them wasn't—and dread what that child's life would be?

Her imagination failed her. She could not conceive of such a life, therefore there was no point trying.

What she could do was indulge her curiosity on a more ordinary level.

"This is delicious," she said by way of an opening. "And last night's dinner was superb. His lordship is very fortunate to have you."

Mrs. Mulroon pinkened. "'Tis kind of you to say so, miss."

"Have you been with him long?"

"Nigh on ten years now. The same's true of all the staff here except for that Mrs. Dickinson. She was taken on in London when it was decided to open the house here." Mrs. Mulroon paused meaningfully before she added, "She'll be returning there now."

"Oh, is she leaving?" Morgana asked. Mrs. Mulroon seemed disposed to chatter. Morgana saw no reason to discourage her, but Sebastian might feel differently. Morgana cast a cautious eye in his direction, but he seemed absorbed in the local paper he was reading. His face was studiously blank.

"Why, of course, miss," the cook went on. "She failed in her duties. His lordship never tolerates that."

Of course, Morgana thought with a hint of exasperation. Heaven forbid that his lordship should be displeased in any way. "Does that mean you'll be needing a new housekeeper?"

"I expect so, miss," Sebastian said, folding the paper. "It would be difficult to manage without one."

Morgana hesitated. She had already brought Owen into the household, however inadvertently. It seemed a bit much to suggest his lordship's taking on someone in addition. And yet . . .

"There is a lady in the village, a Mrs. Gareth. She came here to care for her elderly mother who has since died. Prior to that she was housekeeper to a family in Bath. She seems extremely capable."

"Would she be interested in the position, miss?" Sebastian asked.

"I think so. She is accustomed to working and appears to be somewhat at loose ends."

In fact, Elizabeth Gareth had confided to Morgana that as much as she loved Gynfelin and longed to stay there, she feared she would have to return to England to find work. Her mother had left scarcely a pittance, and Elizabeth had far from enough saved to support herself without constant employment. For her to be hired on at Montfort would be a piece of luck without parallel.

"I shall inform his lordship," Sebastian said gravely. Morgana thought she glimpsed a twinkle in his eyes, but she was undoubtedly mistaken. She finished her breakfast a short time later and prepared to take her leave.

"Would it be possible for me to have a word with Owen before I go?" she asked as she fastened her cloak. It looked like new, as did all her clothes, Lenore having brushed and cleaned them with an effectiveness Morgana herself could never manage. Even her battered old boots gleamed thanks to what must have been a half dozen or more coats of polish.

"Of course, miss," Sebastian replied. "He was up well before dawn this morning and seemed very eager to work. As his lordship didn't quite say what his duties were to be, I took it upon myself to interview him briefly before deciding how he might best apply his considerable energy."

Morgana could not resist a smile. She suspected that far from not quite saying what Owen's duties should be, his lordship had given no indication at all. Certainly, he hadn't done so in her presence. True to his calling, Sebastian had relieved his master of the need.

"What did you decide?" she asked.

"I was most impressed by the boy's knowledge of ancient languages. He seems quite fluent in both Latin and Greek, and informs me this is due to yourself."

From his considerable advantage of height, the butler peered down at her. "Without being presumptuous, might I ask how you acquired such knowledge? It is highly unusual in a woman."

"My father taught me. He loved the classics and wanted me to share that pleasure."

The previous night, when she had said the same to his lordship, the result had been a spirited, not to say provoking, discussion about the proper role of women in society. Sebastian, on the other hand, merely took it in stride.

"Very laudable of him. At any rate, given the boy's abilities, I thought he might be able to assist in the library. The catalog is sadly out of date. His lordship has mentioned the need to do something about it."

"I'm sure Owen will be a great help," Morgana said, thinking that nothing better could have been found for him. Owen would be in ecstasy to be let loose among a veritable treasure trove of books. So he appeared when she entered the library a few moments later. Morgana blinked rapidly at the sight of him. The thin, bedraggled and altogether pitiful child of the day before was gone. In his place was a slender, upright boy whose face was flushed with excitement.

"Oh, miss," he said when he saw her, "have you ever seen any place more wonderful? Books from floor to ceiling about every subject you could imagine, just there for the reading. Mr. Levander says his lordship's been buying books ever since he was my age. He brought them all here when he came so he'd finally have a chance to study them."

"Fascinating," Morgana murmured. She was having a hard time seeing the dark warrior who had subdued Trelawney so effortlessly and swept her off her own feet immersed in the world of learning. But who was she to say?

She went up to the boy and laid a hand gently on his arm. "Are you all right, Owen, truly? Everything happened so suddenly yesterday, and there was no chance for us to talk. His lordship seems to mean well but—"

"Not seems, miss, he truly does. He spoke with me this morning before he went riding. Very kind he was. Said I could stay here and work so long as I also continued my education. Can you imagine that? A job *and* I can keep on learning. He also asked about my music, you must have told him about that, I suppose. There's a harpsichord in the music room that hasn't been touched in an age. He means to restore it and the harp that's there, as well. Truly, he knows about everything—books, music, everything."

Morgana hid a smile but beneath it was a twinge of concern. Clearly, the marquess had won himself an ally. Owen was safe, happy and well-employed. Moreover, he had already found a measure of acceptance with the marquess that his own father had always denied him. Was it any wonder he sang the man's praises so lavishly?

And while on the subject, was that perhaps a twinge of envy she felt that her prize pupil should so quickly replace her as mentor and guide? Shame on herself for so unworthy a thought. Truly, the marquess brought out the worst in her.

"I'm glad you are well, Owen," she said softly. "If you have need of anything, send word to me and I will do whatever I can to help."

He thanked her gravely with a new maturity she found endearing. There were tears in her eyes as she made her way out of Montfort by a side door and began the walk to the village. She had politely rejected Sebastian's offer of a carriage, knowing the stir that would create. The sooner she got back to her normal way of life, the better.

And yet she could not resist a last look over her shoulder at the proud manor house riding on the crest of the hill, all white and golden against the rising sun. It was as something out of a dream, which she would do very well to remember. The real world lay down that rocky, winding road, where she belonged. Determinedly, she turned her gaze straight ahead.

Near the crest of the hill, mounted upon his black steed, David watched the slender, cloak-wrapped figure until it was out of sight. Only then did he turn away, going slowly through the bracken on the hillside, letting the stallion find its own way. He had ridden hard since shortly after dawn. Some of the fierce energy that had kept him sleepless through the night was eased, but not all. He still felt the need to be in motion, if only in flight from the thoughts that gave him no rest.

He desired Morgana Penrhys. The fiery-haired schoolteacher with her tart tongue and reformer's zeal stirred him in a way he had not experienced before. He wanted her not in the safely anonymous way he was accustomed to, in which all beautiful women were essentially interchangeable. Oh, no, that wasn't good enough anymore, it seemed. He wanted her specifically, the spirit and will of her as well as that lovely, slender body the potential of which he was sure she did not remotely suspect.

All of which was quite caddish of him. Good old-fashioned word, he thought. *Cad.* Not the sort of thing he would ever have expected to be said about himself, but then a good many of his expectations had proven to be ill-founded. Still, his dealings with women had always been straightforward. They might not like the limits he set, might indeed strive greatly to change them, but they could never claim they had been misled.

Was he misleading Morgana? He had mocked her notion of propriety despite knowing that it was well-founded. She was right to suspect he had, as he had so quaintly put it, designs on her person. All things being equal, he would have liked nothing better than to strip her of those horrible clothes, lie her down on the thick Araby carpet in the library and proceed to sate himself with her beauty.

But one couldn't do that sort of thing and retain any claim to being an English gentleman.

The thought amused him, and he laughed as the stallion paused momentarily to sniff the air. He had no such claim, having left it behind in the mud and gore of the Crimea. What moral compass he still possessed was strictly his own. Morgana was vulnerable to him by virtue of her position in life and her inexperience. Paradoxically, that protected her. He loathed the notion of taking advantage of the weak, and despised men who did so. Yet *weak* wasn't a word he would use to describe Morgana. Never mind her position or experience, she had strength, determination and courage. All of which, paradoxically again, made her fair game.

He sighed and shook his head ruefully. Sunlight pouring over the eastern hills glinted off his thick, ebony hair. He had left the house so early that morning that he had neglected to shave. His square jaw was dark with a night's growth of beard. The stock of his shirt was undone. He looked far less the noble lord than the dangerous brigand. Yet for all that, and for all his thoughts of Morgana, the beauty of the morning did not escape him. The sun in glory pouring over the hills, the soft gurgle of silvered springs, the scent of wildflowers on the balmy air and, far off in the distance, the boom of the sea with its siren call of infinite possibilities all reminded him of his own great fortune in being there.

Against almost inconceivable odds, he was alive. Perhaps it was time he began to act that way.

Along the road, walking briskly, Morgana suddenly paused. She was swept by a frisson of pleasure like warm, sweet honey flowing through her. Her eyes widened in surprise. She had never experienced anything like that.

It passed, and she forced herself to move on. The road sloped down toward the village. She could feel the sharp pebbles through the soles of her boots. The tiny, almost inconsequential jabs anchored her to reality. Whatever that was she had just experienced, only the memory lingered. Her pace quickened. Her cloak fluttered around her, trailing like the wind-filled wings of a bird in flight.

For an instant, she thought she heard a horse's hooves and jerked her head around. But there was nothing, only the wind and the far-off cry of a bird turning in lazy circles in the air. Ahead lay the neat, whitewashed cottages of Gynfelin nestled in the cleft between two hills. Her own was among them, and not far from it the school. She picked up her skirts and doubled her pace. By the time she reached the small, dearly familiar building, she was running.

Chapter Five

Morgana arrived at the school early the following morning, intending to have a little time to herself to plan the day. She was prevented from that by the discovery of an unwanted, if not unexpected, visitor.

Winnifred Armbruster was already there, seated in the chair behind Morgana's desk, busily going through her drawer. She glanced up when Morgana entered but made no attempt to conceal her activity and showed not the slightest embarrassment.

Her only concession to the irregularity of her actions was to look at Morgana accusingly and say, "You're early."

Morgana bit back the comment that sprang most immediately to her lips and shut the door quietly behind her. Fortunately, the first of the children would not be arriving for another half an hour or so. With luck, they would be spared a distasteful scene.

"But not early enough to welcome you," she said as she came around the desk and deliberately stood close to what was, after all, her place. Mrs. Armbruster scowled but made no move to relinquish possession.

"I have been going through your records. You are teaching thirty-seven children instead of the allocated thirty-two. This has happened before, and you have been called to account for it. Children whose parents refuse to pay the fees are not supposed to be in school."

"No parents refuse to pay," Morgana replied. She thought she was showing admirable restraint in holding on to her temper. But then it would avail her nothing to lose it. "Any parent who can pay does. But there are some very poor families in this village."

She did not add that this was something the minister's wife should know full well. There was no point. Mrs. Armbruster had made her disdain for the poor more than obvious. However, that did not mean Morgana had to accept such unbending harshness.

"Surely," she said pointedly, "you don't believe they are any the less deserving? After all, Holy Scripture itself teaches us that the poor are blessed. Our Lord lived among them, preached to them and cared for them Himself. Are we to do less?"

Mrs. Armbruster turned a shade of red to rival a healthy beet, which she not incidentally resembled, being extremely round in all directions. Whatever her failings, the lack of a healthy appetite was not one of them.

"I believe you are not reluctant to break rules that were set for a very good reason," she snapped, furious to have her piety called into doubt by a chit of a schoolteacher. The poor indeed! If everyone went around making such a fuss about them, nothing would ever get done.

"If you take every child regardless of ability to pay," she said firmly, "the school could be overrun. Children as far away as Glamorgan could be knocking on your door seeking to be educated."

"And wouldn't that be a shame?" Morgana demanded scathingly. She could tolerate many things, but the unwillingness to help children climb beyond poverty and hopelessness to a better life was not one of them. "Imagine, children wanting so badly to learn that they will beg for it. What will this country come to if we permit that? Why, in no time at all, we might actually have a learned, aware populace that could, among other things, question why others live so much better than them while doing so much less."

"That is quite enough!" Mrs. Armbruster declared. She stood up stiffly and glared at the younger woman. "As usual, you overstep yourself. Be warned, Miss Penrhys, there is a limit to the patience the decent people of this village are willing to show you. The squire and Lady Kennard are the very souls of kindness, but even they have limits. Unless you mend your ways, you may very well find yourself without a position."

It was on the tip of Morgana's tongue to point out that only the marquess—who after all owned all of Gynfelin and whose employee she was—could dismiss her. But she stopped herself just in time. She was hardly in the mood to open up any such topic with Mrs. Armbruster. On the contrary, all she wanted was to see the back of her.

"The children will be arriving shortly," Morgana said. "Perhaps we can discuss this at another time."

"There is nothing to discuss," Mrs. Armbruster said. "Your own stubbornness will be the unmaking of you, mark my words." She stomped toward the door, pausing for one additional glare. "I said you were too fancy for this job when you applied, and I am more sure of it than ever. Mend your ways, Morgana Penrhys, or say farewell to Gynfelin!"

On that note, she departed, leaving behind her a certain lingering sourness that did not dissipate until the first child came bouncing in, cheerfully oblivious, and presented Morgana with a handful of wildflowers found beside the road. They were all muddy-stemmed and dripping, yet Morgana found them lovely. She thanked the child and went to get a bucket for the flowers. By the time she was back, the school was full and the day begun.

The hours sped past, as they always did. Morgana had scarcely time to think or sit down as she moved among her pupils, explaining a fact here, offering encouragement there. The children sopped up learning so eagerly, like blossoms turned to the sun. She never failed to marvel at their enthusiasm, especially in circumstances that were far from ideal. The school lacked so much. The building was crumbling, books were scarce, and she had to scramble even to find chalk to write with.

Yet the children learned, from the smallest to the oldest, and when the long day at last ended, they lingered still around her until she sent them on their ways with promises to be there again for them on the morrow.

When they were gone, she lingered a while longer, tidying up as she always did. This quiet time at the end of the day was precious to her. It gave her a chance to sort out the previous hours, to recall those things she needed to take note of and store them away for the future.

But on this particular afternoon, her usually peaceful interlude was broken. It seemed she was not yet done with Armbrusters. This time it was the good reverend. In contrast to his robust wife, he was a small man with rounded shoulders, a soft, pale face and the inevitable squint of the midnight scholar. In his late fifties, with most of that time having been spent in the pursuit of the finer points of medieval genealogies, he tended to find the modern world bewildering in the extreme. ''Dear Winnifred,'' as he called her, was forever fussing over him, insisting that he didn't have the sense of a baby lamb. In fact, he had great sense. He just didn't get much use out of it.

His flock consisted of the local gentry—minus the marquess, who had yet to make an appearance in the pleasant, gabled church and who, truth be told, wasn't really expected—and a few of the village elderly. As for the rest of Gynfelin's residents, he saw little of them. At university, he had cherished the notion of honest, well-scrubbed peasantry trooping off to church of a Sunday, the backbone of the nation and faithful forever to its God.

The reality was different. Gynfelin's residents attested their loyalty to the church well enough, they just didn't think of attending it. His early efforts to draw them out had failed utterly, undoubtedly due to his own ineptitude.

In recent years, he had given up, submerging himself even further in the research that was his truest love. But since Miss Penrhys's coming, he had been increasingly uncomfortable with his own lack of higher purpose. He had begun, however tentatively, to involve himself, supported by her discreet encouragement.

"Ah, you're still here," he said as he puffed up the half dozen steps to the schoolroom. "I was hoping to catch you." He gave her a gentle smile, but his eyes were shadowed. "I've been thinking about the problem with the Trelawney boy. Perhaps I could speak with his father. I know I haven't done much of that sort of thing, but it wouldn't hurt to try. After all, something must be done."

Morgana put away the last of the readers on the shelf near her desk. "That's very good of you, but the problem seems to be solved. Owen has found employment with the Marquess of Montfort."

"My heavens, are you serious?"

"Absolutely." She couldn't help but feel a twinge of satisfaction at the reverend's amazement. After all, what had happened was rather extraordinary.

Armbruster sat down abruptly on one of the wooden benches that faced her desk. In one corner of the small room was a wood stove that provided grudging heat as well as boiling the kettle Morgana used to make the children's tea. She provided that meal from her own pocket and did so as generously as she could, knowing it might be the only decent one some of them would get in a day.

Besides the benches, desk and stove, the room's only furnishings were the shelves where she stored the supplies she hoarded and the three oil lamps suspended by chains from the rafters. In the dark winter days, the lamps were essential, but with the coming of spring, they could be left unlit.

That relieved Morgana of the chore of keeping them filled and cleaned. Similarly, she no longer had to chop and split so much wood for the stove. She smiled inwardly. No wonder she liked spring so much.

"The marquess," Armbruster murmured. "How did you... That is what did you... My heavens, I can hardly conceive of such a thing!"

Morgana smiled. Her own encounter with the marquess had been so unsettling that she had not really had the chance to appreciate the feat of legerdemain to which she had been party. One moment Owen was the abused son of a drunkard and destined for the grimmest of futures, the next he was elevated to membership in the household of Gynfelin's lord and master. The reverend could be excused for feeling as though the world had turned upside down.

"I went to see Trelawney yesterday," she began.

"You didn't! Child, that man is dangerous. You could have been hurt."

"I was," Morgana admitted. She touched a hand lightly to the bruise on her cheek. It was much improved, the pain gone and the swelling all but vanished. Only the discoloration lingered.

The reverend peered at her more closely. He gasped, "I didn't realize… You mean Trelawney… That is too much, he must be reported to the magistrate. That any man should—"

"His lordship took care of it," Morgana interjected, anxious lest the reverend work himself up into a fine fever of outrage. "He came along at the best possible moment to see that Trelawney wasn't a responsible father. Owen made a good impression on him, and the marquess offered him a position."

"Astonishing. Truly, there are times when we see the work of providence directly before our eyes. That may provide me with a theme for this Sunday's sermon. I shall have to think on it. At any rate, the boy is safe. But you say you met the marquess. How extraordinary. No one else here has, you know, although everyone has been angling to do so. Squire Kennard is in fits because his lordship hasn't been in when he calls, nor have any of the invitations to Throckmorton been accepted. All returned with regrets, they say. I'm not sure what's wrong with that, but dear Winnifred informs me it isn't the thing."

"Perhaps his lordship merely values his privacy," Morgana suggested dryly, thinking how wise he would be to do so.

"I'm afraid there is more to it than that, my dear. It is to your credit that you are too involved with your charges to pay heed to the gossip concerning his lordship."

Morgana hesitated. She could hardly admit to an excess of curiosity, yet neither could she pretend a total lack of interest. Cautiously, she repeated, "Gossip?"

"Lady Kennard had it from her sister who resides in Dorset. It seems the sister is wife to a former member of the Royal Fusiliers. Her husband visited London recently and heard the story from members of his company with whom he dined."

"I see," Morgana murmured. Apparently, it wasn't only old genealogies that fascinated the good reverend. He had a nose for the odd bit of news, as well.

And odd it must be to have come so circuitous a route. "Surely, facts become garbled when communicated through so many different parties," she said.

"No doubt. Well, I must be on my way. Very good about young Owen, a great relief. You amaze me, Miss Penrhys, truly you do."

"Wait," Morgana called out. "You didn't say... That is, the marquess..." She was starting to sound like the reverend.

"Refused an order," Armbruster said, "at Balaklava, I believe it was. He would have been cashiered, but apparently influence was brought to bear and it was hushed up. Still, he wouldn't be received in society, not in London at any rate. Apparently, that's why he's come here."

"But he has no interest in our society," Morgana pointed out. It was the most reasonable response she could make just then. The reverend's declaration was shocking. The refusal of an order under any circumstances was a grave offense. For it to occur in the heat of battle made it equivalent to treason.

She had spent only a few hours in his company, scant time for assessing a man's character. Yet she was convinced he was many things—arrogant, tough, demanding, with the careless selfishness of his class, yet with a streak of compassion he could not escape no matter how much he might try to deny it.

She closed her eyes for a moment, remembering how he had looked when he spoke of the Crimea. That wasn't fear she had seen in him then, but simple horror at the obscenity of war. If he had refused an order, and that remained very much in doubt, it would not have been out of cowardice.

But in the final analysis it didn't matter. Whatever he had or had not done, he was master of Gynfelin. They would all, the Reverend Armbruster and Squire Kennard included, be wise to remember that. Morgana had little experience with men and virtually none with a man such as the marquess, but she was quite certain of one thing—he did not take kindly to being crossed. It would be interesting to see what happened if they tried.

After the reverend left, she finished straightening the schoolroom, then put on her cloak to walk the short distance to her cottage. It was a small, ramshackle affair consisting of a single room beneath a rough-hewn loft used in the not too distant past for the storing of hay. Against one wall was a rudimentary kitchen centered on a small fireplace. Nearby, a narrow bed took up all of a tiny alcove. There was a battered table with two straight chairs, a large shelf for books and a single dresser.

Some of the furniture came from her parents' home, the rest she had picked up here and there. The brightly hued rug was a special find, bartered from the Gypsies in return for teaching their children whenever they happened to be in the area, which she gladly did even though she knew it earned the disapproval of some of the locals. Dried flowers and herbs further brightened the small room, as did the curtains she had sewn.

Ordinarily, she should have been boarding with the local family best able to accommodate her, in this case the squire and his good wife. But Rosalind Kennard had taken one look at Morgana and found it inconvenient to keep her under her roof. Instead, she hit upon the cottage, owned by the squire but vacant for several years, as the perfect solution. Never mind that it was almost derelict, it would simply have to do.

Three years later, it did. As she stepped inside for the first time in more than a day, Morgana breathed a soft sigh of relief. With the door closed behind her, she felt as though she had shut the world out. Her pantry offered little encouragement, but she made herself a simple dinner and ate it before the fire.

The evening had turned cool. She lit an oil lamp and read for a short time before her eyes grew heavy. As she undressed for bed, she thought ruefully of the cosseting she had received the night before. It was just as well she was the independent sort or she might have missed it.

But when she was beneath the covers, the lamp extinguished and silence wrapped all around her, the weight of solitude pressed down on her. She turned on her side, drawing her knees up and curling tight just the way she had done as a child when confronted by something she felt unable to cope with.

Loneliness was not precisely unknown to her, but she encountered it rarely. She was simply too busy and too involved with the children to dwell on her solitary state. At least she had been up until now. The dinner shared with the marquess appeared to have had an unexpected cost. Suddenly, she was no longer sufficient unto herself. She needed something—no, be truthful—someone else.

Madness, that's what it was. Desperately, she willed sleep to come and bring forgetfulness, if only for a time. It did—and did not—for in her dreams a dark stallion pawed the air with hooves of slashing steel, and all around her the wind murmured ancient, half-understood incantations.

The next several days passed slowly. Morgana had a slight cold, which added to her lingering sense of fatigue and befuddlement. Her nose ran and turned red. She drank quantities of tea, assured the children she was fine and tried to convince herself it was true. By the end of the week she was recovered enough to welcome a visit from Owen. He came after school let out, appearing suddenly at the door with a shy smile and a basket heavily laden with goodies from Mrs. Mulroon's kitchen.

"I'm sorry I didn't come before," he said as they walked together toward her cottage. Morgana kept casting sidelong glances at him, amazed by the change in his appearance.

He was still small and slightly built—a few days of decent treatment wouldn't change that—but he carried himself with his head high and his shoulders back, making him seem bigger. His skin glowed with ruddy color, his eyes were bright, and he smiled more readily than she had ever seen him. He was also far better dressed. When she commented on the good-quality shirt and trousers he wore, he flushed.

"Mr. Levander said I had to dress proper. These are supposed to be for a footman, but they cut them down for me."

"Are you enjoying the work?" Morgana asked softly.

"It's wonderful! You can't imagine the books his lordship has. There's dozens just on botany alone, and that's only one subject. So far I've counted half a dozen languages. His lordship reads French and Italian as well as Latin and Greek. His particular interest is map making, there are at least a hundred books on the old explorers. He told me when he was a boy his family was staying down in Bath, he got hold of a small boat and set out to sea, thinking he'd see for himself what the Americas looked like. He got ten miles down the coast before a fisherman plucked him out. Imagine that."

"I see," Morgana murmured. Owen had never been a very talkative boy but apparently that, too, had changed. He also seemed to have developed quite an admiration for the marquess. She prayed it wasn't misplaced.

"Do you see a great deal of his lordship?" she asked as they entered the cottage. Owen put the basket down on the table as Morgana went to open the windows. It had been cool that morning when she left, but now the air was turning pleasantly warm.

"Not really. He's out a good deal, riding over the estate. He was at Cardovan yesterday talking with the shepherds, and the day before that he went down to Flynnelin to check on the fishing."

Both of those were villages within the Montfort demesne, smaller than Gynfelin but important to the manor's economy. Still, it was odd he hadn't started closer to home.

When she said as much, Owen explained, "Mr. Levander says his lordship is already well acquainted with Gynfelin, having familiarized himself with the account rolls and suchlike before he came here."

Morgana frowned. "The account books? That's hardly a way to get to know a place. He needs to get to know the people."

"Perhaps he doesn't want to. I shouldn't say this, but between us, the squire's been making a nuisance of himself. He keeps trying to call on his lordship and when that failed he sent him an invitation to the spring fete Saturday evening." Owen laughed. "Mr. Levander already knows about the squire's two daughters so I guess his lordship does, too. He says, Mr. Levander does, that the marquess is an old hand at avoiding such snares."

"Indeed," Morgana murmured. Her mouth tightened. Personally, she didn't care a fig for the squire or his daughters, but they were still a part of Gynfelin. The marquess seemed determined to give the entire village short shrift.

Owen rattled on about this and that as they un-packed the basket. Morgana would have been less than human not to be delighted by the still-warm tea breads, the freshly-churned butter and the small ket-tle filled with delectable soup.

"This was very kind of Mrs. Mulroon," she said.

"She'd like you to visit when you have the chance."

"I'll do that," Morgana promised, thinking she would pick a time when the marquess was away. "How is Mrs. Gareth settling in?" Elizabeth Gareth had come to call several days before, all atwitter over being summoned to the manor house for an interview and profusely grateful for Morgana's help. The re-sults being mutually satisfactory, she had taken up her new post immediately.

"She's doing fine," Owen said, "and she also said she would like you to call since she's so busy and fears she won't get down to the village for awhile. Mrs. Dickinson left something of a mess."

"I'm sure Mrs. Gareth will have it straightened out quickly enough," Morgana said. She sliced one of the tea cakes and put an extra large piece on a plate for Owen. He wolfed it down and didn't demure when she offered another. At the rate he was going, his spindly thinness would soon be a thing of the past. Other remnants of his former life might linger, though.

Softly, Morgana asked, "Have you heard anything from your father?"

A shadow passed behind Owen's gray eyes, but it was gone almost at once. "No, but Mr. Levander told me he has left the neighborhood. He said they could try to track him down if I wanted, but I didn't see any point. It's not as though we ever got on together.''

''No,'' Morgana said, ''it's not.'' She laid a hand gently on his arm. ''We all carry our pasts around with us, but that doesn't mean we have to be burdened by them. You are yourself, Owen Trelawney, and from where I sit that's saying something.''

He gave her a quick, shy smile. ''Thank you, miss. That's so inadequate to say, but I don't know how else to put it. If you hadn't stood up for me, my life would have been over.''

In the back of her mind, Morgana thought that her standing up for him had almost cost him his life. She had a vivid memory of the elder Trelawney standing over his son, the hoe gripped between his hands, ready to strike. Only the marquess's swift, implacable intervention had prevented a terrible end to a young and promising life.

There was a lesson for her in that, she realized. Good intentions weren't enough. They needed strength to back them up. She lacked that strength, but the marquess possessed it in abundance.

Long after Owen left to return to the manor, Morgana sat at the table, thinking. When twilight gave way to darkness, she roused herself long enough to light the lamps but she did not pick up a book or a piece of needlework to while away the evening, as she usually did. Instead, she forced herself to confront what was before her eyes.

The children of Gynfelin had desperate needs she was not managing to meet. Oh, she did a good enough job by the usual measure, but it did not remotely satisfy her. There were so many of them who were so bright, so deserving of something better than a life of poverty and hopelessness.

The marquess had the means to change that. All he lacked was the understanding and the will. Those she could provide in ample measure. The problem was that she would have to seek him out, talk to him, convince him to take a greater interest in the school.

In other words, she would have to put herself directly in his path.

The thought dismayed her yet she couldn't reject it. To see such an opportunity and walk away from it out of fear was intolerable. She would simply have to steel herself to the task and bide her time until she found the right moment.

Two days later, the moment found her.

Chapter Six

Coming out of church Sunday morning, Morgana was surprised when Rosalind Kennard beckoned to her. Ordinarily, the squire's wife did no more than barely acknowledge that Gynfelin possessed a school-teacher, and that only with a glance that seemed focused somewhere over Morgana's shoulder.

She had been away from the village when Morgana applied to be teacher and had therefore missed the opportunity to prevent her from being installed in that position. That decision, made jointly by the squire, who had an unfailing eye for a pretty woman, and the reverend, who for once in his life failed to heed the advice of dear Winnifred, still rankled Lady Kennard.

She was one of those women who automatically viewed with suspicion and dislike any member of her sex who was younger, more attractive, wittier or more charming than she or her two unfortunate daughters. Since that encompassed most of the females presently alive on the planet, her ladyship had ample targets on which to hone her nastiness.

Still, Morgana remained one of her favorites. Worse than all her other sins, in Lady Kennard's eyes at least, was Morgana's refusal to be properly deferential. Much as Mrs. Armbruster fancied herself a good woman when she was anything but, Lady Kennard liked to think of herself as a scholar. Oh, not a bluestocking, to be sure, but possessed of an above-average mind, gifted with rare insights and a talented authoress, to boot.

She had, on one unfortunate occasion, gifted Morgana with a selection of her poetry. When, upon being pressed to comment, Morgana characterized it as "flowery," the battle lines were drawn. The two had said barely a civil word since. Yet there her ladyship was, laced into a day dress of navy blue silk trimmed in yards of white poplin that might have been better suited to a younger and more slender woman, a beribboned bonnet framing her stern face.

"Miss Penrhys," she said in the slightly nasal tone she affected, believing it to be a mark of the gentry, "you are well?"

Morgana gripped her prayer book more firmly, hoping the spirit of tolerance would seep into her from it, and inclined her head. "Quite, Lady Kennard, thank you. And yourself?"

"Tolerable. As you know, I have a delicate disposition not suited to the rigors of life in these uncivilized parts, but I make the best of it."

In fact, the squire's wife had a disposition roughly equivalent to that of the average ox. She would have done better—and probably been a good deal happier—helping to farm a smallholding with a gaggle of children at her knees. Instead, she languished, forbidden by her social position to do much of anything. With so much idle time and surplus energy she had become one of those little tyrants whose throne room is the front parlor and whose army is a ready supply of slander.

Still, she was tolerably well behaved as she faced Morgana. Indeed she almost managed to smile, quite a feat considering how rarely she attempted it.

"I do hope you will be joining us tomorrow evening," she said.

"Tomorrow?"

"Why of course, for the spring fete. You did receive your invitation, didn't you?"

Of course she hadn't. In the three years she had been in Gynfelin, Morgana had never received an invitation to the spring fete or, for that matter, to any other social event given by the local gentry. Ordinarily, the schoolteacher would have been included as a matter of course. Morgana was not, because Gynfelin's social dragons, the formidable mesdames Kennard and Armbruster, were united in their determination to keep her in her place.

"I'm sorry," Morgana said with dignity, "but I did not."

"That stupid girl of mine, I really don't know why I keep her on as secretary. Never mind, you're invited now. Eight o'clock at the hall. Don't worry about dressing. No one expects you to make a show." She glanced down the considerable length of her nose at Morgana. "In fact, what you have on now is quite suitable."

What she had on now was a no-nonsense brown serge skirt and matching jacket worn with a plain white blouse. Her hair was gathered in a bun at the nape of her neck and covered, at least on top, with a small straw hat. She looked perfectly presentable for church, also perfectly plain or as near to it as she could ever get.

"Thank you," she said, thinking that she would move heaven and earth to avoid arriving at the Kennard's doorstep in such an ensemble. As it happened, she needn't have worried. Several years before, Morgana's mother, well-intentioned lady that she was, had made a brief effort to find Morgana a husband. She had given up in the face of her daughter's blatant disinterest, but a few remnants of the attempt still lingered. One of them was a gown hanging in the far back of the cottage's tiny closet.

Morgana took the gown out when she got back from church, removed its cotton covering and laid it carefully on the bed. She stared at it for a long time, wondering if she would have the nerve to wear it. Not that there was anything immodest about the gown, far from it. Its neckline came up to the throat, which was framed by a ruffle of tea-hued lace that matched the lace panels in the bodice and skirt. Not immodest at all, but the most beautiful and feminine dress Morgana had ever possessed. Wearing it, she felt almost like a different person.

That evening, she pressed the gown carefully, heating the iron on her tiny stove. It was tedious work but at last she was done. She hung the dress at the front of the closet where it would not wrinkle. All the following day, as she worked, she kept returning to it in her mind. Wearing it would win her no approval from the dragons. Indeed, they might well seize upon it as an excuse for being even more suspicious of her. Her Penrhys blood rose at the thought. Let them—she was who she was, and she wasn't going to pretend otherwise.

Yet for all that imagined confidence, nerves threatened to overcome her as the hour of the fete drew near. With the shutters of the cottage closed and the door securely locked, she tugged the tin tub in front of the fireplace. Back and forth she went to the stove, laboriously sloshing in bucket after bucket of heated water.

Baths were almost her sole indulgence, and she enjoyed them enough not to mind the work involved. When the water was scented with lavender still potent with the perfume of the previous summer, Morgana removed her clothes. She folded them neatly and set them on a nearby chair. A long sigh of delight escaped her as she lowered herself into the bath. She stretched out full length and closed her eyes. All the tension and worry of the past few days melted away. For a time, at least, she was free.

She stayed until the water cooled too much to be comfortable. Only then did she rise reluctantly and towel herself dry. Wearing a chemise, lace-trimmed drawers and a light corset, she considered herself in the small mirror on the wall opposite her bed. The mirror showed only her shoulders and head; she had no way of seeing the rest of herself. But perhaps that was for the best. She was anxious enough without having to confront the results of her daring.

Her hair presented a problem. The moist heat of the bath had left it in tangled curls that steadfastly refused to be brushed into anything that resembled order. The maid, Lenore, perhaps could have done something with it, but Morgana could not. She gave up finally and left it down, secured away from her face by a length of black velvet ribbon that stood out darkly against the riot of Titian tresses.

Getting into the dress proved a bit awkward, but she managed it well enough. As the delicate silk and lace settled around her, she was swept by piercing doubt and almost changed her mind. But the Penrhys courage held. With a toss of her head, she gathered a pretty shawl around her shoulders, took a firm grip on her reticule and left the cottage.

The evening shoes she wore, bought to go with the dress, were hardly meant for walking along country lanes. Fortunately, the squire's residence was only a little distance away. A stolid house of yellow brick set behind overgrown hedges, it offered little in the way of elegance or warmth. The previous year, Lady Kennard had conceived a fondness for topiary after being advised by a friend in London that it was all the rage among the nobility. The result was a disconcerting menagerie of bears, giraffes, geese and whatnot frozen like so many leafy statues at odd intervals around the house.

Morgana brushed past them and walked up the path to the main entrance. Several carriages were disgorging their passengers. She nodded cordially to those she knew and tried hard not to notice their startled glances or the sudden murmur of conversation springing up behind her.

Chin high, she climbed the half dozen stone steps to the ornately carved double doors. They stood open, spilling light into the gathering darkness. Beyond lay a high-ceilinged vestibule with an elaborate marble mosaic floor better suited to a noble residence. The hall was furnished with overstuffed brocade settees and stern-faced portraits, presumably of the Kennard ancestry.

Morgana surrendered her shawl to a majordomo hired for the evening and continued gingerly into the large gallery at the back of the house, a place Lady Kennard insisted on referring to as the ballroom although, in fact, it was too small for so grandiose a function. It was large enough, however, to accommodate the sixty or so guests gathered there, sipping punch and chatting among themselves as they waited for the music to begin.

Morgana had tried to time her arrival to draw the least possible attention, hoping that most everyone would already be there and involved with one another. She was right in one sense, the evening was already in full swing, but wrong in another. Barely had she set foot into the long gallery than eyes turned in her direction. Morgana refused to flinch under the weight of their scrutiny.

Never mind the scowls from more than a few of the women or, worse yet, the sudden smiles from the so-called gentlemen. She was dressed perfectly properly, she was behaving exactly as she should, and she had, after all, been invited. Although now that she thought about it, she had to wonder why. What had inspired her hostess to suddenly desire her company? Before long, she had her answer.

The Reverend Armbruster was, when all was said and done, a kindly man. Seeing her so alone and vulnerable, he approached swiftly and offered his arm.

"My dear, lovel, to see you. Do come join us."

Grateful for his intervention, she allowed herself to be spirited off toward a corner of the gallery where Lady Kennard was holding court. She eyed her young guest with undisguised surprise.

"Why, Miss Penrhys, what a lovely gown, and quite in fashion, too, several seasons ago. I had no idea you possessed such a wardrobe."

"I don't," Morgana said bluntly, ignoring the sting in the back of her throat. She wasn't normally so thin-skinned, but so much unfortunate attention was beginning to affect her. She wished herself back in her cottage without delay even as she knew that was impossible. Having come this far she had no choice but to stick it out.

"Naturally," she went on, "I wouldn't dream of offending you by coming improperly dressed. After all, you've gone to such impressive effort yourself." Her gaze skimmed the plump, bejeweled woman so tightly laced that her face glowed red and tiny beads of sweat showed along her upper lip.

Lady Kennard's gaze focused on the bright mane of Morgana's hair, which seemed to particularly offend her. Still, she forced a chilly smile.

"Do sit down, my dear. I don't believe you've met—" She rattled off a series of names attached to the dozen or so ladies and gentlemen hovering around her. Some Morgana knew, they were people of middling affluence from the surrounding area. Others were strangers, friends seemingly of her ladyship and every bit as supercilious in their regard.

"We were just discussing the marquess," Lady Kennard informed her. "He insists on being so frightfully mysterious. No one has been permitted to call since he arrived, and of course, he has called on no one. But wait, that isn't quite correct, is it?" She turned to Morgana with a gesture that had all the spontaneity of a heavy pudding. "You've met the marquess, haven't you, my dear? Do tell us about him."

Feeling for all the world as though she had been called on to sing for her supper, Morgana stifled a groan. Surely this would teach her to be more cautious in the future. Of course Lady Kennard had had a motive for inviting her, perhaps even two. She could gain information about the marquess and at the same time cast the bold schoolteacher into disrepute.

"There is really nothing to tell," Morgana said softly. It didn't help that her audience leaned forward, the better to hear her. Not even the reverend could hide his curiosity.

"Nonsense," Lady Kennard said briskly. "Why, you spent the night under his roof."

A delighted inhaling of breath informed Morgana of the general response to this morsel of malicious innuendo. What had promised to be no more than an ordinary evening's entertainment was suddenly enlightened with the sauce of scandal.

The reverend looked aghast while his good wife appeared grimly satisfied. Hadn't she always known or at least suspected that Miss Penrhys was not all she should be?

"You didn't," she murmured even as her tone said she was quite certain Morgana had. Indeed, she wasn't surprised at all, it was just the sort of thing a wild-haired hussy would do, and to think they had entrusted her with the souls of their tender young. No wonder the world was going to hell in a hand basket.

"It was very late," Morgana replied firmly, "and the weather was poor. His lordship kindly invited me to stay until morning."

"I must say," Lady Kennard declared, "I've never heard of a young, unmarried woman accepting hospitality under such circumstances. However, who are we to judge?"

Everyone, if her expression was any indication, Morgana thought. Lady Kennard was perfectly comfortable as judge, jury and hangman. Delighted by how well her little entertainment was proceeding, she prepared to deliver the coup de grace.

"I understand he brought a very small household with him, all intensely loyal. Is that correct?"

"Not quite," Morgana said. "There was some difficulty with the housekeeper."

"Oh, yes, that's right. She's been replaced by Mrs. Gareth, hasn't she? At your recommendation, I understand." She paused for good effect, allowing her listeners to relish the notion that the schoolteacher had already, after only a single night under his lordship's roof, acquired such influence with him. That could be accounted for in any number of ways, but they knew which one they preferred and grasped it happily.

"Really," Mrs. Armbruster sniffed, "when I was a young woman such things simply were not done."

"Now, now," Lady Kennard said, "we mustn't demand too much of dear Miss Penrhys. We all knew her background when she came here. It was hardly regular."

Morgana had done quite well so far controlling her temper, but effort carried a price. Now, when she most needed it, her patience snapped.

"There is nothing whatsoever wrong with my background," she said. "I am very sorry to hear you think otherwise." She stood, magnificent with her flashing eyes and the fire of anger burning her cheeks. So much better than the insipid blush of embarrassment and so much more suited to her character. "If you will excuse me," she said, "I will be going."

"Now, my dear, don't—" the reverend began.

"Really, I can't imagine—" Lady Kennard interjected.

"Harrumph," Mrs. Armbruster said, thoroughly satisfied. The chit was just as she'd always suspected, and she was getting exactly what she deserved.

The others, familiar faces and not, bent close together, murmuring eagerly. She was an amusement to them, Morgana realized, nothing more. Her reputation, her fate, her very life did not exist for them. That all of it might lie in ruins as the result of Lady

Kennard's viciousness would not cause any of them a moment's unease.

Tears stung her eyes. She blinked them back furiously and turned to go. A stir rippled down the long gallery, born on excited voices. The crowd parted as naturally as the fabled sea, cleaved neatly in two by the sudden appearance of the man standing at the top of the steps. He was dressed in black but for the glint of silver buttons on the cuffs of his velvet frock coat. Silver, too, glinted in the dark mass of ebony hair and in the relentless gleam of his eyes. The hard line of his mouth curved slightly in a sardonic smile. He walked, strode, really, through the hall as though it were empty, taking no notice of anyone except—oh, no, surely she was wrong! It was Morgana upon whom all his considerable attention seemed suddenly focused.

He was, she realized in that shattering instant, much bigger than the other men. His shoulders and chest were immense, his legs long and taut. He moved with the easy grace of a man readied for battle and not in any way dreading it. All he lacked was a bejeweled sword in his hand to complete the image of a barbarian returned to boldly claim the present.

"Oh, my," whispered Lady Kennard in a tone altogether different from the one she had used scant moments before.

Morgana might have said the same except speech was beyond her. So, it seemed, was any possibility of escape. She stood motionless, a slender figure in fragile lace and silk with her wild hair streaming around her, as the distance between them closed inexorably.

"Miss Penrhys," the marquess said as he stopped at last directly in front of her. His smile deepened but in his eyes was something altogether different, the fierce light of tender battle, which she should not have been able to recognize but did all the same.

Her took her hand, she did not offer it. Holding the fingers curled in his own, he raised them to his lips. His mouth was warm, his touch fleeting, the merest brush of his lips, and she was released. But the effects lingered, burning down the length of her spine, resonating deep within her.

His eyes held hers a moment longer before, mercifully, he deigned to acknowledge his hostess.

"Lady Kennard," he said cordially, accepting the hand she promptly thrust at him, but merely bending over it with rigid correctness.

"What a delightful surprise, your lordship," she simpered—there really was no other word for it. She acted like a nervous twit fresh from the nursery. "We had no idea you were coming although, of course, you are most welcome. Most welcome indeed. Isn't that so, my dear?"

Summoned to play his role, the squire did his best. He puffed out his chest, his ruddy face agleam, and said solemnly, "Yes, indeed, most welcome. Great honor, what? Glad to have you."

"You must let me introduce you to everyone, your lordship," Lady Kennard said, hardly able to contain her excitement. To shepherd the Marquess of Montfort, deciding who he should and should not meet. Ecstasy!

"Perhaps later," David said smoothly. "Actually I came to have a word with Miss Penrhys. If you'd excuse us."

Without waiting for an answer, he turned aside. His eyes claimed Morgana even as he took her arm in a gesture that not even she could mistake as anything other than possessive. "Perhaps you would like some punch," he suggested, guiding her away.

Morgana didn't even try to hear what was being said behind them. She could imagine it well enough. His lordship had just provided sufficient fodder to keep the gossipers at work for a very long time to come, curse him.

She tried to pull away, but without success. His grip tightened insufficiently to hurt her, but quite sufficiently to leave no doubt that she couldn't detach herself without a struggle that would only attract even more undesired attention.

"What are you doing?" she demanded.

He looked at her in mild bemusement. "Why, getting you some punch, of course. You look as though you could use it."

"This isn't funny," she insisted, for the smile had returned to his lean, burnished visage. He really was a devastatingly handsome man. It was most unfair. Had she really been thinking so confidently about using him to her own ends? She would need all her wits and then some merely to survive the encounter.

"You have deliberately given everyone here the wrong impression," she went on. "I do not enjoy being made the subject of malicious gossip."

"Of course you don't," he agreed with perfect reasonableness. "But from what I understand that was happening anyway."

Morgana stopped before the table where the punch was set out and stared at him. "What do you mean?"

He frowned. "You don't know?" When she shook her head, he went on. "Sebastian informed me there was some talk in the village. Apparently he learned of it from Mrs. Gareth, who is concerned about you. Lady Kennard and the reverend's wife have been spreading tales."

Morgana's eyes widened. She could not dispute him, not after the comments made by her hostess a short time before. But to think that sort of thing had been going on for several days and she had been oblivious to it.

"I have never paid much attention to gossip," she said, thinking she should have.

"Obviously not." He smiled again as he released her arm. In the gesture was confidence that she would not again try to leave. A nervous footman handed him a crystal goblet of punch, which the marquess handed to Morgana. He declined any for himself.

"Come," he said, leading her a little distance away. She went, acutely aware of the attention they drew. He, on the other hand, showed no sign of noticing it. They might as well have been completely alone so far as the marquess was concerned.

In fact, that wasn't completely true. David would have liked very much to be alone with the lovely Miss Penrhys, and he regretted that wasn't the case. She had surprised him, a rare enough occurrence to be worth noting for its own sake, but particularly so given the nature of the surprise.

Sweet lord, she was beautiful. He had recognized that at their first meeting when not even the awful clothes she wore succeeded in disguising the radiance of the woman within. But now the full extent of that loveliness struck him forcibly.

Walking beside him, slender and graceful, she reminded him of a magnificent lily crowned in glory. Such thoughts were not his customary fare; he was a plainspoken man with little tolerance for poetry and far less for romance. And yet he seemed caught in currents he could not deny even if he had been able to muster the will to do so.

Near a pair of French doors leading to the garden was a narrow bench built more for show than for comfort. Morgana settled herself on it gingerly. The marquess remained standing. This required her to look up at him, a position she found annoying, so she stared straight ahead instead.

"I want to talk to you about the school," he said. Well, he had to say something, offer some explanation for seeking her out as he had done. Even he, who heaven knew had never paid much attention to the proprieties, realized how he had violated them. The plain truth was that he wanted to see her, to convince himself that the woman he kept returning to in his thoughts was not so extraordinary as he remembered. So much for that. He was more thoroughly caught than before and had to make the best of it.

Her head jerked up, her eyes meeting his. She had the unsettling sensation that he was, and might always be, several steps ahead of her. "The school?"

He smiled inwardly, savoring the small triumph. Prickly Miss Penrhys might want to keep her distance from him, but she could not. He understood too well that her greatest strength, the fierce love she had for the children of Gynfelin, was also the chink in her armor.

"Indeed, I have been speaking with Owen about it. A very bright boy, by the way. He adores you."

Morgana blinked. Was he suggesting Owen's brightness led to his adoring her? "Owen is my friend," she said simply.

The marquess's steely eyes turned opaque, but beneath them thoughts tumbled. Her affection for the boy touched him deeply. It might even be said that he envied Owen. The notion was disturbing. He pushed it aside and said, "I would like to see the school."

Morgana struggled to contain her amazement. Such august personages as the marquess never set foot in the humble schoolhouses where people like her struggled to educate the great bulk of the population against almost insurmountable odds. He would be as out of place there as a glorious hawk set down among starlings. The experience might be good for him.

"As you wish," she said.

He had expected more enthusiasm, even—poor fool that he was—gratitude for his interest. Not this measured acceptance that had an almost regal quality, like a queen granting a favor she was under no obligation to bestow.

"Tomorrow," he said, seeking to regain the upper hand, this presuming he had ever had it.

Morgana inclined her head. "As you wish." She set her glass of punch untouched on a nearby table and rose. "Now if you will excuse me, I was leaving when you arrived."

"So soon?" he asked, his voice sounding to him as though it came from a great distance. He caught the scent of lavender on her skin and felt—he swore he did—the heat pouring from her fiery hair.

"It was a mistake to come."

God send him an honest woman, for her price was above pearls. He threw back his dark-crowned head and laughed.

"Excuse me," he said when her startled glance had shot clear through him. "I did not expect that."

"Yet you knew I was having some ... difficulty."

"Did the old harridan cut you to ribbons?" he asked, good humor gone.

Morgana sniffed and tilted her head so that her delicately curved chin took on the aspect of stone. "Of course not. She was merely rude."

Somewhere in this girl's past, he decided, there were princesses, beautiful daughters of the royal Welsh houses who danced under the swollen moon at the ancient festivals of life and rebirth. Nothing else explained the perfect look of disdain that flitted through her eyes.

He laughed, he couldn't help it. Poor Lady Kennard had no idea what she had taken on. But then perhaps the same could be said of him.

"Allow me to see you home," he said.

She hesitated. Strictly speaking she should refuse outright. And yet...

"That isn't necessary," she said. "I'm sure you would prefer to remain awhile."

"I will make the sacrifice," he told her dryly.

Morgana laughed, a sound as beautiful as sunlight on water, or so he thought, he who had no poetry or romance in him. Such are the misconceptions men cherish about themselves.

"Not on my account," she said firmly. "It really wouldn't do."

He shrugged and stepped back, allowing her to pass. A little surprised by her ready victory, Morgana stifled a surge of disappointment. She really was a fool to be tempted by something that could never be.

Ordinarily, she would have made her farewells to her hostess, but under the circumstances they seemed unnecessary. Having reclaimed her shawl from the majordomo, she made her way down the gravel path to the lane. The last remnants of twilight were long gone, and the moon had risen. It hung, a sickle cleaving upward, shedding its bounty over the undulating land. The night air was soft and fragrant. It entered into Morgana, quieting her troubled spirit. By the time she reached her cottage, she had put much of the evening's turmoil behind her. Snug within her own walls, she prepared for bed.

Outside, near the shadows of the protective yew
trees, a flame glowed for an instant and was gone. The
marquess stood, leaning against one of the trees,
smoking a cheroot. He waited until Morgana's light
went out. Only then did he turn away and leave her to
her solitary slumber.

Chapter Seven

Morgana did not tell her pupils that the marquess would be paying them a visit. For one thing, she wasn't sure he would really do so. In the stark light of morning, the previous evening's encounter had a certain unreal quality to it. But even if he did intend to come, she had no confidence it would be anytime soon. Her admittedly limited experience with the gentry—she'd had none at all before then with the aristocracy—suggested that they were casual at best in their commitments, especially to those they considered inferior.

So it was with great surprise that she looked up, barely half an hour into the morning's work, to find him standing at the schoolroom door. A night and more had passed since she had seen him last, but it seemed like scant moments. There was a simple explanation for that—she had dreamed of him, shadowy dreams she didn't want to remember but couldn't quite forget.

"My lord," she said. Behind her the children were shocked into silence. They were well behaved in ordinary times, knowing how precious was the chance to learn, but now they seemed frozen between astonishment and fear. She saw their small faces, suddenly white, upturned toward him, and moved quickly, as though by instinct, to place herself between the children and the tall, implacable man who held such immense power over them all.

"You are welcome," she said gravely, though her expression put him on notice that the welcome was conditional. He was expected to behave himself.

The notion amused David. So did the transformation she had managed from the evening before. Her hair was restricted in a demure bun and her clothes were plain to the extreme. He frowned slightly as his keen eyes took in the slight fraying on the white cuffs of her blouse. The black wool skirt she wore was shiny in places. He glanced down at her ruthlessly practical shoes. They were polished but clearly worn.

He raised his head slowly and looked around the schoolroom. He saw perhaps four dozen children ranging in age from five to thirteen or so. All were pale and thin, dressed in clothes no better, and in some cases worse, than those Morgana wore. They sat on benches, lacking any desks, and clutched small slates in their hands. A few books were in evidence, but not very many. There was a small stove, cold at the moment, with a pile of kindling in a pail beside it. Gas lamps hung from the ceiling. The air was filled with the smell of dry wood, wool and something else—fear.

His gaze narrowed. For the first time, he really looked into the faces of the children. What he saw appalled him. They were terrified of him.

Why? Surely he had never done anything to these scraps of humanity. On the contrary, they must know by now about Owen, one of their own, snug and safe under the marquess's roof. But that didn't seem to matter. Perhaps Owen had been too far beyond their own aspirations that they could apply the lesson of kindness to themselves.

"Thank you for allowing me to visit, Miss Penrhys," he said quietly and watched as their eyes widened. He was thanking her, their teacher, their protector, their window on the world. Here and there a smile flickered, shy and tentative but with the potential for far more.

"No thanks are needed, your lordship," she replied with grave formality. "You are welcome here."

Even as she spoke with such confidence, Morgana's thoughts tumbled over each other. What was she to do now? The children were still far too nervous to recite, and it would be cruel to ask them to do so. Yet they could hardly just all sit there, staring at him.

"It is time for a story," she said and closed her eyes for an instant, summoning inspiration. On a breath of sound she began.

"Long ago in the dawn time Bran, the great raven, was flying over the land of Cymru. He came to a river where a small boy was fishing. When the boy saw Bran, he was very afraid, for he recognized the great raven for what he was. 'Have you come to kill me?' he asked Bran. The raven was surprised, for though he knew men associated him with death he did not think of himself that way. To him, life and death were separated by no more than a cobweb, and he didn't understand all the fuss about passing from one to the other. He told the boy this, and then he dived into the water. In his beak he caught a great flashing salmon, which he brought to the bank and gave to the boy. Then he flew off, his wings blotting out the sun. The boy took the salmon home to his parents and told them how it had come to him. At first they were afraid to eat it, thinking that perhaps they should dedicate it to the old gods people believed in back then. But the boy insisted it should be eaten because it was the gift of Bran, who believed men should not fear anything, not even death. They ate the salmon and were nourished by it. Long after the boy grew, he remembered what Bran had told him. He told it to his children who told it to theirs. So it was that great courage was born in the land of Cymru, and people learned that what they fear the most is never so terrible as they think.''

''Who was the boy?'' one of the children asked.

''Arthur,'' another said promptly. ''Bran came at Merlin's summons to instruct him.''

''If it was Arthur, the story would say so,'' another chimed in.

''It was Llywelyn Olaf,'' said one, naming the last of the Welsh kings, martyr to British might but as alive in memory as he had ever been during his brief time in this world. And still inspiration for those who dreamed of free Wales.

''What is it you seek to teach them?'' the marquess murmured. ''Ancient legends, magical ways, rebellion?''

He said the last almost as if it amused him, yet Morgana was not misled. He had cut to the heart of it, this black-garbed Englishman with his sardonic smile and relentless eyes. Yet he had it wrong. It wasn't rebellion she sought to teach the children, but pride. Pride in their own heritage, not that imposed on them by a conqueror. Pride that had to take root at the core of their being if they were ever to make more of their lives than fate seemed to decree. Pride could not exist hand in hand with fear.

Softly, she said, "I want to teach them to know themselves."

He stared at her for a long moment, trying to reconcile what she said, and apparently so firmly believed, with what little he knew of teaching. His own education had followed the usual pattern, a tutor at home until he was eight then off to Eton, his father's school and his father's before him, as it had been for uncounted generations of Harrells. In the beginning, he'd hated the place and done his best to be sent down. But gradually he had learned to appreciate that under the bullying and enforced mediocrity lay some redeeming features. He had, as Morgana said, learned to know himself. Much later, on the blood-soaked fields of the Crimea, that had turned out to be indispensible, for him and for his men. The only problem was that of all the hallowed ranks of old Etonians, he seemed among the very few to have learned that single and ultimately simple lesson.

The same lesson this woman was trying to impart to the children of peasants in a rudimentary one-room schoolhouse hard by the Welsh wild lands. On the surface, it should have seemed absurd, but he had met Owen, and more importantly he had spent time with

Morgana, enough to know she was neither deluded nor naive. She was merely very serious.

"A worthy objective," he said slowly, "but wouldn't it be more easily accomplished in better surroundings?"

She stared at him, her face the mirror of her thoughts. Surprise warred with anger. Was he mocking her, stating what was obvious and the daily source of her frustration and fear, that when all was said and done she would not succeed?

He didn't seem to be, for his face had lost that hard, impenetrable look she was already coming to know well. He was suddenly more open, even approachable.

Daring greatly, she said, "Of course it would. Sadly, the Gynfelin school has very little money."

"So I surmise. We will have to discuss that. Perhaps you would do me the honor of coming to tea this afternoon."

Morgana took a deep breath to steady herself and let it go. Along with it went her doubts, her caution and her hard-won attempts at the claustrophobic propriety her society insisted on. Damn them all if she seriously had a chance to improve her school.

"I would be delighted."

So was Mrs. Mulroon when she heard Morgana was coming to visit. She outdid herself preparing tea. When the marquess saw it he laughed out loud. That earned him a chiding glance from Sebastian, who paused in the midst of laying out plates heaped with exquisite sandwiches and small pastries.

"Cook was very impressed with Miss Penrhys."

"So I see," David said. "I don't recall her ever going to such lengths before."

"Like everyone else, she needs inspiration."

"Is that how she finds Miss Penrhys, inspiring?"

Sebastian straightened and surveyed the table. He nodded once, approvingly. "I would say that is apt, wouldn't you, sir?"

The marquess made a noncommittal sound. He settled himself to wait. Morgana arrived precisely on time. Sebastian allowed himself a small smile as he showed her into the library. The doors to the outside were flung open, admitting the fertile scents of the awakening garden. Sunlight fell gently over the gleaming leather bindings of the books, across the polished mahogany furnishings, pooling at the feet of the man who rose, tall and powerful, as she entered.

"My lord," she murmured.

"Miss Penrhys," he replied. He could have said anything, so distracted was he by her appearance. She was dressed as she had been that morning in the schoolroom, which was to say badly. But the walk to the manor had dislodged strands of her willful hair and brought a bright flush to her cheeks. She looked vividly alive, entrancingly female and thoroughly, utterly desirable.

"Won't you sit down?" he suggested. She didn't seem to hear him at first. Indeed, their distraction appeared mutual. But after a heartbeat or two, she sank gracefully onto the high-backed leather couch.

Sebastian poured, which was just as well, since neither of them thought of it. He hovered, offering plates of this and that, and when they were at last provided for, saw himself out.

David set his plate aside, ignored the tea and looked at Morgana. He had the odd sense that he could go on doing that for a very long time. But she avoided his eyes, and the flush to her cheeks had taken on a hint of embarrassment. He did not want her to be uncomfortable. That much he knew. What he *did* want wasn't so clear to him, but perhaps time would remedy that.

"About the school," he said.

"Yes, the school." She seized on it with relief. "Were you really serious about helping?"

"Of course. Did you think otherwise?"

"I did wonder," she admitted. "Men of your standing don't often take an interest in educating the so-called lower classes."

"So-called?" he repeated, his eyebrows lifting. He had never thought much about class distinctions, but then he didn't have to. He was neatly situated at the top of the pile, and what went on below hadn't concerned him overmuch. At least not until now.

"They are lower only in the sense that their opportunities are so restricted and they are taught to have such low expectations for themselves. If you tell a child often enough that he isn't very bright and can't amount to much, he will believe you, even though it simply isn't true. These children are as intelligent and capable as any you could find in far more favored circumstances."

"I have very little experience with children of any sort. If you say they are intelligent, then so they are."

Morgana stared at him, momentarily at a loss. She had expected to argue this point in detail, certain that he would oppose the idea that the children of peasants were no different from those his own class spawned.

"More tea?" the marquess inquired pleasantly. Since she had yet to touch her cup, it was clear he was amusing himself, but she couldn't object. So far everything was going wonderfully.

"The school needs everything," she said, having already decided that this was a classic case of in for a penny, in for a pound. "As you saw, there are no desks, only benches, and those are so crowded that by the end of the day some of the children are sitting on the floor. The building is in disrepair—several windows are broken and the walls are in need of caulking. As for the outhouse, I will say only that it is desperately overdue for a cleaning. In addition, we have few books, almost no writing materials, and nothing at all with which to teach them about the wider world."

The marquess frowned. "I checked the ledgers after I came back this morning. While the money allocated for the school hasn't been precisely generous, it seems as though it should have gone farther."

Morgana took a deep breath. It was now or never. "Perhaps it would have if Squire Kennard had not placed himself in charge of its disbursement. He has repeatedly rejected my requests while insisting that parents with children in the school pay higher fees. The result is that there are several children who should be attending but can't. Meanwhile, the school itself is going to rack and ruin.''

''It seems the squire and I need to have a chat,'' David said softly. The mildness of his tone made it all the worse. A tremor ran down Morgana's back as she glanced at him. His expression was perfectly controlled, but beneath it she caught glimpses of anger so deep it frightened her.

''There is nothing unusual about him,'' she said, seeking some way to minimize what she seemed to have inadvertently provoked. ''Many people would behave the same way.''

''Perhaps, but that isn't the point. He did it here and now, to *my* people, and for that he will have to answer.''

When she started to say something more, he raised a hand in a gesture as natural as it was commanding. ''You will prepare a list of everything needed. Don't stint. If you think it would be useful, write it down. So far as repairing the building is concerned, from what I saw this morning it wouldn't be worth the effort. Work will begin immediately on a new one.''

Was she dreaming? Morgana resisted the temptation to pinch herself, and nodded instead. Later, when it all sank in, she would be overjoyed. But for the moment all she could think of was what a huge difference money and power made. Anger stirred in her. Life really was shockingly unfair.

''What troubles you?'' the marquess asked.

''Nothing.''

''Nonsense, something has you irked. Come for a walk in the garden and tell me all about it.''

Morgana shook her head. "I have a list to make."

"Surely it can wait a few minutes. Besides, what sort of host would I be if I let a guest leave so obviously displeased?"

"I am not at all displeased," Morgana insisted even as he rose and held out a hand to her. What wayward self lurked in the hidden parts of her mind? Before she could stop herself, she rested her fingers in his and allowed him to draw her upright.

Allowed might be too strong a word. She had the impression no one allowed the marquess to do anything. He released her when they stepped from the house into the garden. She was grateful for that, as it let her make some pretense of normality.

Long ago, the manor's gardens had been laid out with care and foresight, and formal flower beds were interspersed with gravel paths and here and there a pretty fountain. Neglect had thrown much into disrepair, but already the effort to reclaim could be seen. Several old men whom Morgana recognized as being from the village were hard at work, pruning and weeding, their gnarled hands etched with soil.

"Do you really intend to stay on here?" she asked. The question was impertinent; his plans were none of her affair. Yet she asked all the same, driven by a curiosity she could not control.

The marquess shrugged. He did not appear to see the beauty of the gardens bathed in the bright radiance of the day. "One place is as good as another."

"That isn't true," she said promptly. "Many places, probably most, are far worse than this. London, for instance. It's crowded and grimy with hardly any air to breathe and no end of noise.''

"You've been there?"

"Well, no, not actually. But I've heard.''

"London isn't all bad. It has great vitality.''

Morgana eyed him dubiously. She wasn't a city person. "If you say so.''

He smiled faintly. "You would enjoy London if you gave it a chance.''

"That is hardly likely to happen. Do you find Gynfelin too confining, too ordinary?''

"No,'' he said and was honest enough to admit, if only to himself, that he might if he hadn't been able to pick up and go at any moment. "Do you?''

"Sometimes,'' she admitted. "It's too easy to forget about the wider world here. Events that are really of no importance take on false significance.''

"Your experience of yesterday evening, for instance?''

"It was very petty,'' she admitted. "I would just as soon forget about it.''

"Presuming you are allowed to. In my experience, women like Lady Kennard nurture grudges the way those old men over there nurture flowers. Unfortunately, the results are far less benign.''

"She doesn't frighten me,'' Morgana insisted. "All I care about is the school, and she cannot deny me that.''

The marquess did not reply directly. Strictly speaking she was correct. He paid for the Gynfelin school, therefore he controlled it. It didn't stretch credence too far to suspect Morgana was reminding him of that deliberately. But he also suspected that she underestimated her own vulnerability. Lady Kennard could make life very unpleasant for her. It was definitely past time for a chat with the squire.

But first he could enjoy a few stolen moments strolling with Morgana in the garden. For all her fire and will, there was a reservoir of peace deep within her. Looking at her, he felt as though he was gazing into a great well of quiet strength. Odd given the fragile exterior, but there it was all the same.

In a tree high above them, a lark burst into song. Morgana turned her head to look at it. Sunlight caught the curve of her cheek and slid caressingly down the slender line of her throat.

The marquess resisted the urge to follow that same path. He was powerfully drawn to her, there was no sense even trying to deny that. But he also held hard to a code of honor that made it impossible to take advantage of anyone dependent on him. In a very real sense, and whether she liked it or not, Miss Morgana Penrhys was under his protection.

Not for the first time, he considered that fate had a damnable sense of humor. If there was a god, and he'd had ample reason of late to doubt that, he was surely laughing at the cosmic joke he'd perpetrated when he created hapless mankind.

Women were a different story, of course. Whatever god had created them had been deadly serious. Which was why, when it came down to it, they seemed to have all the advantages.

If men agreed on anything at all, it was that women must not know how disconcerting they could be.

Composing himself as best he could, the marquess began a discussion of the garden that continued until the sun began to slant westward and Morgana took her leave. She went with more reluctance than she cared to admit. When she regained her cottage, she made herself a cup of chamomile tea mixed with a hint of rosemary, a remedy she had found infallible for clearing muddled heads. Up until now.

The tea sat beside her on the worn table, pale curls of steam fading haplessly away, as she struggled to make her list. The neat black rows of script accumulated slowly. In between came thoughts of the man who could hold a flowering anemone so tenderly in his hand that not a single petal was damaged and yet who could act with such deliberate violence to subdue a brute like Trelawney.

There was much contradiction in him, she decided. A small voice in the back of her mind murmured that the same could be said of her. She ignored it and concentrated more firmly on her list. It was midnight before it was done. She sat back and regarded the sheets of paper with some surprise. Had she really thought of so much? If the marquess agreed to half, the Gynfelin school would be the best of its kind in Wales if not in all of Britain.

And why not, she thought with a faint smile as she tumbled, weary but exultant, into bed. With him, all things seemed possible.

That tempting thought followed her into sleep and made of her dreams a marvel she would not, no matter how hard she tried, manage to forget.

Chapter Eight

Even as Morgana moved swiftly to insure that her students would benefit from the marquess's unexpected generosity, someone else in the village of Gynfelin was also acting without delay. Lady Kennard bested her own record for destroying reputations. The day after the spring fete, while she yet reclined in bed recovering from the excitement of it, she received several of her women friends. They clustered around like so many overstuffed magpies, picking up the glittering bits of slander she tossed their way.

"They left together," Lady Kennard said, "or the next thing to it. Really, I can't get over how blatant it was. Has all decency and propriety gone out the window?"

A hum of pleasant excitement assured her of her audience's full attention.

"Shocking," Mrs. Armbruster proclaimed. The reverend's good wife sat in the place of honor, an ornate armchair drawn up beside the bed within easy reach of the pot of chocolate on a nearby table. Her round face was flushed, and her eyes gleamed with satisfaction. She had never liked the snooty Miss Penrhys and resented her husband's fondness for the creature. Whatever she could do to aid and abet Lady Kennard would be not merely her duty but her pleasure.

"One can't really blame the marquess," Lady Kennard went on smoothly. "For all his rank, he is only a man."

Heads swiveled as the dozen or so women exchanged meaningful glances. Such a shame, all things considered, for the marquess was a handsome figure of a man and devastatingly rich, to boot. No, he wasn't to blame at all. It was that hussy, that insufferable Morgana Penrhys who was always going on and on about the poor as though anyone really gave a fig for them. Being among the gentry ought to mean being comfortable and secure, complacent in the knowledge that all was right in one's own little world. She robbed them of that, forcing them to acknowledge the injustice that lurked around every corner. It was time for her to pay.

"I do think matters will have to be taken in hand," Mrs. Armbruster said. "We can't expect the lower classes to comprehend what is going on since their own morals are, shall we say, shaky?"

Lady Kennard sipped her chocolate and nodded. "We shall have to guide them to a proper understanding. Obviously, they cannot leave their children in that woman's care."

"Obviously," Mrs. Armbruster agreed.

"Obviously," the assembled ladies chorused.

Lady Kennard sat back against her lace-tufted pillows and smiled her satisfaction. All was going exactly as she decreed. She couldn't think of when she had enjoyed herself more.

Morgana presented her list to the marquess the following day. She called at teatime, half hoping he would not be in. When Sebastian assured her that not only was he on the premises but that he would be happy to receive her, she had to resist the impulse to thrust the list into the butler's hands, mutter her excuses and run down the road. That was really too absurd. She was a grown woman, secure in her spinsterhood and, moreover, imbued with a mission. Propriety could not be allowed to stand in her way.

Sebastian, she promptly discovered, was prone to exaggeration. Strictly speaking, his lordship was not on the premises. He was in the stables, looking over that huge black stallion he had been riding when he came out of the mist to terrify Trelawney. The horse snorted as Morgana entered the low, whitewashed building. She hung back near the doorway, trying not to notice how perfectly horse and man suited each other. Both were magnificent creatures, large, well muscled and endowed with proud spirit. The stallion raised its head, eyes flashing red, and stared directly at Morgana. The marquess turned and looked in the same direction.

"Miss Penrhys," he said, his voice low and slightly rough.

"I am sorry to disturb you," she said quickly. "Mr. Levander sent me down here, but he didn't say you were busy."

"I'm not," David replied. He gave the stallion a final pat and walked toward her through streaks of sunlight filled with dancing dust motes.

He glanced at the papers in her hand and smiled. "You've been busy."

"I was afraid you would change your mind." She frowned suddenly. "You haven't, have you?"

"Not at all," he assured her, thinking again of pearls. Her skin had a fine translucent hue tinged with the softest pink, like the first light of dawn. Her lips, he couldn't help but notice, were full and soft. She had managed to achieve some order in her hair, but already tendrils were slipping loose. He resisted the impulse to catch one in his hand and reached for the papers instead.

"This seems quite comprehensive," he said dryly. If she had forgotten anything, it hadn't been invented yet.

Very much on her dignity, she replied, "I believe in being thorough."

"Good. Now do you have an estimate of cost?"

"No," Morgana admitted. "Since I've never had an opportunity to buy such things before, I'm not really sure how dear they are." She hesitated, looking at him. "I suppose I should have thought of that."

"Not at all. I will be going into Glamorgan on Saturday." He named the nearest large town to Gynfelin. "I can begin making inquiries then. Perhaps you would care to accompany me." The invitation was offered on the spur of the moment, but he saw no reason to withdraw it. He had business in Glamorgan apart from the school. She could visit the several bookstores in the town and begin ordering the materials herself while he attended to other things. It was an efficient use of both their time.

"That is very kind of you," Morgana said when he had explained his purpose. "I teach a half day but the rest is free."

They would have spoken further, but Sebastian stuck his head in a moment later to announce that Squire Kennard had come calling. The marquess grimaced. He inclined his dark head to Morgana. "Saturday."

She nodded, watching as he strode toward the manor. Sebastian gave her a quick, almost conspiratorial smile and trotted after him. Morgana repressed a spurt of pity for the hapless squire. She took the long way back to the road, well away from the house, not wishing to hear anything that might be going on within.

As it happened, she received a full report from Elizabeth Gareth. The new housekeeper was waiting for her when Morgana returned from the school the next day. It had been an unusually quiet day with several of the children absent. Typically, this time of year brought fewer ailments, not more. If the absences kept up, she would have to contact the parents to find out the cause. But for the moment she could concentrate on welcoming her friend.

"Come in," she said as she opened the cottage door. Elizabeth was a slender woman with a pretty, if mild, face and hair gone prematurely gray. Although she was referred to as "missus" she had in fact never married. The title was given automatically to any woman of a certain age. Morgana supposed that she herself would receive it before very much longer.

Mrs. Mulroon had provided another basket crammed with the best from her kitchen. Morgana's stomach rumbled at the good smells. She laughed and shook her head ruefully. "I am becoming very spoiled."

"Oh, I doubt that," Elizabeth said. She smiled gently at the younger woman. "You've been working all day. Sit down and let me get the tea."

Morgana hated to admit it but she was tired. Of late, she'd had too little sleep, and what she got had been hardly restful. The thought of that darkened her cheeks. She was glad that Elizabeth had her back turned and couldn't see.

By the time the other woman returned with the tea, Morgana had recovered herself. She sliced fragrant poppy-seed cake as Elizabeth poured. When the two were settled, Elizabeth took a delicate sip from her cup, set it down carefully and said, "Have you seen the squire lately?"

Morgana shook her head. "Not since the fete." She wrinkled her nose. "And I hardly saw him then. He was too much in his lady's shadow."

Elizabeth laughed. "When you look for him next, you may have to search. I understand he's at least several inches shorter than he used to be."

"What do you mean?"

"Only that his lordship took that much off him and possibly more when they spoke yesterday."

Morgana's eyes widened. For the briefest moment, her conscience twinged. She really should be above this. Fortunately, she wasn't. "What happened?"

Briefly, Elizabeth told her. "I don't know all, of course, because they met in the library and I was upstairs counting linen. But Owen said later—what a lovely boy, by the way—he said that when the squire came out he was white as one of the sheets. His lordship looked the same as always, but Owen heard him say, just as the squire was leaving, that he expected full restitution. Now what does that mean, do you suppose?"

Without hesitation, Morgana said, "He wants the money back that the squire was supposed to spend on the school and didn't."

"Is that the way of it? Oh, my, her ladyship won't like that, not one little bit."

"I'm sure she won't, but it doesn't sound as though the squire will have much choice."

"About the school, what's this I hear about the marquess deciding to make improvements?"

Morgana laughed. "Does anything pass you by?"

"Not really. When you're in service, you learn to keep an ear to the ground. Speaking of which…" She paused a moment, looking at Morgana before she said gently, "Lady Kennard is already very bitter toward you. This will only make it worse."

"There's nothing I can do about that," Morgana said sadly. She had the usual desire to be liked, but she accepted that couldn't always be the case.

"I know there isn't," Elizabeth said, not unkindly. "But you must be careful. Refrain from invoking any more animosity if you can."

That was good advice from a good friend. Morgana wanted to follow it. But other things came first.

By Saturday, fully one third of Morgana's pupils were absent. Her worry for them was compounded by the fact that when she went to call at their homes to find out what was wrong their parents were uncommunicative. Doors were not precisely closed in her face, but they came close to it.

The remaining children were unusually subdued, even Willy Fergus who could always be counted on to liven up a day. Not now, though. He sat glum-faced with his eyes averted and, when she called on him, half jumped out of his skin.

That did it. As soon as school was over, Morgana set off to talk with Willy's mother, Wynne, the egg woman. Morgana found her behind her small but meticulously neat cottage, tending to the hens who were her livelihood. Wynne Fergus was a small, round woman with pale blond hair, worn hands and a strong, cheerful face. Intelligence shone from her. She nodded cordially to Morgana as she wiped her hands on her apron.

"I thought you might be by."

Morgana stepped over a pile of straw and picked up a bucket of feed. Automatically, she helped Wynne see to the cackling hens who pecked and pranced around their feet. When they had been properly cared for, the two women walked a little distance away. They sat down on a large stone fallen in the shade of an oak tree. Once the stone had been part of a standing circle, the remnants of which could still be seen around the village. Now it was no more than a convenient bench.

"I'm concerned about Willy," Morgana said.

Wynne smiled fondly. "What's the little hellion done now?"

"Nothing, that's the problem. He was very subdued today, even sad. Has something happened to cause that?"

Wynne looked at her steadily, as though weighing her judgment. "Aye," she said at length. "He overheard the Right Reverend Mrs. Armbruster saying I shouldn't let him go to school anymore, least not while you were teacher there."

"What?" Morgana exclaimed. "Why would she say such a thing?"

Wynne shrugged. "I've no idea except for what else she told me. Something about you being a fallen woman and unworthy to be entrusted with her children." She snorted. "As though she ever cared anything for them. I told her as much when I showed her the door. She won't be back here, but from what I hear, she's having better luck elsewhere."

"My God," Morgana whispered. "I can't believe this is happening."

"You'd better believe it, lass," Wynne said gently. "Lady Kennard's the one calling the shots. She's determined to have you out, and that old harridan Armbruster's only too happy to help."

"But why? I haven't done anything!"

"Wouldn't matter if you had. You're a damn fine teacher, and anyone with any sense knows it. The trouble is that enough people in this village are dependent on the squire for their livelihood that they don't dare go against him or his wife."

Morgana shook her head wearily. She felt overwhelmed by the realization that so much anger and vitriol could be turned against her. Perhaps she had been naive, but she had never really thought it possible.

"What am I going to do?" she murmured.

Wynne put out a large, capable hand and patted hers gently. "Whatever you have to, lass. That's the way of the world." She paused delicately before adding, "'Tis the squire people know, him with his ties to the mines and able to get men work there when they're desperate enough." Bitterness crept into her voice for her brothers had walked that path. "But 'tis the marquess who rules, even though he's been little seen so far. People need to be more aware of him, then they wouldn't be so inclined to fear Squire Kennard."

"I'm going to Glamorgan on Saturday with the marquess," Morgana said.

Wynne's eyes brightened. "Are you then? That's fine. You can put a bug in his ear."

Morgana laughed at the notion, but it was undeniably tempting. He could solve her problem so easily. Why should she hesitate to involve him?

Because there was some small degree of truth to the accusations against her, that was why. She realized it deep within. Not that it justified what Lady Kennard and Mrs. Armbruster were doing, but it did make her defense more difficult. Appealing to him for more than better financing for the school meant effectively asking for his protection. She suspected he would give it, but at what cost to them both?

With Saturday rapidly approaching, Morgana mulled over what to do. The number of children at the school seemed to have stabilized at just over half its normal enrollment. Visits to parents continued to be unproductive. Late Friday afternoon, as Morgana came out of the butcher shop, she saw the Reverend Armbruster across the street and considered going to speak to him. But he saw her first and scuttled away. Back to his old books, no doubt, where he felt a good deal safer.

She bit back a sigh and went on her way. Several people on the winding village street glanced at her kindly. She even received a few shy smiles. But she was also the target of averted eyes and even cold glares. Gynfelin seemed about evenly split on the subject of its schoolteacher. Some of the residents were only too happy to see her as a fallen woman. Others, remembering her kindness to their children, felt differently. The trouble was that they were neither numerous nor bold enough to make a difference.

Morgana slept badly that night. The following morning, she took the children on a nature walk through the field near the school, then brought them back and dismissed them early. She went to her cottage to ready herself for the trip to Glamorgan. Shortly after noon, the rumble of carriage wheels on the path drew her to the door.

His lordship had apparently decided that the fine day called for an open phaeton, which he drove himself, holding the reins of a fine pair of matched grays. The equipage would have been well suited to the nobler streets of London. In little Gynfelin, in front of the schoolteacher's cottage, it had a fairy-tale aura.

Feeling almost like Cinderella, except for her sensible brown boots, Morgana allowed herself to be helped into the high seat. The marquess took his place beside her. He grinned when he saw her surprise.

"Did you expect a nice staid brougham?"

"Perish the thought," she murmured.

He laughed and spurred the grays on. They left Gynfelin amid swirling dust and sharp-eyed glances.

Chapter Nine

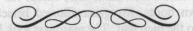

Glamorgan was a grimy town in the center of what had once been a verdant valley of the same name. Generations of Welsh men and women had farmed it lovingly until the coal barons arrived. Then the land was torn open, its bounty ripped from it and the stark white scars left scattered over the valley like bones whitening in the sun.

Those scars were about the only part of Glamorgan that remained white. The rest bore tracings of the coal dust that hung in the air and settled on every surface. Even the laundry hanging outside the tiny workers' houses they passed had a dingy look to it.

"Now I remember why I never come here," Morgana murmured.

The marquess frowned. His ownership of vast tracts of nearby land did not make him any more familiar with the area than a man who had no connection to it at all. He had, in his ignorance, presumed Glamorgan would be a smaller version of the industrial towns he had seen in the south of England. To a certain extent it was, but the coal stamped everything with its own inescapable reality.

"It is dirty," he said as though to himself.

"Can you imagine what it is like to live here day after day?" Morgana demanded. "To never see the sun except through a haze of coal dust? To never really be clean?"

"No," he said, before she could continue. He was in no mood for a political debate, no matter how well-intentioned. "We will stop here," he added, drawing up before an inn that looked at least middling respectable. A stable boy rushed out, all agog at the phaeton, and took the horses' leads with commendable respect.

"See that they're watered and brushed," the marquess said, "and there'll be another for you." He flipped the boy a guinea, which caused the lad's eyes to bulge.

"Right you are, sir. Tad's my name, and I'll take proper care of them, that's for sure." He shot them a grin made all the more engaging for the lack of two front teeth. "If you and the lady be looking for lodgings, the Bluebird's the best in town. The beer's never watered, the food won't kill you, and the beds are pretty much clean."

"And people claim civilization hasn't penetrated this far west," the marquess said after they had left the boy. "Who could ask for a better recommendation than that?"

Morgana decided the question required no answer and held her tongue. It seemed the wisest course under the circumstances. The notion that she and the marquess might have been looking for a place to stay together unsettled her. She was still resolved on her mission, proper or not, but she was beginning to realize how they might look to other people.

"I have the names of several bookstores," she said when they had emerged onto the street in front of the inn. "As you have other matters to attend to, I will take my leave. What time would you like to meet?"

He smiled faintly and handed her a card on which an address was neatly penned. "Be there in three hours. Will that give you enough time?"

She nodded, staring at the card. "Who is this?"

"A builder I intend to engage for the new school."

"Oh, I see."

"I thought it might be wise for you to be present at our discussion."

"That is very thoughtful of you."

His smile deepened. "Don't sound so surprised. It wounds my vanity. Oh, by the way—" He held out a thick leather folder.

"What is this?" she asked.

"Money. You can't buy anything without it. Whatever you do select, tell the merchants they are responsible for delivering it to Gynfelin. I don't want to find you struggling under a load of bundles, understand?"

"Perfectly," Morgana said under her breath. She took the wallet gingerly.

"Don't flash it around," the marquess cautioned.

"I'm not a child. I know how to take care of myself."

He looked at her doubtfully. "And don't lose the address. I'll see you in three hours."

Morgana bridled at his arbitrary tone, but that was no more than a reflex, quickly gone. Far more important was his generosity. Because of him, she held within her hands the means to help her students.

"Thank you," she said softly.

He frowned. "Enough of that. Get started or you won't have enough time."

She hesitated an instant more, wishing he would leave first, but he held his ground. She had no choice but to walk away, vividly conscious of his eyes on her back. Conscious also, as she had never been before, that she swayed as she walked. How was it she had not noticed that before? Trying to control the motion only made it worse. She was bright red by the time she rounded the corner.

The marquess released a sigh. The more time he spent with the sharp-tongued Miss Penrhys, the more he realized that she presented a significant problem. He seemed to have worked his way into a corner in his feelings for her. On the one side was desire, on the other honor. At the moment, they appeared irreconcilable.

That being the case, he did what any sensible man would do. He turned his mind to other things. His first appointment was to look over farming equipment he was thinking of acquiring. It had not escaped his notice that his tenants still relied on methods that were at least a generation or two out of date. They might not accept change readily, but he was determined to guide them to it.

He found the equipment supplier without difficulty and was shortly involved in a detailed discussion about the attributes of various types of plows. Six months before such a conversation would have been inconceivable to him. Now he found it genuinely interesting.

Morgana had similar success at the bookstores she visited. Once their owners realized she was serious about buying—and in quantity—they fell all over themselves to accommodate her. Some items on her list would have to be ordered from elsewhere but a gratifying number were immediately available. She arranged for their delivery to Gynfelin.

It was midafternoon when she left the last store. She was tired and thirsty. Spying a small tea shop across the street, she headed toward it when a man suddenly appeared before her. He was of medium height and had a slender build. His square face might have been handsome but for the layer of grime etched into it. His hair appeared gray, but that was from the pervasive coal dust. His clothes were shabby and reeked of the sulfurous smell associated with the mines.

Morgana took a quick step back, intending to go around him. The man held out his hand. "Wait," he said. "Be you Miss Penrhys?"

She nodded slowly. The man was unknown to her, she was sure of that. How had he recognized her?

"Hugh Dawkins is the name," he said. "My sister be Wynne Fergus over to Gynfelin. She sent word you were coming into town today and said I might find you here."

"Oh, of course. I'm sorry, I thought—"

"I know what you thought, but I'm no cutthroat, I promise." He managed a smile that transformed his worn features. Morgana realized that he was younger than he first appeared. More seriously, he added, "I need to talk with you, Miss Penrhys. It's important."

"All right," she said. "I was about to have some tea." She gestured toward the shop.

Hugh Dawkins laughed. The sound wheezed in his throat and turned into a cough. He turned his head away for a moment. When he turned back, his look was somber. "I can't go in there, Miss Penrhys. They wouldn't serve me. It's a lot to ask, but I know a place just around the corner. It's a working man's pub, not fancy but respectable. They could probably manage a pot of tea."

"That will be fine," Morgana said.

He looked surprised by her ready acceptance. "My sister said you were different."

"I'll take that as a compliment."

He laughed again. "Wynne always was a good judge of character."

They walked a short distance to the pub. It was as Dawkins described, plain but clean. He showed her into the lounge reserved for women and men prepared to behave themselves. The bar was strictly for men and attracted the rowdier sort. It was separated from the lounge by a long wooden counter. Behind the counter was a very fat, very cheerful woman who gave Morgana an open-mouthed stare.

"A pot of tea for the lady, if you please, Winnona," Dawkins said. "And I'll be having my usual."

"Pot o' tea?" the woman repeated as though she had never heard of such a thing. She continued to stare at Morgana until abruptly recalled to herself. "Oh, aye, of course. Have a seat then. Pleased to have you, miss. Tea won't be a minute."

"Winnona's a good sort," Dawkins said when they had found a table set in a small alcove that afforded some privacy. "She won't say anything about your being here."

Morgana nodded. She couldn't pretend that her behavior was at all commonplace.

"I can't stay long," she said as she settled into her place. "I have to meet someone."

Dawkins took the chair across from her. He stared at her so closely that she shifted slightly. "The marquess?" he asked.

"What makes you think that?"

"Wynne said you were coming in with him. She says he's helping to make the school better. Is that true?"

"Yes, it is."

"Why's he doing that?"

"To be kind, I suppose, although he denies it."

"Nobs are never kind," Dawkins said firmly. "They just do what suits them. Don't have to tell you to watch yourself, do I?"

"No, Mr. Dawkins, you most certainly do not."

He grinned again. "Don't get riled. If he wants to help, that's fine. More important question is do you trust him?"

"Yes," Morgana said so promptly that she surprised herself. Apparently, she didn't even have to think about it. "Yes, I do."

"Why?"

"I'm not sure exactly." How to explain about the gentleness with which he had cared for her injured cheek, the excitement that coursed through her when he appeared at the fete, the sense whenever she was with him that something hitherto missing from her life was suddenly found?

"He took in a boy I was trying to help," she said, settling for that. "His name is Owen Trelawney. He's very intelligent and could have a good future, but his father was going to send him to the mines."

"Father? Would that be Thomas Trelawney?"

"It would. You know him?"

"Of him. He's gone to work for Lord Westerley."

"The mine owner? What is Trelawney doing for him?"

"Security, they call it. Oppression is what it really is. Trelawney got hired on by Jack Farr. Farr's job is to make sure the workers stay in line. Nothing's allowed to interfere with Lord Westerley bleeding this land white and everyone in it as well."

Morgana was aware of Lord Philip Westerley. He owned most of the mines in Glamorgan, although he was never seen in the area. Rumor had it he lived in a palatial mansion outside London from which he rarely strayed except to visit his equally luxurious town house in the city. Farr was his enforcer, the man who made sure nothing interfered with the smooth flow of profits into Lord Westerley's avaricious hands.

"I'm not surprised," she said slowly. "That's the kind of job Trelawney would be well suited for."

She broke off as Winnona arrived with the tea and a small whiskey for Dawkins. Setting both in front of them, she allowed herself a quick, all-encompassing glance before disappearing behind the bar.

Morgana poured herself a cup as Dawkins lifted his glass. "To better times," he said.

She caught the sadness in his eyes that suggested he feared they would never come, but behind that sadness was the dark flash of buried strength.

"You said there was something important you wanted to talk about," she prompted.

"Aye, there is. We've trouble here, bad trouble. It's never been pleasant working in the mines but of late it's become much worse. Farr's put the squeeze on. Every man's quota has been upped, we're expected to work at a faster pace than ever, and there's no regard at all being given to safety. It's only a matter of time before there's a serious accident, unless something changes quick."

"I see," Morgana said slowly. She had always known that conditions were grim in the mines, hence her struggle to keep Owen and the others from them. But now it appeared that struggle was more essential than ever. "Do you have any idea why Farr is doing this?"

Dawkins shrugged. He took a sip of his whiskey before he said, "There's only rumors, but they all have to do with Lord Westerley's gambling debts being so heavy that he's frantic for funds. The only way he can get them is to take them out of our hides."

"How do you imagine I can help? Mind you, I want to, but what can I do?"

"You can speak for us to the marquess. If he's smart enough to know that our people need better education, maybe he'll also realize that in the long run there's more money to be made by treating us decent. Men who are beaten down and without hope can't work as well as men who see a chance for themselves and their families. Somebody's got to get through to Westerley, to stop him. We can't do it but maybe the marquess can."

Morgana sat back against the cracked leather bench and stared at him. By all appearances, Hugh Dawkins was serious. He believed there was at least a chance that she could convince the marquess to consider the miners' plight.

Was there? She had persuaded him about the school, although truth be told that hadn't been very difficult. But that was a very small matter compared to what Dawkins had in mind. Besides, Westerley was of the same social class as the marquess, and such things tended to count more heavily than any other consideration.

"I don't know," she answered. "I can try, but I'm not sure he will agree."

"Just ask him to let me speak with him, that's all. One meeting is what I'm asking. If I can't persuade him then, I'll forget the whole thing."

"Forget Farr and what he's doing?" Morgana asked skeptically.

"No," Dawkins admitted. "I mean forget the chance that this can be worked out peacefully."

Her eyes widened in alarm. "What other alternative is there?"

He leaned forward across the table. Their eyes met. In his, she saw the fierce light of implacable resolve. "A strike, Miss Penrhys, that's what there is."

"Strikes are illegal. Every time someone has tried to call one, the police and the army have crushed it ruthlessly."

"Aye, I know, and I understand that could happen here. But there comes a time when a man simply has no other choice. We're at that point, unless the marquess can offer another way."

"That's a bit much to expect of someone who isn't even directly involved, don't you think?"

Dawkins shrugged. "Probably, but I still have to try."

And so did she, Morgana decided. She could not let Dawkins and the miners he represented go down the bloody road to a strike without exerting every ounce of effort she could muster to stop them.

"I'll speak with him today," she promised.

"Good. You can get word to me through Wynne."

They left the pub a short time later. "I'd walk you to where you're going," Dawkins said with a smile, "but I've involved you enough already."

"I'm glad you did," Morgana said honestly. As worried as she was, she would rather know what was happening than remain in ignorance.

She glanced at the watch pinned to her jacket. "It's later than I realized. I must go." He bade her farewell and disappeared down a back alley behind the pub. The swiftness with which he went drove home to her the care he must have to take. If Farr got wind of what

Dawkins was doing, his life would be in terrible danger.

Morgana reached the builder's offices a short time later. They were in a pretty Georgian building along Glamorgan's main street. The builder was obviously well-off, but even here the effects of the coal dust could be seen. The building must have once been the creamy stone popular in the area; now it was gray.

The marquess was already there. He rose as she entered. "You're late."

"I lost track of the time. Please excuse me."

David frowned. She was breathing more rapidly than normal, as though she had been running or at least walking very fast. Her cheeks were flushed, and her eyes were unusually bright. She looked very lovely, but he sensed an air of preoccupation about her that aroused his concern.

"Is something wrong?"

Morgana caught herself before she could reply too quickly. How could he possibly know?

"Why would anything be wrong?" As though to demonstrate how silly the notion was, she turned a dazzling smile on the young man who had risen from behind the desk.

"I do apologize. It's been some time since I was last in Glamorgan, but that's no excuse for being tardy. I hope I haven't caused a problem?"

He shook his head slowly, staring at her all the while with the wide-eyed, unblinking look that suggests the viewer has been confronted with something that is both unexpected and delightful.

"Not at all," he said, coming from around the desk. He was tall and well built, hardly so dominant as the marquess, but a good figure of a man if she had been disposed to notice such a thing, which truth be told she was not. All her attention remained focused, despite the direction of her eyes, on the dark man beside her. The other, lighter both in coloring and spirit, hardly existed as more than an insubstantial shadow.

But he, of course, did not know that. Taking her hand, he mustered his most engaging smile. "I am Charles Whitcomb, Miss Penrhys. It is a great pleasure to make your acquaintance. His lordship indicated you would be helping to plan the new school."

"I'm not sure I said exactly that," the marquess intervened, his tone just on the near side of chilled as though to hint at far icier winds banked and waiting. "It will be a simple building. Little planning is required."

Charles had the good sense to hear some, if not all, of what lay behind the words. Had his life up until that moment been different he might have heard it all and behaved more wisely. But he was the youngest son of loving parents, cosseted from birth, endowed with the best education and advancement money and influence could buy. For all that, he was not without talent and qualified genuinely as a pleasant man. That availed him nothing, however, when confronted with the far more complex and ultimately dangerous nature of the man who watched both other occupants of the room through narrowed eyes.

Morgana, on the other hand, heard it perfectly. She should not have, for strictly speaking she was of even less experience and worldliness than Charles Whitcomb. But hers was a far older spirit, endowed with lessons he was very far yet from learning.

Gently, she removed her hand. "Thank you, sir," she said. "But the marquess is quite correct, the building is simple, and truth be told, I fear I have little to contribute to its design."

She glanced at David as she spoke and saw the flash of satisfaction that sped across his stone-carved features. Insufferable man! Did he really expect to be toadied to like that? If she hadn't feared, for just a split second, that he might inflict some actual harm on the hapless Whitcomb, she would never have indulged him like that.

It was a foolish thought, really, for what harm could occur in a builder's office on the main street of a perfectly proper Welsh town on a perfectly pleasant afternoon?

The question lingered in her mind as they took their places around the table at the far end of the room. Several large sheets of paper were spread out, each showing a different view of a simple but elegant building.

"When you contacted me, sir," Charles explained, "I took the liberty of drawing up a few elevations. As I haven't actually seen the site, these will need adjustment. But I think the general design is well suited to its function."

"Novel idea, Mr. Whitcomb," the marquess said. His mood seemed to have improved in the past few minutes. He even gave Morgana a small smile in passing. "Too few architects seem to take any note of function at all. We have factories that look like palaces and are as uncomfortable as any of those ever built, churches that resemble warehouses with steeples unaccountably stuck on top of them, and town houses that appear intended as mausoleums rather than a place for the living to go about their ordinary tasks.''

''Indeed, your lordship, I couldn't agree more,'' Charles exclaimed. No toadying here, Morgana thought sourly, he was perfectly sincere. ''That was my great failing when I studied architecture. I could not absorb the idea that purpose mattered not at all, that all building was merely to glorify whoever happened to be paying for it.''

''Still someone must pay,'' the marquess pointed out. ''You recall I said you were not to stint. The best materials are to be used and fair wages to the laborers.''

''Absolutely, my lord. I can recommend several very good men. If we could begin immediately, the structure would be completed before summer.''

''Does that suit you, Miss Penrhys?'' the marquess inquired.

She sat straight-backed in the leather chair and looked anywhere but at him. ''Perfectly.''

Chapter Ten

They left the office a short time later and walked in the general direction of the inn. Morgana did not speak, nor did the marquess attempt conversation. But he did moderate his naturally long stride to better accommodate her. They walked, she thought, as though they were at ease in each other's company, when in fact nothing could be further from the truth.

Still, she had to find some way to overcome the prickly self-consciousness he provoked in her. Whatever her personal concerns, events demanded she put them aside.

"I must thank you again," she said, very properly. "My visit to the bookstores was very successful. New supplies should begin arriving in a few days. As for the new school building, it is more than I could have dreamed."

Her gratitude made him uncomfortable. He slowed his pace even further and glanced at her. "It's done, you don't have to go on thanking me for it."

"There's nothing wrong with thanks. If people were more appreciative of what they had, we would all be better off."

"Is that what you tell your students, or do you encourage them to strive for more?"

"Both," she said honestly. "I will never tell them to accept their lot in life, not while I'm so sure it can be improved."

He looked at her thoughtfully. "What about yourself? Does the same advice hold?"

Morgana hesitated. The question took her by surprise, but then so much about this man had the same effect that she really shouldn't be surprised by anything he said or did, if that made any sense, which she doubted, since making sense out of anything seemed to be slipping beyond her capabilities. It was such a simple question, two actually. The sort someone might ask out of mild interest, no more. Why then did they seem so fraught with meaning to her?

Was she content with her life? A week ago she would have said yes. She was doing work she loved and considered important. Despite its frustrations, she was achieving enough success to convince her that her hopes for the children were not at all unrealistic. Moreover, she had managed to stand against the almost irresistible tidal pull of convention that decreed women her age should be kept under the authority of an appropriate male. To a remarkable degree, she had achieved independence.

But that was all a week ago, and in the meantime a great deal had changed. Moment to moment, she was increasingly forced to acknowledge all that was missing from her life.

Love, for instance. Not the tender nurturing she felt for the children, but the passionate, enduring love of a woman for a man. And speaking of passion, the less said of it the better. Her dreams were eloquent enough on the subject.

"Is one ever truly accepting?" she asked, equivocating. "Yourself, for instance. Is there nothing in your life you would change?"

"A great deal," he said bluntly. She waited, hoping he would continue, but he did not. They reached the inn in silence. True to his promise, Tad had cared well for the grays. The boy accepted his second guinea with a broad smile. He raced off as though fearing his benefactor might have a change of mind.

They were beyond Glamorgan, on the road leading to Gynfelin, when Morgana said, "I need to speak with you." She had been thinking how to approach the subject of Dawkins and decided that directness was the only choice. The problem was how to find the opportunity. Once they reached the village, they would go their separate ways. She could hardly invite the marquess into her cottage, and to accept his hospitality at such an hour would invite questions she did not care to answer.

"We have been speaking," David pointed out. He glanced at her out of the corner of his eye, taking in her sudden paleness and the stillness that sat so unnaturally on her. "I was right, wasn't I?"

"What do you mean?"

"Back in what's-his-name's office when I asked you what was wrong."

"His name is Mr. Charles Whitcomb," Morgana said chidingly, "which you know full well. And yes, much as I hate to admit it, you were right."

"Why do you hate to admit it?"

"Because, to be perfectly frank, your arrogance needs no encouragement. It is quite sufficient unto itself."

He laughed, and for an instant looked at her so appreciatively that she felt herself warm. "By all means, be frank, Miss Penrhys. It is remarkably refreshing. Now tell me, what happened?"

Morgana looked at her hands, neatly folded in her lap. She searched for composure without any great success. "As I left the last bookstore, a man approached me. His name is Hugh Dawkins. He is the brother of a village woman who is my friend. Mr. Dawkins asked me to intercede on his behalf to arrange a meeting with you. I told him I was reluctant to do so and expressed doubt as to any effectiveness I might have, but he insisted that this was his only hope. Therefore, I agreed to try."

David drew back on the reins. He halted the grays in the middle of the road and turned his full attention on Morgana.

"Do you make a habit of being approached by strange men?"

"Of course I don't! What an awful thing to say."

"I didn't say, I asked, and I did so because there seems to be a certain pattern here. First I go out to inspect my property, the weather turns foul, and I head for home and hearth like any sensible man only to find myself suddenly riding to your rescue. Then Mr. Charles Whitcomb, who at our first meeting appeared to be a perfectly serious young man intent on his profession, turns out to be a blithering idiot who can't seem to do anything but stare at you. And now there's this Dawkins fellow. You do see my point?''

"No, I don't! This is absurd, not to mention highly insulting. You make me sound like some...some flirt, which is patently ridiculous. I am a schoolteacher and a spinster. My behavior has always been above reproach. How dare you suggest that—''

"Hush, Morgana.''

"What...?''

David sighed. He really shouldn't do this; it was absolutely wrong. He knew that right down to his aristocratic veins. But in those veins ran the blood of warriors, generation after generation of them, all well accustomed to taking whatever it was they happened to want. He wanted her, prickly Miss Morgana Penrhys, schoolteacher and—so laughable, this— spinster. God help him, he wanted her more than he could remember ever wanting anything.

His dark head moved swiftly, blotting out the sun. Her mouth was warm, infinitely soft and pliant. He was still in sufficient possession of himself not to deepen the kiss. It hinted at the barely banked fires of passion rather than revealing them.

He sat back slowly, surveying her. Her eyes were wide and luminous, her cheeks slightly flushed. Interestingly, she made no attempt to struggle, nor did she protest. She merely looked at him assessingly.

"Morgana," he said softly, "there's nothing to be afraid of."

Quite clearly, her voice just a shade high, she replied, "Don't be silly, of course there is. Not for you, perhaps, but certainly for me. Let us at least be honest about that."

The marquess had faced the savagery of battle. He had brought his men through if not hell, the closest thing on earth to it. He had faced down terror, dread, horror, shock and rage. But he had never confronted shame before, despite what all the rumors might suggest. The experience was singularly unsettling.

She was right, of course, and they both knew it. She had far more at risk than did he. The fact that she didn't immediately retreat in high offense, but stayed to consider the situation more or less calmly, said a great deal about where they stood with one another.

Much later, the marquess would realize that it was at that precise moment he banished any thought that he could enjoy a pleasant little fling with Miss Morgana Penrhys. She was made of much more serious—and sterner—stuff than that. Ah, well, he decided, it happened to the best of men. They coped; he could, too.

"I'm sorry," he said gently, "but I cannot remake the world."

Their eyes met. It seemed to him that she looked directly into him, as though seeking out the bright, immortal light that he had felt at rare moments at the center of his being. What she saw must have satisfied her for she nodded once, as though to herself.

"We must still speak of Mr. Dawkins. I did promise him."

"That was rude of me," the marquess admitted. It was as close as he would come to an outright apology, still not being convinced that he was in the wrong. She was a damnably attractive woman whether she realized it or not.

Morgana let it go. Under the circumstances, she had little choice. Her heart was beating so quickly she thought he must surely see it under the neatly buttoned jacket of her sensible brown serge suit. A part of her, standing off somewhere on the sidelines, marveled that she managed to appear so calm and self-possessed when inside she was anything but.

The world had just changed, suddenly and irrevocably. Somehow she had to find a way to deal with this new existence in which she found herself. Dawkins linked her to the old reality, the one that was all she had known up until a few moments ago. She grabbed hold of him, figuratively speaking, with both hands, and did her darnedest not to let go.

"Mr. Dawkins works in the mines," she said. "I gather he is one of the unofficial leaders who have arisen among the men there. He wants to speak with you because he is very concerned about conditions. They have always been bad, but recently they have become much worse." She paused, drawing on her courage. "He says there will be a strike unless something changes quickly."

"A strike? He's mad. Doesn't he realize what that would lead to?"

"I think he does," Morgana said softly, "but he is desperate. So are they all."

David shook his head wearily. He had heard all this before, desperate men proposing desperate solutions that could only bring them even greater suffering. The British government from the crown on down was united in its determination to protect the rights of the rich and powerful. Social unrest of any sort was seen as intolerable. The government would do anything necessary to crush it.

"Your Mr. Dawkins is courting disaster," he said.

"He isn't *my* Mr. Dawkins, and as for disaster, if he is right, that is going to happen anyway."

The marquess picked up the reins again and chucked them lightly across the backs of the grays. As the phaeton moved forward, he asked, "What does he imagine I can do to prevent it?"

"I don't know," Morgana admitted. "Apparently, he heard about your willingness to improve the school and thought that might indicate a general concern for the welfare of the less fortunate. Still, even if that is the case, I have to admit you would be very limited in any influence you could bring to bear."

David shot her a narrow glance. Reluctant as he was to admit it, he liked sparring with her almost as much as he would undoubtedly enjoy other pastimes. With a handful of words, she put him on his mettle to prove that he actually did care about others and that his influence extended beyond the narrow reaches of Gynfelin. Nicely done. He took a moment to wonder if she played chess before replying.

"Indeed," he said. "Did you tell your Mr. Dawkins that?"

"No," she admitted. "All I said was that I would try my best." She fell silent, waiting for what she expected to be his refusal. Men of his class simply did not associate with the likes of Hugh Dawkins. They most especially did not side with such men against the overwhelming forces of the British establishment. The gulf was too big, the chasm too wide, the—

"All right," the marquess said. "I'll see him."

"You will?" Morgana exclaimed. She could not hide her amazement. "But why?"

"Perhaps because I'm not quite as insensitive as you credit me. I happen to know something about Lord Philip Westerley who, the last I heard, owns the Glamorgan mines. The man's a poor gambler and a worse tippler. He should be kept on a very short lead."

"I never said you were insensitive," Morgana pointed out as she digested the rest of it. He knew Westerley and he had a bad opinion of him. There might actually be hope after all.

"That's true," the marquess acknowledged. "You didn't." He permitted himself the smallest smile of satisfaction before urging the grays on.

Wynne Fergus made Morgana repeat herself three times before she believed her. When she did at last, she sat down on the stump of a tree, her apron twisted in her hands, and shook her head.

"I don't know what to say. Hugh's taking an awful chance."

"I know," Morgana said softly. It was Sunday. She had just come from services. Although she tried not to let it, the scene at the church still preoccupied her.

She had been snubbed, plain and simple. No one, not a single person, had so much as nodded to her. Even the Reverend Armbruster from his perch at the altar had managed to keep his eyes from wandering to her. He stumbled more than usual during his sermon, and he looked undeniably relieved when she didn't join the line after services to exchange greetings with him. As for the rest, they gifted her with a variety of ugly looks, sneers and mutterings she would remember for a very long time.

All of which was unfortunate, but she must not allow it to distract her from the more important matters at hand.

"Mr. Dawkins is doing what he must," she said. "I admit to being surprised when the marquess said he would speak with him, but that is a step in the right direction."

"Aye," Wynne replied. "Maybe his lordship can talk some sense into that stubborn head. I swear I was never able to."

She stood up, holding herself stiffly to contain her fear, and said, "I'll get word to him right enough and I thank you for your help. Take a nice dozen eggs home, won't you?"

Morgana agreed reluctantly because she understood that pride was involved. A debt had been incurred, some recompense must be offered. To do otherwise would shame Wynne, who had little more than pride to armor her life.

Later, when she had returned to her cottage, Morgana cooked herself a frugal dinner and ate it methodically, all the while keeping her thoughts at bay. Not until her stomach was properly filled did she sit down in front of the small fire and force herself to confront what she must.

Her time in Gynfelin might be coming to an end. What Wynne had told her about the attitude among the gentry could no longer be avoided. If it continued, she would lose her ability to help the children in any meaningful way. Her new school, her fine materials, would all be for naught.

Her eyes burned. She blinked hard and told herself not to be a ninny. The situation was as it was. She had to deal with that rather than waste time wishing for what could not be. The scene in the phaeton kept coming back to her. Beyond the kiss itself, what stunned her was her own reaction to it. She had not offered the least resistance or even the pretense of surprise.

Surely the marquess, as experienced as he was, could not have been left in any doubt that she was, at the very least, susceptible to him. Yet he had made no attempt to take advantage of her. On the contrary, to be fair, he had dealt with her far more gently than she had any right to expect. He had even gone so far as to agree to meet Dawkins, although truth be told, she had rather pushed him into that.

Now she was in his debt and, like Wynne, she would have to do something to settle her account. Deeper and deeper, she thought wearily as she poked the fire. With each passing moment, she seemed more firmly enmeshed with the formidable marquess and more in danger of losing all that had been until very recently at the center of her life. Whichever way she looked, disaster seemed to loom.

The fire sputtered and crackled, wood falling into ash. Morgana sat in her chair for a long time, watching it. She stared into the flames as she always had done as a child when beset by any difficulty. Her father had teased her about that, but her mother had taken a different view. Once—once only—she had mentioned that in the old time people believed fire could open paths for those gifted and courageous enough to follow.

"There's Otherlife in flame," she'd said, using an old Welsh word for things unseen, "not like us but from the one beginning all the same."

Part of Morgana, the part her father had trained in the rigorous life of the mind, rejected such thoughts. But another, stronger part knew them to be true. There were aspects of existence that could not be readily described. They were not seen or heard or touched. They simply were. At most, a person might feel them in a tremor up the spine or along the back of the neck, in a sudden wave of apprehension or exaltation, in those moments when the boundaries between worlds slipped and all things became possible.

Otherlife. The life before and beyond this. The beginning and the re-beginning, for there never was an end. Nature could be many things, but she was never wasteful. Nothing was ever truly done with.

Not even the wood burning brightly in the fire, being transformed into heat and smoke. And light. Dancing, shimmering, beckoning light.

"There are those that fear what lies beyond," Morgana's mother had said, "and I don't question why. They've the sense not to venture from the here and now lest they become lost. But you, you're different."

Holding her daughter on her lap, for Morgana had been very small, she stroked her fire-hued hair and smiled wistfully. "You've an old soul, child, as the wise ones used to say. And like all of them, you'll find your place in this world. But that's not to say it will be easy. Where your spirit leaps, you'll follow even though it land you on rocky ground."

Her mother always smelled of lavender, Morgana thought. She smiled sleepily, safe and content. The scent of lavender was all around her. She could feel her mother's hand gentle on her hair and knew again the piercing sweetness of being totally loved.

Without warning a well of sorrow opened inside her She knew again the anguished grief she had known five years before when her mother died. But the sorrow was fleeting. Hard on it, overwhelming and erasing it, was that recaptured sense of love. Her mother was so near, so very near. She had only to reach out her hand and she would surely touch her.

Her eyes opened. Her hand, pale and slim, was stretched toward the fire. Not close enough to be burned but near enough to feel the heat. She drew back, trembling slightly, and closed her eyes. When she opened them moments later, there had been a sift in the pattern, a refocusing of sorts. The world was back in place. But the memory of her mother's closeness lingered.

She did not remember going to bed but she must have done so for she woke as usual in her small alcove. Turning her head slightly, she looked out at an inverted bowl of blue untouched by the slightest cloud. It was a day of astonishing clarity when all debate seemed meaningless and only decisions remained.

She rose, dressed herself and went out into it.

Chapter Eleven

That day, the first of the supplies Morgana had ordered began to arrive. Eventually everything would have to be moved into the new building, but for the moment the children, those who were still coming, would be able to have their own books and writing tablets. She worked late into the afternoon putting everything away and was still at it when Owen burst in upon her.

"You're here," he said, struggling to catch his breath. "I couldn't find you at the cottage. I—"

"Owen, what's wrong?" She went toward him, her face wreathed in concern. Despite the better treatment of recent days, he was still only a slip of a boy, and his exertions had taxed his strength to the limit and beyond. "Here," she said as she pushed a bench under him, "sit down. What on earth has happened?"

"It's the marquess—" he began.

Morgana stopped breathing. For a blinding instant she was aware of the world only through a shimmering veil of the most acute pain she had ever experienced. It eased, thankfully, for it surely would have killed her if it had not. But she was still left weak and trembling.

She sat down on the bench next to Owen, took a deep breath and said, "Tell me."

"That man, Dawkins, came first thing this morning. He and his lordship were alone in the library for several hours. When he left, everything seemed fine, but a few hours later someone else came galloping up on one of the sorriest horses you've ever seen. He was shouting that Dawkins had told him to get word to his lordship that Farr had killed a worker in the mines and the rest had gone out. His lordship told Sebastian, Mr. Levander that is, to saddle his horse right away, and he went racing off to Glamorgan."

"Gone out," Morgana repeated. "On strike?"

Owen nodded. He swallowed hard. "Aye, miss, a strike. In Glamorgan. In the mines. I never thought I'd see it."

"Neither did I," she murmured, praying that somehow it would still prove not to be true. They had been so close, with David agreeing to see Dawkins and— David. Oh, God, when had she started thinking of him so familiarly, and more to the point, what was happening to him right at that moment? He'd gone to Glamorgan, which must be in turmoil. Yes, he was big and strong, proven in battle, but he was only one man. Anything might go wrong.

"I'm going," she said suddenly as she jumped up from the bench.

Owen stared at her, dumbfounded. "Miss?"

"You heard me. We're going to the manor together and you're going to find me a horse. I can't ride very well but I'll manage. I must get to Glamorgan."

"You can't, miss! There'll be rioting there. The militia will be called up. It'll be as bad as if a war had broken out."

"Stop talking," Morgana said. She took a firm grip on his shoulder and urged him up. "I got his lordship into this. Do you expect me to sit in my cottage, twiddling my thumbs, while all hell breaks loose?"

Perhaps it was her choice of language, or the determination that turned her eyes to stone. Whichever, Owen stopped arguing.

"I've a horse outside," he said. "That's how I came."

Morgana beamed him a smile. "I always said you were a resourceful lad, Owen Trelawney." She grabbed her shawl and ran for the door. Fortunately, Owen was no more confident around horseflesh than she was. The mount he'd selected was a placid gelding, strong of limb but docile of temperament.

"Help me," Morgana said urgently as she reached up to grip the pommel.

Owen obliged, making a stirrup of his hands so that she could pull herself up. When she was settled in the saddle, indelicately astride since this was no time to think of appearances, he said, "I think you should reconsider, miss. If his lordship gets wind of this, there's no telling what he'll do."

"I'll take that chance." She dug her heels into the gelding's flanks, bent her head to the wind and was gone.

Which is overstating the facts just a bit. Actually, the gelding was not so much swift as persistent. He could be urged to a gentle canter but no more. Morgana tried to be grateful for that. Left to her own devices, she would have urged him to a gallop and probably gotten herself killed in the process. As it was, she just managed to hold on as they crested the ridge of hills and came down into the scarred valley.

Glamorgan was burning. That was her first impression, and it terrified her. Great plumes of inky black smoke shrouded the town. A scream rose in her throat. One man dead, a strike called, terrible danger, but not this, not this sudden and overwhelming sense of disaster.

The gelding also sensed it. He stepped, hesitating, and went on only with Morgana murmuring encouragement.

Two days before, she had walked the main street in search of tools to instruct the children. Now she rode it seeking someone, anyone who could instruct her, who could say what had happened and where she should go in the hope of finding the man she sought. But she found only shuttered shops and empty doorways. The residents, wherever they were, were not in evidence.

Finally, in desperation, she made her way to the pub Hugh Dawkins had taken her to. As with everywhere else, it was securely shut, but by dint of pounding on the door, she managed to call attention to herself. The door opened a crack and a face peered out.

"Please," Morgana said quickly, "I'm trying to find someone. His name is Dawkins, Hugh Dawkins."

She offered the strike leader's name, judging that his whereabouts were far more likely to be known than those of the marquess. In this she was not disappointed.

The door opened a shade more. The small brown eyes of Winnona, the barmaid, met hers. "You're the lady he brought, the one who drank the tea."

"That's right," Morgana said quickly. "I came as soon as I heard what is happening. Is the strike still going on?"

Winnona shrugged. She did not open the door farther or suggest that Morgana enter, but she did spare a glance for the horse.

"Come on your own, did you?"

"As soon as I heard," Morgana repeated. "I must find Mr. Dawkins. Do you know where he is?"

"In heaven or hell," Winnona said. She cracked a gap-toothed smile and shrugged again. "Who knows? Maybe he's even still on this earth, although I wouldn't put money on that. First thing Farr would do with a strike called is go hunting for Dawkins."

A chill ran through Morgana. She thought of the desperate but still proud and determined man she had met, and she thought of Wynne, who always seemed so self-sufficient, and yet who would surely mourn her brother.

"You don't know that he's dead, do you?"

"No," Winnona admitted, "but they say a dozen or so are. There's been fighting since morning. The fires started an hour or so ago."

"Where are they coming from?"

"A couple of the mine shafts, I think. Some say the strikers lit them, some say it was the company men. Who knows? As for Dawkins, there's still a mob fighting down by the entrance to the mines. That's to the west of town. Maybe you'll find him there, but if you've any sense you won't look. Head back where you came from and thank your stars you're not involved."

"I can't do that," Morgana said. She drew the gelding over to a mounting block outside the pub and clambered into the saddle.

Winnona eyed her dubiously. "Suit yourself." She disappeared behind the door. It closed with a heavy thud.

West she had said and west Morgana went, through the empty street where the only sounds were the clip-clop of her horse's hooves against the paving stones. The smoke thickened. She pulled the scarf from around her neck and tied it over her mouth. From a distance, she began to hear a dull roar. At first it sounded like breakers crashing against a rocky coast, but soon that changed. The sound became almost a living thing. She had a sudden, flashing image of the legendary Welsh dragon, scales licked by flame, nostrils distended with searing smoke.

The gelding shied under her. Morgana drew rein and looked around quickly. There was a small shed behind the building nearest to her.

"Come on then," she said, turning the horse toward it. He went willingly enough, seeming to sense that she meant to protect him. When he was secure in the shed, safe from at least the worst of the smoke, she patted him gently. "I'll be back," she promised. He rolled his eyes at her and nuzzled her hand. His whickering followed her as she hurried to the road.

Now she went more slowly. Amid the dragon's roar she began to hear human voices, most shouting, some screaming in pain and fear. A woman ran toward her out of the smoke. Morgana stopped in shock. Blood dripped from the woman's forehead. Her clothes were filthy, and one of her arms hung uselessly at her side.

"Wait," Morgana cried. The injured woman shot her a look of pure terror and ran past. Morgana was tempted to follow her. This was far worse than anything she had envisioned. But that only made it more necessary for her to continue. Mustering all her courage, she plunged on.

What greeted her as she came around the last corner and looked directly toward the mines was a scene of pure pandemonium. It might have been conceived by Dante in one of his darker moods. Surely the circles of hell had little worse to offer than what was happening in Glamorgan.

Everywhere she looked men and women were running, screaming, fighting, falling. Some wore the uniforms of the local constabulary, and they were moving through the crowd wielding clubs and cutting down anyone who came within reach. Others appeared to be thugs brought in for the occasion and free to wreak whatever savagery they chose. For an instant, Morgana thought she saw Thomas Trelawney among them, using his beefy fists to beat a much smaller man, but she couldn't be sure.

Indeed, she couldn't be sure of anything as she was tossed this way and that, unable to move in any particular direction and knowing that at any moment she might fall victim to club or fist. She was just beginning to think that perhaps she really had made a mistake in coming when that seemed irrevocably confirmed. Her foot slipped, she lost her balance, and before she could draw a single breath, she went down.

Before her eyes, the world turned into a dark, whirling mass of feet and legs, all pressing against her. She could not get up no matter how frantically she tried. A scream bubbled up in her throat, but there was no breath to free it. A foot or perhaps a knee rammed into her ribs. Pain engulfed her. A red mist moved before her eyes. For a single, horrible moment she felt herself falling away into smothering darkness.

Iron seized her. Iron, wrapped around her waist, pulled her upward to the light and air. Iron, warm and hard, cursing mightily.

Wait. Iron wasn't warm, it was cold. She still retained enough of her senses to know that. And as for the cursing, it had an oddly familiar ring to it.

She opened her eyes. The red mist was gone. More's the pity, that, for there was nothing at all to protect her from the enraged glare of the Marquess of Montfort. Had she said iron? Say rather steel, shooting through her in remorseless shards, tearing away the tattered remnants of her defenses and leaving her helplessly exposed and vulnerable.

"You are the most damnable woman who has ever lived," that so-familiar voice declared.

Morgana thought she really ought to defend herself, but the words would not come. Nothing would except the blinding realization that as close as she had come to death—and as precarious as her situation remained—she was filled with overwhelming, incandescent happiness. Just to see him, to be with him, to know that he was safe—absolutely enraged, of course, but safe. It was sheer bliss.

She shut her eyes for a moment. So this was madness. It wasn't at all as she would have expected. On the contrary, there was a stillness at the center of it that was most appealing.

"I'm sorry," she whispered.

David pulled back slightly, the better to glare at her. "What for?" He broke off, shaking his head so that a lock of ebony hair tumbled across his soot-stained brow. "What am I saying? Of all the many things you have to be sorry for, which prompts your sudden repentance?"

"What do you mean, many? I'm only sorry for involving you in this, not for anything else."

"I rest my case," he muttered. He stood suddenly—she hadn't even been aware that he was kneeling beside her—then scooped her up and began striding off in some direction she could not determine.

"What case?"

"That you are the world's most damnable woman. You are sorry for involving *me*? What about involving yourself? For God's sake, Morgana, you could have been killed. If I hadn't reached you when I did—"

"I know," she said. The pain in his voice astounded her. He was angry, she could still feel that coming off him in great waves. But underneath it was something else that seemed very much like relief.

Was it possible the incandescent madness was not hers alone?

That thought tumbled through her mind, turning over and over like the bright, glittering balls she had seen in a book of fairy tales her father gave her. Fairy playthings they were, not of the real world. And yet...

"Where are we going?" she asked for want of anything else to say. Not that plenty else didn't occur to her, but she did have a small store of sense still to call upon. Her position was precarious, to say the least. But also oh, so sweet, heaven help her.

"Where do you think?" he demanded, unhelpful man.

"Paris," she suggested on the spur of the moment because she had always wanted to go there.

He looked down at her warily. "How much smoke did you breathe?"

"A paltry amount. I put my scarf over my face." She said it proudly as though to drive home the point that she was not, whatever he claimed, a fool.

"I know," he said grimly. "It slipped off while you were being tossed around by the mob. If you could see your face, you would realize how ineffective it was."

"What's wrong with my face?" Morgana demanded.

"It's filthy. So is the rest of you."

"Oh, dear," she said, glancing at herself. He was quite right. "My best suit."

"It won't clean."

"How would you know? I'd wager you've never cleaned anything in your life."

"It won't because I won't let it. I heartily dislike that suit."

That stopped her, at least for a bit. Anything else she might have said went clean out of her mind. He had opinions about her clothes. Firm opinions, by the sound of it. Also, she couldn't help but notice that he carried her effortlessly. The tensile strength of his arms and the rock hardness of his chest communicated themselves clearly through the hated suit. Oh, dear.

"Wait," she said. "My horse."

"What horse?"

"Yours actually, a very sweet gelding. I rode him here. He's in a shed... There, that way." She pointed.

"My horse," the marquess grumbled. "You rode a horse of mine here? How did you manage that?"

"I don't have a horse of my own," she said reasonably.

"I know that! You went to the manor, and Sebastian actually let you have a horse, even though he must have suspected where you'd be going? What in hell was he thinking of?"

"It wasn't Sebastian." She hesitated, eyeing him cautiously. He was still very angry, but the worst of his rage seemed to be easing. "Owen came to tell me where you had gone." Hastily, she added, "You mustn't blame him. He's only a child and he's already devoted to you. Please."

The marquess sighed. It was a sound generations of long-suffering males would have recognized. Truth be told, all those warrior ancestors would have, too. The Harrell line had bred for strength in the female as well as the male.

"I don't blame him," David said as they reached the shed where Morgana had left the gelding. "I wouldn't have really blamed Sebastian if he'd been involved. I can't even muster much anger at Dawkins, who is, after all, only one more hapless man."

He set her down, a tad roughly, she thought, and opened the door to the shed. The gelding whinnied a greeting. At least she'd had the sense to care for the horse, the marquess thought. Too bad she didn't show the same sense when it came to herself.

"Do you really want to go to Paris?" he asked as he led the horse out. His hands closed firmly around her waist. She was sideways in the saddle, with her legs properly covered, before she could answer.

"I can't ride like this," she said.

"Why not?"

"It isn't a lady's saddle, and besides, I never learned to ride any way but astride." She looked away, aware that under all the grime she was blushing. "Turn your head."

The beginnings of a smile crept over his face. "Why?"

"Because I asked you to and because you are supposed to be a gentleman."

"I won't comment on that." He showed her his back just long enough for her to swing a leg over the saddle and settle in more comfortably. Or at least as comfortably as she could with a good portion of her limbs exposed to his view. She couldn't get her skirt down more than a few inches below her knees.

"About Paris," he said, studiously not looking at the slender calves above high-buttoned boots. She had a well-turned ankle, by the look of it. Her feet were narrow, in keeping with the overall delicacy of her bone structure. She was really quite fragile even though she would move heaven and earth to deny it.

"There is no Paris," she said softly. Something moved between them that was ancient and powerful, a fracture in the order of the world. "There is only here and now."

Their eyes met. Slowly, David nodded. He took hold of the reins. The gelding followed. Morgana held on to the pommel. Behind her she could still hear the dragon's roar, but the screams and shouts had died down. Glamorgan was pausing—battered, stunned, uncertain—to gather its collective breath. And to prepare as best it could for whatever was still to come.

Chapter Twelve

Lights burned in the ground-floor windows of the manor house as they approached. David was mounted on the black stallion with the gelding following placidly behind. Morgana had managed to ride half the way before weariness and shock overcame her. Seeing her swaying in the saddle, the marquess had wasted no time lifting her in front of him. She nestled in the crook of his arm. Beneath the curve of her cheek, she could feel his heart beating. The rhythm almost, but not quite, lulled her into sleep.

The sudden flurry of activity in the stable yard jerked her awake, but only slightly. Dark shapes surrounded them. Someone was speaking, first the marquess, then someone else. She was lifted down in his arms and carried a little distance, up winding steps, to a high place. Softness enveloped her.

"Morgana . . ."

She stirred reluctantly. "Hmm?"

"We're here. Lenore is drawing you a bath. I must go now. I have to talk with Sebastian."

"Hmm."

The marquess smiled ruefully. It was truly marvelous, the effect he had on this woman. She appeared utterly unaware of him.

"Take care of her," he said to the maid, who nodded swiftly and bobbed him a curtsy.

"Yes, milord, as you say, milord."

It would be pointless, he supposed, to hope that Morgana would ever be so agreeable. Indeed, truth be told, he couldn't claim he would want her to be. She was fire and wind, starlight and the merciless eye of the eternal moon. She was made to bedevil a man, not to make his life serene.

He took it as a measure of his own magnanimity that he no longer felt the urge to strangle her. Other urges, however, were an entirely different matter.

He reached the library and thrust open the door, only to be startled by a sudden movement in the pale light. Owen turned to face him, his face washed of all color and his eyes dark smudges of concern.

David was very tired. Although he would not have admitted it to anyone, his shoulders ached where a chunk of burning wood had fallen across them while he was pulling Hugh Dawkins out from under a mob of bullyboys intent on killing him. He'd managed to avoid serious injury but he was still feeling a bit battered. It would have been very easy for him to dismiss the boy, perhaps even with the promise of a scolding later when he felt more inclined to give it.

Instead, he said, "It's all right, Owen. Miss Penrhys is fine. There's no harm done."

The relief that shone from that young face was almost painful. Yet the dignity the boy mustered said much of the man to be. "I was very worried, my lord."

"Of course you were. So was I. Now it's late and you look as though you could do with a rest. Miss Penrhys will be here in the morning. You can see her then."

Owen murmured his thanks and withdrew swiftly, but not before bestowing a smile of such appreciation on the marquess that he felt gifted by a stray ray of sunlight, somehow set wandering through the dark and smoky night.

Hard on it came Sebastian and with him matters of a decidedly more practical sort.

"Are you hurt, sir?" he asked, looking pointedly in the direction of the marquess's broad shoulders.

"Not at all. But I could do with a brandy if it wouldn't be too much to ask." He was sounding testy, but he couldn't help it. Sebastian was a master of the disapproving presence. Without a word or a flicker of expression, he let his master know what he thought of his behavior.

"At your elbow, sir. It was already poured."

"You spoil me."

"As you say, sir. I have ordered a bath as well as a light supper. Will you require anything else?"

David nodded. "Send one of the stable boys to find a woman named Wynne Fergus. Mrs. Mulroon will know of her. He's to tell her that her brother is injured but not seriously and is being brought to her. I expect him to lie low until I can decide what to do about this matter."

Sebastian inclined his head gravely. "As you say, sir. A very regrettable business."

"And likely to become even more so." The brandy was warm and sharp on the tongue. He swallowed a good measure of it. "Miss Penrhys is staying."

"Of course, sir."

The marquess lifted an eyebrow. "No other comment?"

The butler thought for a moment. With suitable gravity, he said, "Only that I find her to be a most unusual but also a most admirable young woman. We all have a very high opinion of her."

"A few hours ago, I could have cheerfully wrung her neck."

A smile twitched at the corners of Sebastian's mouth. "I can see how she might have that effect, sir. But her heart is in the right place, and she has the courage of her convictions. There is a great deal to be said for that."

"She is a thorn in my side," David muttered. He finished the brandy in a single swallow.

"Your lady mother had a great fondness for roses. But she would not permit any to be used in arrangements unless they had been stripped of their thorns. I never said so, of course, but I always thought that a rose denied its thorns developed a cloying, unpleasant scent whereas those in their natural state are far more appealing."

The marquess rose a shade unsteadily. The brandy was hitting him hard, but more than that he really did need to rest. First, though, he said, "After all the years we've known each other, Sebastian, I really think you should feel free to state your opinions. You are far too reticent.''

"I presume you are being sarcastic, sir?"

"I am doing my best."

"You are tired. May I assist you?"

"No, damn it, you may not. Send the supper to my room and the stable boy to Mrs. Fergus. Then get out of my sight for awhile. I have thinking to do."

"Sir," the butler said and bowed himself out. David considered another measure of the brandy but thought better of it. He made his way upstairs to find the fire blazing in his chamber, the bath drawn and supper laid out. Muted sounds reached him from the room next door. Lenore would be bustling around, doing whatever it was maids did. What she was thinking was less difficult to imagine. David had, quite consciously, taken Morgana to the room directly beside his own, the one linked to it by a connecting door.

He stared at that door for awhile as he lay in the steaming tub. When the water began to cool, he rose, toweled himself dry and put on the old silk robe he'd had forever. Suddenly hungry, he devoured the supper. When Sebastian came to remove the tray, he found his master stretched out in the armchair, staring into the fire.

"Will there be anything else, sir?"

David's eyes remained focused on the dancing flame. "First thing tomorrow, send a message to the London house. We will be going there directly."

The marquess's eyes drifted toward the heavy oak door connecting the two rooms. The intensity of his gaze was almost enough to make Sebastian ask who exactly *we* was. He restrained himself.

"I am in your debt," Hugh Dawkins said the following morning. The marquess was seated in the breakfast room. The day was clear and inviting. The mood within was somewhat less so.

"How do you intend to repay it?" David demanded. His mood was dark. Honor, however necessary to life, made a cold and unsatisfying bedmate.

Dawkins hesitated. His face was bruised and there was an ugly cut under his left eye, but for all that he was in far better shape than he had any right to be. That his continued health was a direct result of actions taken by the man before him raised certain problems he had yet to come to terms with.

"I'm not sure what you mean," he began.

David made an impatient gesture. "Sit down. Have you eaten?"

Dawkins nodded, a bit dazedly. "Aye, my sister saw to that. I meant what I said, I owe you a great deal. The entire movement does. But as to payment—"

"Movement? You mean that unholy melee I witnessed yesterday? Two were killed, by the way, and at least a dozen others injured. There would have been more if your people hadn't fled as quickly as they did."

Dawkins grimaced. He hadn't known of the deaths, but he had surmised there must have been some. It was impossible to confront such overwhelming force and emerge unscathed. Still, as the marquess said, it could have been worse.

"We knew that the price would be high when we began," Dawkins said. "No one wants to die, but then none of us is truly living. When a man has nothing to lose, he will take great risks."

He expected a quick rejoinder from his host but he got only silence. Slowly, David said, "There's truth in that."

Dawkins sensed an opening. He did not hesitate to press it. "You sound as though you speak from experience."

"I was in the Crimea," David said. "There were a great many mistakes made there but one that was not. I was ordered to take my men into a position that was hopeless. It served nothing, not as a feint or a holding action, nothing. Virtually all of them would have been killed."

Dawkins sucked in his breath. He was learning that the responsibility of leading men could be crushing. "What did you do?"

"As you say, I considered the situation, decided I had nothing more to lose, and refused."

"What happened?"

"My men lived." Nothing more, only that. No word about the rage he had faced as a result of his actions. Almost any other man would have been broken. Only the knowledge in the highest quarters that he was right prevented it. That and the awareness that the Marquess of Montfort would not go quietly. He had threatened, quite simply, to take the government with him. The men who knew about such things had believed him capable of it.

Dawkins let his breath go slowly. This put a different complexion on things. The marquess was not merely an ally but one who knew the ways of power better than any Welsh miner ever would.

"What payment do you seek?" he asked.

"Your patience," David said promptly. "Lie low, draw no attention to yourself. You can stay here, if you wish, just so long as Farr can't find you. Send word to your men to do nothing more. They must return to work prepared to bide their time."

"To what end? I can't send men back into hell without giving them a damn good reason for going."

"Tell them they are fighting the wrong enemy. It isn't Farr or anyone like him. The world's full of jumped-up toadies who imagine themselves in authority because someone higher than them tells them it's so. The real problem is Westerley."

"He's beyond our reach."

The marquess smiled. He spoke with perfect pleasantness. "But not beyond mine."

"Your what?" Morgana asked. She came into the breakfast room without warning, having found lingering outside too wearing on her nerves. Never mind that the men were involved in a conversation they clearly considered their private preserve. She wanted to know what was afoot, and she didn't mind letting them know it.

"My reach," David said on a note of deliberately strained patience. Never mind that she looked delightful in the soft white lace gown Lenore had found for her. Her fiery hair tumbled around her shoulders. There was still a hint of slumber in the heaviness of her eyelids, giving her the air of a sleepy child. One who was determined to play with the grown-ups.

"Good morning, Mr. Dawkins," Morgana said. "I am relieved to find you well."

"My thanks to you, miss," he replied as he stood up, "and to you, my lord. I will take your advice and visit with my sister for awhile. If things get too hot for that, your hospitality will be most appreciated."

"Come at any time," the marquess said. "Sebastian will see to you."

That same gentleman paused in the act of setting down a tray laden with Mrs. Mulroon's best cinnamon buns. "Sir?"

"Mr. Dawkins may be staying here while we are in London. Should that be the case, I entrust him to your care."

"Of course, my lord." The butler glanced from one face to the other, the two grave men, each strong in his way, but the marquess by far the stronger, and the young woman, Miss Penrhys, looking very lovely and composed except for a cool dart of moonlight behind her eyes.

Moonlight? It was bright morning. His eyes were fooling him.

"I am to stay then, my lord?"

"Indeed, there will be nothing for you to do in London."

To his credit, Sebastian did not flinch although he certainly wanted to. Most gentlemen of the marquess's standing would not dream of going farther than the nearest crossroads without their gentleman's gentleman, much less to the most elegant and exacting capital in the world. True enough, there was a skeleton staff left on at the London house, but they were hardly up to Sebastian's standards. Still, there was nothing to be done about it.

Which, of course, begged the question of who exactly *we* was.

"To where?" Morgana said. It was an hour or so later. Breakfast was done, the dishes whisked away, and her own departure delayed by the marquess's insistence that she was not well enough to return to work. He had, he informed her, sent a message to the Reverend Armbruster telling that worthy that he would have to take charge of the school for the day. Miss Penrhys had suffered a shock and was in need of rest.

"London," he replied, quite calmly. "You mentioned Paris, but London is more in the cards at the moment. I have business there."

"You want me to go with you to London." Perhaps if she said it often enough, it would begin to make some kind of sense. At the moment, it made none. Wasn't her life already in sufficient shambles without bringing it down entirely?

He leaned back in his chair, looking for all the world as though they were discussing nothing more important than the weather, and said, "You're an honest woman."

It wasn't a question, and she didn't mistake it for such. "Why do I think I am about to perceive that as a weakness?"

His eyes narrowed in amusement. "Because you are too suspicious. Not that I blame you; life has a way of schooling us in that direction. However, to return to the matter at hand, tell me honestly, haven't you ever wished that you could step out of your life into a different existence if only for a brief time?"

"Perhaps," Morgana said slowly. Her common sense told her she should not be having this conversation. Indeed, she should flee from it with all speed, and would have, had not she become inexplicably glued to her seat. The light in those silvery eyes was simply too enticing to resist. She would stay a small while longer, allowing herself only that much indulgence. Surely, it could not hurt?

"Whatever gain might come from such an interlude," she said, "would have to be weighed against the consequences. *Honesty* forces me to admit that they appear overwhelming."

"Do they? Let us examine the matter. If you come with me to London, what is likely to happen?"

"I am likely to never be able to return here because the good people of Gynfelin would tar and feather me if I tried."

"You exaggerate. Besides there is no reason for them to know you have gone."

Morgana's eyebrows rose. What game was this? "No reason?"

The marquess shook his head. "So far as anyone is concerned, you would be staying on here to recuperate from your ordeal in Glamorgan. I would not be present, having gone to London."

"That would be a lie."

He shrugged, hoping she did not stick too much on this point, for she was right, of course, it was a lie. The question was how much would she care? "It is a subterfuge," he said, "a small one to allow you what I believe you most desire."

He observed with interest the hectic flush that spread over her cheeks. Perhaps they were not so far apart in their thinking after all.

"And what," Morgana said tautly, "do you imagine that to be?"

She held her breath waiting for him to answer and let it out slowly when he said, "A bit of freedom. A small part of life that isn't confined beneath all the restrictions you place on yourself. Society's restrictions are bad enough but yours seem tougher still."

"That is my conscience you are discussing."

"Not at all. I have no argument at all with your conscience. If I did, I wouldn't give you my word that should you decide to accompany me to London, we will go as no more than friends." He smiled gently at her open skepticism. "I would pledge to regard you in a purely brotherly fashion, but that wouldn't be true. I am well aware of you as a woman and a very desirable one at that. But I really do want you to see something of the wider world beyond this small village and the confines of your life. Therefore, I will put my own desires aside and tell you that your safety in all regards will be both my privilege and my duty."

Morgana stared at him for a long moment. Softly, on the merest breath, she said, "For truth, you are the devil's own."

David laughed. He took no offense for he was too wise for that. "Which devil do you mean? Surely not that pitchforked caricature swathed in tinsel red like some trollop run amok? I looked for him in the clash of battle, but he was nowhere to be seen. Not surprising, really, for he's a recent creation, as you must know, and doesn't hold up well under close examination." He paused, holding her gaze with his own. "But I think you mean something older, a poor fellow not deserving of the condemnation he's received of late. It seems he never asked for anything except to be left alone to dance under the moon and make music on his pipes."

"I never knew anyone to speak of such things," Morgana said, "save for my mother and one or two others. It is curious that you do so. I suppose it results from your devotion to books, for I have noticed you have a number of titles relevant to these matters. However, be that as it may, you misstate the case. Your dancing piper is no more real than the pitchfork fellow. The reality was far different, far more powerful and significant, and is still—I think—with us."

Deliberately, she did not look at him just then, fearing that if she did so she would see, for an instant out of time, the true face of unbridled male strength, husband to the earth, essential to her renewal, the other half of herself without which all life would wither and die. Say rather that he was merely a man, although an exceptionally clever one at that.

"Your word?" she murmured.

"Most solemnly." He rose and, reaching out, took her hand. She was drawn up beside him, there in the golden morning light at the first birth of spring.

His voice was soft, even caressing, but also implacable. "I promise you, Morgana, that I will never do anything to bring you harm."

She looked into the silvery eyes, into the proud, hard face, into the battered but still valiant spirit beneath. Heaven help her, she believed him.

Chapter Thirteen

"**W**hen a man is tired of London," Samuel Johnson wrote, "he is tired of life." Perhaps so, Morgana thought, but more recently the poet Shelley had observed, "Hell is a city much like London—a populous and smoky city." An argument could be made that they were both right, but at the moment she was too distracted to manage it.

Peering through the carriage window—truth be told, she was half hanging out of it—she watched the array of people and buildings as they passed and wondered if anything in the history of mankind had ever been quite so daring.

London. All her life she had known of it but now, seeing it for the first time, she understood that she knew nothing about it. Not how big it was—did anyone know how many millions of people called it home?—or what went on in it—every back alley and lane seemed to guard a secret—or where in the remorseless tide of events it might be going. All that mattered was that it *was*, magnificently, improbably, defiantly, and that she was there to enjoy it.

"Incredible," she murmured as she at last drew back and settled herself once more against the tufted leather carriage seat. It was a temporary withdrawal, merely to catch her breath, but it required her to face the man who sat across from her, observing her every movement with scarcely concealed amusement.

Not that she could blame him. What a spectacle she must be, with her hair in tangles—of late it had proven even more unmanageable than usual—her cheeks flushed—that seemed to have become their permanent appearance—and her eyes aglow with the marvels she had seen.

And yet to give him credit, he was proving himself the perfect gentleman. No, that wasn't regret she felt. On the contrary, it was relief. She had trusted him, and her trust was not misplaced. How could that evoke anything other than appreciation for the high-mindedness of his moral principles? Regret, indeed! What an idea.

"Did you sleep well?" David inquired, ever the soul of courtesy. They had stopped at an inn overnight, one of the better class to be found along the main road. Morgana had seen little of the place, having been shown up a private stair to an equally private room where a young maid served her supper and returned the following morning with her solitary breakfast. The marquess was, in addition to everything else, perfectly discreet.

"Very well," she said, stretching the truth enormously. What was sleep? She couldn't quite remember, but she was sure it bore scant resemblance to the uneasy thoughts and half-acknowledged longings that had become her nightly companions. "And you?"

"Superbly. Country air has that effect on me."

Did that mean he slept less well in the city? Never mind, it counted for nothing. How he slept, where he slept, with whom he slept, all meant nothing to her.

"Do you think," she asked, "that it becomes easier to lie with practice?"

"Probably," David agreed, wondering what had prompted that. The single lie, that she remained at Gynfelin in his absence, was behind them. There were no others, were there?

"What makes you ask?"

"Nothing," she said, deciding it was easier, and turned away to examine the turbulent cityscape.

Mayfair was a revelation. It came out of the turmoil, emerging as an island of relative calm sparkling with marble-fronted mansions, greenswards, and everywhere cleanliness, so noticeably absent in the grimy mayhem they had passed through. The carriage drew up beside a three-story building of notable grace and elegance. Immediately, the door was opened by a liveried footman who hurried down the steps to greet them.

David descended first, then handed Morgana down. He tucked her hand into the crook of his arm, smiled reassuringly and led her into the house. It was all done so quickly that any final qualms she might have felt, however belatedly, never got a chance to proclaim themselves.

Her first impression was that the beauty and luxury of the Welsh manor had somehow been condensed into this smaller but no less impressive residence. Marble floors, plaster moldings, gleaming chandeliers, polished brass and gleaming mahogany all combined to drive home the impression of unbridled wealth in the service of unlimited comfort.

And then there were the servants. A half dozen of them were lined up, bowing and bobbing, to greet the marquess. First there was the butler, stern and impressive in his morning coat, then two liveried footmen, including the one who had rushed to receive them, then a plump cook whose girth advertised her skill, and lastly two housemaids with eyes so large their faces seemed hardly able to contain them.

"This is Miss Penrhys," the marquess said to the butler, and by extension, to all of them. "Has the blue room been prepared, Fenwith?"

The butler—Norman Fenwith by name, a distant cousin of Sebastian's whom even that taskmaster admitted wasn't a bad sort—nodded quickly. "Indeed, sir." He took a step forward, gesturing to one of the maids as he did. "If you would come with me, miss."

The marquess stepped back a pace so that Morgana could pass him. Distantly, she thought they might have been in the midst of an intricate dance, master of the house back, butler forward, everyone smiling and nodding, for he had with those handful of words clarified her presence as much as he was likely to do. The blue room was, although she didn't know it then, the traditional abode of honored guests. It was situated on the middle floor at the farthest end of the hall from the marquess's quarters. Several decades before, the hapless prince regent had stayed in it one night when, having lingered late at cards, he found himself with a belly too much of gin and a disinclination to risk the suddenly stormy night. That event sanctified the room, so to speak, and made it appropriate only for those whose reputations placed them above the slightest reproach.

At least, that was how the servants reasoned. On a more mundane level, they also knew that they were fortunate to have good positions in which they were well paid and fairly treated. If his lordship chose to bring a young woman with him from Wales, who were they to have an opinion about it? She would be shown every courtesy, but beyond that she was to all intents and purposes invisible.

That suited Morgana perfectly. After all, this wasn't real life. It was an interlude, a time out of time, a holiday from being herself. She was happy enough to flit through it as though her feet didn't quite touch the ground.

The journey had tired her more than she realized. After a warm bath and a pleasant tea, she was glad enough to accept the maid's suggestion and slip into bed for a rest. Alone, she lay for a short time gazing around the room. It really wasn't blue, being mainly furnished in a combination of greens, yellows and here and there a splash of crimson. She wasn't surprised. At some time in its past, the room had undoubtedly been blue, and the name had stuck while the color scheme changed. What had been would always be, at least until someone thought better of it.

She drifted, skimming the surface of sleep, occasionally slipping deeper. The day waned and gentle evening light suffused the room. A soft knock drew her to full attention. The maid entered, bearing fresh juice in a glistening pitcher, and suggested it was time to dress for dinner.

Morgana went down the stairs carefully. Her caution had two sources. First, the situation was enough to give her pause, and second, there was the gown she wore. It had arrived over the maid's arm, a frilly concoction of lace and silk in a shade of blue that precisely matched her eyes. This last part must be a coincidence, for the dress had been ordered from a seamstress only a few days before—by the same letter, it was worth noting, as he notified the house staff to expect their master's imminent arrival. Such confidence! Such effrontery!

Such a lovely dress, so soft and feminine, so yielding against her limbs, everything, indeed, that she herself must not be.

She should have refused to wear it but such nicety, though suitable enough in its place, had struck her as the height of hypocrisy under the present circumstances. For she was not any longer Miss Penrhys, schoolteacher and spinster. Rather she had become, for however short a time, simply Morgana, named for la Fey, in whom the ancient ways ran deep indeed.

She stepped from the stairs onto stone, the cold marble announcing itself through the delicacy of the evening slippers she wore, their color a precise match for the dress. The entry hall was chilled, but across it double doors were flung open and through them she caught the welcome leap and crackle of fire and, somewhere near it, not quite in her sight yet sensed all the same, her host.

Impulsively, she moved toward them both.

The marquess was nervous. No, that was too strong a word. Anxious, perhaps, or more conscious of himself than was his norm. He wanted very much to please her but that was a complex matter involving as it did holding his own desires in strictest check while endeavoring to give hers free rein.

He had put himself in this position and was determined to make the best of it, but he wasn't quite prepared for the vision she presented as she walked—wafted?—into the room.

Morgana indeed, la Fey to the bone and proud of it.

A tremor ran through him. He had been right that instant in the phaeton when for the first time he tasted her sweetness. Right, then, to plot so audacious a course, and right to stick with it, no matter what the cost. That was cost to him, of course, not to her, for he stood hard by his word. He would do nothing to hurt her.

What she chose to do was another matter altogether.

"Come in," he said and added for good measure, "you look very lovely."

"Thank you," she replied, all grave schoolgirl politeness, but there was nothing of the schoolgirl in the flashing eyes that raked him, then were gone behind the screen of her mystery.

He cleared his throat. "Fenwith thought we would be more comfortable dining here." A small table was drawn up close enough to the fire to be pleasant on the cool spring evening. A damask cloth, slightly too large for the table, was billowed in soft white waves against the muted carpet. Fine china and gold gleamed in the light of two thick white candles set in intricately turned silver sticks.

"How nice," Morgana murmured. The silk of her dress was cool against her skin. Its soft susurration followed her as she moved. "Oh, and thank you for the dress, but you really shouldn't have gone to the bother."

"As my sainted mother would have said, had I had a sainted mother, you pay for the dressing."

"What was she like, your mother?" Morgana asked as she took the seat he held for her. There was no sign of servants. Warming dishes were set on a tea trolley beside the table, easily within their reach. They could dine without interruptions—or observers.

"I have no idea," David said. He sat down opposite her and filled their glasses with crisp, golden Chablis from the wine cooler next to him.

Morgana's eyebrows rose. "None at all?"

He shook his head. "The only time I ever saw her she was either coming from or going to a party. You can't really form an opinion of a person under those circumstances, can you?"

Privately, Morgana thought that not only could you do so, you were virtually compelled to. However, she resisted saying so.

She took a sip of the wine, found it delightful and promptly resolved not to touch it again. Setting her glass down, she looked at him directly. "Did you really mean what you said about giving your word?"

"If you thought I didn't, would you be sitting here?"

"No, but I have wondered. It is all so...improbable."

He laughed. "Indeed. Perhaps it is time to confess that I have an ulterior motive. Salmon?"

"What?"

"Salmon in dill sauce. It's quite good, actually. Here, try some." He set a piece on her plate, poured a dollop of sauce over it and smiled encouragingly. "I brought you along to keep me on the straight and narrow."

Morgana took a forkful of the salmon. It melted on her tongue. Whatever else, she wouldn't starve. "Would you mind awfully explaining that remark about an ulterior motive?"

"Of course. I've come to London to beard Lord Westerley in his den, so to speak. Since I have little patience for such things, I thought it would be prudent to bring along a reminder of exactly why my presence here is necessary. With you here, I can hardly forget Gynfelin, can I, or my responsibilities there?"

"I see," Morgana said slowly. "So I'm some sort of conscience minder then? A hair shirt, as it were?"

His eyes narrowed, silver in the shadowed light. She thought he smiled. "I could make some comment about the aspect of having you close to my skin, but being a gentleman, I will not do so."

"You're right," she said as she dug her fork into the salmon with more force than was strictly necessary. "This is delicious."

"Do you know anything about Westerley?"

"Only what you told me, that he is a gambler and drinker."

"And he does both badly."

"Yet he has great wealth and power."

"He *should* have," the marquess corrected, "for he was born to both. But the wealth is being squandered, and without it power tends to melt away. He is heavily in debt, but despite that he has always refused to sell the Glamorgan mines because they are his last source of ready income. He uses them to hold his creditors at bay, if only barely."

Morgana took another bite of the salmon, finding it as delicious as the first. She was embarrassingly hungry. He had that effect on her.

"If that is the case, how do you intend to change his mind?"

"By breaking him," the marquess said pleasantly. "Salad?"

"Thank you. You do that quite well."

"Do what?"

"Manage without servants. I imagined you were used to having someone else do everything for you."

"Not quite everything," he said dryly. "I'm actually quite good at fending for myself when the occasion demands."

"Did you learn that in the Crimea?" She was daring greatly now and knew it, for surely if there was anything he did not want to talk about, it was his experience in that charnel house.

"No," he said and meant to make that the end of the matter, but something prompted him to go on, to explain himself to her. "When I was a boy, I lived apart from my parents most of the time. I would be at school or in whichever residence they didn't happen to be using. At school, there were people who were technically servants, but they wielded more actual power than the masters themselves and made sure no one forgot it. Elsewhere—'' He shrugged. ''Sebastian looked after me, but he also insisted that I learn to care for myself.''

Appalled at the picture of family life that he painted, Morgana said the first thing that came into her mind. ''I'm sorry.''

''What for?''

''I'm not sure, exactly, but your childhood seems to have been very barren compared to mine.''

''You said yourself that there was no money and your mother was constantly having to make do.''

''Yes, but she did make do, you see. When I was growing up, I had no real sense of being poor. Considering how little we really had, that was a great accomplishment for her. Later, when I found out how rough it had been, I still had a sense of richness that came from all the time we spent together and the things we did together.''

''What kinds of things?'' he asked, genuinely curious, for he had no experience with such matters.

''Cooking, making clothes, visiting the sick, taking care of the young children. The things women normally do.''

''You don't find that boring?''

She shook her head, thinking how sad that he had grown up knowing only people who turned their backs on the best of life. ''No,'' she said softly, ''I don't. In fact, I can't imagine life without those things that give it genuine meaning."

"Hmm." He said nothing more, at least not on that subject, but changed it quite deliberately. "What would you like to do tomorrow?"

"As I know nothing of London, it is difficult for me to say."

"Shopping, perhaps. London is known for its shops."

Her nose wrinkled. "I have everything I could want for the school, and other shopping doesn't interest me."

"Museums, then. London teems with works of art."

"I'm sure that would be wonderful, but do you know what I've just thought of, something I heard of years ago." She hesitated, suddenly uncertain. "Perhaps it is too ordinary for you."

"Tell me anyway," he encouraged.

"I would love to go boating on the river. It is, after all, the heart of London and probably the best way to comprehend the city."

David hesitated. "True enough, but it might not be as you imagine."

"How so?"

"Everything in London comes to the river eventually."

"Oh, I know that. It has always been so. During the years immediately after the Norman Conquest, there were people who said the fish taken from the Thames were unusually fat because of all the bodies in the river. A great many people took their own lives, you see, because they were so filled with despair."

He had forgotten. This was the woman who faced down Owen Trelawney, who waded into the melee at Glamorgan, who, for that matter, accepted his own challenge to jettison all she had known of safety and security. The river would suit her well.

"Fine," he said, "we will go tomorrow. I will show you where they took the young Elizabeth through Traitor's Gate into the Tower, where Sir Thomas More went to tell his king he could not conspire in the great divorce, and where in earlier times there was a thriving market in oysters that men spoke of as far away as the Mediterranean."

"The perfect guide," she said, smiling. But she was thinking something else altogether. How handsome he looked in the flickering candlelight, how sweet the sound of his voice, how she found herself looking at his hands and wondering what they would feel like on her. The river, by all means, where the heart of England ran to meet the sea, where reality and dream flowed together until no one could say where one began and the other ended.

Chapter Fourteen

Despite David's warnings, the outing on the river proved perfectly pleasant. They rented a skiff complete with a boatman who claimed his family had been rowing on the river back to the time of the Conqueror himself.

"Saw him come, they did, my forebears, when there be nothing here but a Saxon stronghold. He raised the White Tower there and subdued rebellion throughout the land. There's plenty who followed him but we seen them all, King and commoner, come and go. Still, nothing changes along the river."

"What do you think of the present monarch?" David asked pleasantly.

The boatman hesitated. The pair were simply dressed and seemed pleasant enough. The woman was beautiful, no doubt of that, and the man looked like no one he would ever want to cross. But his interest appeared genuine.

"She's a fine lady," he said. "We're lucky to have her after some who've been in her place. But—"

"Aye?" the marquess prompted. "But?"

"She could pay a mite more attention to the common folk. I know it's hard, with her living in palaces and all, but she doesn't seem to have much sense of how it is to hold body and soul together in this world."

He looked at them cautiously to gauge their reaction but neither seemed offended. On the contrary, the woman was nodding. "We need a truly representative parliament," she said, "with power vested in the Commons, not the Lords, and everyone allowed to vote, including women."

The two men shared a speaking glance. Never mind all that separated them, they were united in their common bewilderment at this notion. "Women?" David asked.

"Absolutely," Morgana replied. "Women have just as much at stake in our society, if not more so, for we are responsible for the children."

"Power in the Commons?" asked the boatman, retreating to more solid, if still startling grounds. "Would the Lords ever agree to that?"

"Only if they had to," Morgana said and sat back, satisfied to let them mull that one over.

The boatman found it prudent to turn his attention to his oars. They skimmed along, moving downriver with the tide, until they came to a landing several miles south of the city. There they left the boat and walked a short distance to a pretty inn where they took lunch sitting on the terrace overlooking the water. A stage brought them back into town in late afternoon. They came sun-warmed and slightly disheveled. Morgana's light cotton frock was dusted with pollen from the newly blossomed daffodils they had strolled past.

David had undone his stock and taken off his morning coat, draping it over one shoulder. He looked younger than she was used to seeing him, and well relaxed. The day had refreshed them both. Unspoken between them was the sense that at least some of the smoke and screams of Glamorgan had been put aside, if only temporarily.

But the pleasant mood was fragile. It shattered when Morgana came downstairs after changing to find David, impeccable in evening dress, preparing to go out.

"Oh," she said, stopping on the last step. "I didn't realize."

The man who faced her was the same person she had spent the day with, yet different. His features were guarded, his manner distant.

"I'm sorry," he said, correct as ever, "I should have mentioned to you that I would be out this evening."

"Not at all," she assured him, striving hastily to adopt some measure of his coolness. "I hardly expect you to entertain me every moment." She mustered a smile that might have fooled someone who didn't know her as well as he was coming to. "Wherever you're off to, have a lovely time."

"I am off to play cards with Westerley," he said bluntly, "and I can assure you, there will be nothing lovely about it."

Restraint was called for here. The impulse to shout hoorah was definitely misplaced. But she was buoyantly glad to know he was set on so grim an errand instead of any one of the hundreds of more pleasant divertissements London could have offered.

He saw it in her face clearly enough and laughed, startling the footman who was standing ready at the door. Morgana laughed, too, tried to stop and, when she couldn't, ended up hiccuping.

"I really am sorry," she said when she was finally able, "my manners are abominable."

"Not at all," he assured her, "merely transparent."

"Why, you—"

He raised a finger admonishingly. "Be a good girl. Eat your supper and go to bed early."

She sorely regretted that they were not in her cottage where she could have found something convenient to throw. There was a vase on a nearby table and she did eye it closely enough to alarm the footman who deserted his post and took a quick step toward it. The marquess chuckled and took himself off in a flurry of black silk cape lined with scarlet, leaving Morgana to soothe the ruffled servant as best she could.

She did that, she ate her supper and she did go to bed, but she did not sleep. She lay awake in the not-blue blue room, mulling all that had happened to turn her life topsy-turvy in so short a time. Owen, his father, the school, the cruel gossip and the inescapable truth.

She loved him.

Ah, well, that was no surprise. She'd felt it coming on from the beginning and was too honest to pretend otherwise. The question was what to do about it.

Friends, he'd said. A time out of her own life. A time for—what? Dreams or something more?

All her life she had been so careful. Granted, she had taken what looked like risks, but they had never felt that way to her. She had always worked toward a particular goal, first to get her education and then to educate others. Everything she did was intended to achieve that.

This was different. It was more risk than she had ever contemplated, the possibility of terrible pain and at the end—what? A handful of memories that would at best be bittersweet?

But if she did nothing, if she denied what she felt so deeply, what would become of her? Would she become one of those tired, dried-up women she had seen, sour in the denial of their womanhood, at odds with all of life?

She could not bear that.

Silently she rose, and on silent feet descended the stairs. The room where they had breakfasted was empty. She went past it, down another flight of stairs and found the kitchen. Wreathed in shadows, it still offered homey comfort in the lingering smells of fresh-baked bread and the soft glow of embers in the big, cast-iron stove. She worked the pump enough to fill the kettle and put it on to heat. The first cup of boiling water went to warm the pot, the rest to steep fragrant tea. She found a tray and set it with a lacy cloth, the pot and a practical pottery cup she would not have to worry about chipping. There had been little time to explore the house, but she found the library without difficulty. It was smaller than at the manor but no less imposing. Settled on an overstuffed couch with the tea to keep her company, she resigned herself to wait.

The clock chimed one, then two, and finally, just as her eyes were growing heavy-lidded, the softer chime signaled the half-hour. A key turned in the lock. Morgana sat bolt upright. She waited a moment more, another, and then came the sound of footsteps in the hall beyond.

She was up in a flash and hurrying toward him. "David, wait."

He stopped, turned, dark and large against the greater darkness of the night. "Morgana?"

"I...I couldn't sleep. I...made tea. Would you like some?" Too late, she realized it would be cold by now, but David was already shaking his head.

"No, thank you. It's very late. Are you all right?"

"Perfectly. I just thought... Did it go well with Westerley?"

David stared at her. She was wrapped in lace that covered her as properly as any dress could have and yet still managed to appear so much more improper, for beneath the frilly confection of nightgown and robe was only Morgana, beautiful, free and right there before him.

"Westerley?"

She nodded. "You went to play cards with him, didn't you?"

"Oh, yes, of course. I lost."

Her face fell. "Oh, no!"

He laughed and took a step toward her. "It's all right, I meant to lose. Lord Westerley is now convinced that I am a poor but eager player with a fat wallet. In short, a pigeon. We will play again tonight but for higher stakes.'' Grimly, he added, ''Higher than he can imagine.''

''You are luring him in,'' Morgana said.

''Exactly. It's a fine old tradition.'' He removed his cape and left it on the banister. Beneath he wore evening clothes of unrelieved black save for his shirt and the flash of white at his throat. ''Did you say tea?''

''I forgot how long ago I fixed it. It will be cold by now. But I could make a fresh pot.''

''No need. I would rather have a brandy.'' He looked at her. ''Will you join me?''

She could say no. She could tell him good-night and withdraw to her room. She could . . .

''Yes, thank you.''

They went into the library. Morgana had lit only a small gas lamp and David made no effort to add to it. He filled two crystal goblets with a modest measure of brandy and handed one to her.

''You are very beautiful,'' he said.

Her breath caught in her throat. ''Oh . . .''

A flashing grin lit his face. ''I don't believe it. Morgana Penrhys at a loss for words?''

''Not at all, merely surprised. I've never thought of myself that way.'' Her brow knit. ''Do you think I talk too much?''

''Only sometimes,'' the marquess said. He set his brandy down. Slowly, so as not to alarm her unduly, he put his hands on her shoulders and drew her to him. She stiffened slightly but made no attempt to pull away.

Huskily, he said, ''There is something I must tell you.''

"What?" Her voice shook, but that was hardly surprising since the rest of her was doing the same.

He looked at her, his face grave. Deep within his eyes, a silvery flame leaped and darted. "My intentions toward you are strictly honorable."

Obviously, she had fallen asleep on the couch and was dreaming. None of this was actually happening. David wasn't here, she wasn't in his arms, he wasn't saying—

"I don't understand."

"My intentions. When I asked you to come to London, I meant what I said about not doing anything that could harm you. Lovemaking by itself isn't harmful, but the consequences of it can be. Have you considered that?"

"Yes," Morgana said, not altogether truthfully, for she hadn't considered much of anything except her feelings for him. Yet it took no great cogitating to understand what he was saying.

"I have been so careful all my life," she murmured. "What happens here still counts, I know that. But I...I care very deeply for you and I can't just turn my back on that."

A moment longer he gazed at her before, very gently, he smiled. "Ah, Morgana, I find it incredible that there was a time when I did not know you, yet still thought myself fully alive. But tell me, what are we going to do about my honorable intentions?"

She took a breath and reached down, down, deep within herself to where the great shining fire of her courage dwelt. That she took hold of, gathering it up as though in her hands, and offered it to him.

"Perhaps," she said, "we can find a way around them."

He made a low sound deep in his throat in the instant before his arms closed irrevocably around her. His kiss was hot, demanding and without quarter. The swift thrust of his tongue sent her senses reeling. She clung to him, her hands digging into the smooth velvet evening coat, as the rest of world fell away.

If he had thought to frighten her, he almost succeeded. But this was not Morgana Penrhys, schoolteacher and spinster in her plain brown serge suit and her sensible shoes. This was Morgana of another name, la Fey was as good as any, and something more, for this was woman being born, fighting her way free of the shackles that had held her, watching them fall away into nothingness.

Her passion surged, overcoming doubt and fear. Her teeth grazed his tongue, drawing him deeper. He pulled back slightly, plunged again, withdrew and came yet again until with that final surge her knees buckled. If he hadn't been holding her, she would have fallen. He lifted her high against his broad chest and carried her swiftly from the room, up the curving steps and down the hall, not to the blue room but to his own.

Fenwith or some other faithful soul had left a lamp burning. In its light, Morgana blinked. The room was unrelentingly masculine. At its center stood a high bed with an intricately carved headboard and four posters supporting a canopy and hangings that had been old before the century turned. There was a chest against one wall and a writing desk, and there, behind the bed, a tapestry of breathtaking beauty in which a woman wreathed in golden hair stood, beckoning gently to a unicorn.

David set her gently on the floor and, still holding her, stepped back a pace. His eyes, molten steel now, looked deeply into hers.

"Are you sure?" he demanded.

Her answer was to reach for him, hands trembling only slightly, as they slipped beneath his evening coat and gently eased it off.

He gasped at her touch but stood still, waiting, giving her the precious freedom to act. Her fingers shook, but she managed to undo the buttons of his vest and that, too, went the way of the coat. Beneath he wore a shirt of white silk, the stock already loose, and below, dark trousers fitted snugly and tucked into riding boots.

The newer shirts were put on over the head and worn heavily starched. David disliked them and, seeing no reason to bow to fashion, stayed with the softer version secured with laces across the chest. These Morgana undid, her fingers brushing the burnished skin lightly roughened with dark whorls of hair. Dimly, she became aware of her breasts suddenly aching, the nipples growing hard. She bit her lip hard and could not take her eyes from him as he yanked the shirt off.

Dazedly, she thought that someone should have warned her that men could be so beautiful. He was perfectly formed, every muscle and sinew articulated by a master creator. Her head fell back, weighted by the heavy mass of her hair. Her eyes were slumberous, and deep within herself she was becoming wet.

Abruptly, he sat down on the edge of the bed and pulled his boots off. When he stood again, a dull flush darkened his cheeks. He reached for her, sliding silk from her shoulders, letting it fall through his hands to pool at her feet. She was left in the nightgown of fragile lace and silk that hinted at more than it outrightly concealed. His breath grew taut as he gazed at the thrusting darkness of her nipples against the fragile veil and between her legs another darkness, soft, beckoning, hinting at fire.

He should go slowly, restrain himself, think only of her, but the fire was rising, burning deeply, and he seemed to be slipping away from himself, into the light that lay somewhere deep within her eyes.

"I want to be gentle with you," he said desperately.

"You will be."

He shook his head. "You don't know what it's like for a man ... for me. I have never wanted anything as I want you." Between grated teeth, he said, "This is too much."

"No, it is exactly how it must be." Where her confidence came from, she could not say, but it gave her the strength to do what was needed.

Holding his eyes, she pulled gently at the pale ribbons that secured her nightgown. Slowly, smiling tenderly, she released them and let the gown fall away.

Like alabaster, he thought, in the first instant of seeing her completely revealed to him. Yet not like it at all, for this was perfection made whole, warm, suffused with life rushing through her. Her breasts were the loveliest he had ever seen, high and full with rosy nipples swollen for his touch. Beneath them her waist narrowed to flare again at her hips. Her belly was almost flat except for the slightly pillowy softness. Her thighs were slender, beautifully curved and between them nestled a thicket of curls like dark fire hiding the innermost secrets of her womanhood.

A groan broke from him. His manhood rose hot and tumescent, demanding release. He fumbled for an instant with the buttons of his trousers, undid them hastily and slid them off. Naked, he came to her, gloriously male, filled with burning need, more magnificent than anything she had ever imagined.

And yet, truth be told, rather more than she had bargained for. Thanks to an enlightened mother and a largely rural upbringing, she had understood the mechanics well enough. But this was a different matter altogether. Her eyes widened as the first tremors of doubt assailed her.

He saw it and moved quickly to soothe her. "Don't be afraid. It isn't as bad as it seems. Your body and mine were made to fit together."

But not necessarily without discomfort or even pain for her. Realizing that dampened his ardor just enough to allow him to regain some shaky measure of control. How long it would last he did not dare to guess. He only knew that he must do everything he could to bring her to a peak of readiness, and to do it swiftly.

"Morgana," he said thickly, "trust me. I don't want to shock or frighten you, but your body must be prepared. There are ways, pleasurable to both.'' Gently, he urged her onto the bed so that she was lying stretched out, wide-eyed, gazing up at him.

He smiled reassuringly and slipped his hands beneath her thighs, urging them apart. Opened to him, she gasped and tried to cover herself but he would not permit it. Slowly, he covered her, holding his weight above her so that she was gently but remorselessly confined. His hands stroked her breasts, the long fingers teasing her aching nipples. She gasped, her head moving back and forth against the silken covers. The heat of his gaze seared her. His head bent, his mouth closing over her, coaxing the rosy peak to even greater hardness as he suckled first one breast and then the other. As his tongue laved her, his hands moved lower, stroking, coaxing, discovering. Nothing was barred to him; he would not permit it. The soft folds of her womanhood knew the thrust of his fingers as he delved within her, judging her readiness.

The barrier of her virginity was unmistakable. He drew back slightly, breathing deeply, and spread her legs farther. When his mouth touched her again, she cried out. Frantically, she tried to fight him, but he would not allow that any more than he would permit her to harm herself. With gentle strength, he held her to his will, tasting and savoring her until the undulating spasms of her body told him of her readiness.

Only then did he move within her, easily breaching the barrier of her virginity and sheathing himself tight within her welcoming fire.

He waited through a heartbeat and another until he could feel her beginning to tighten around him of her own accord. The last tenuous bonds of his self-control broke. With devastating strength, he made them truly one.

Chapter Fifteen

"Wake up, lazybones," a voice said near her ear. Morgana grumbled and tried to turn over, away from the intrusion. The bed was warm and soft, and she was still so tired.

"Go away," she murmured.

The voice chuckled, still very near her ear. She felt the warm brush of breath on her cheek.

"Up," the voice said, commanding, and in the next instant the covers were ripped from her. Chill air engulfed her naked body. She came instantly, vehemently awake.

"Yi! You..."

"Temper," David admonished. He was standing beside the bed, holding the covers and gazing at her appreciatively. And why not? For she was as bare as the day of her birth, every inch of her exposed to his view. With another yelp, she jumped from the bed and grabbed for the robe he thoughtfully held out. Fumbling into it, she said, "You are no gentleman."

He laughed and dropped the covers. His eyes slid over her fondly and with the unmistakable stamp of possession. "I was gentle last night. You said so."

She flushed so scarlet that for a moment her skin and hair seemed to blend into one another. Last night did not bear thinking about, and she most certainly was no longer the abandoned creature who had reached for him again and again.

"David, we..."

"No," he said, "let's not start in. We did fine once we stopped talking. Besides, we don't have time."

"What do you mean?"

"It's simple, sweetling," he said, taking her by the shoulders and steering her toward the dressing room. "Madame Chanon is getting up early just to meet you, and it would be impolite to keep her waiting."

Morgana dug her heels into the carpeting and refused to budge. "Who is Madame Chanon when she's at home?"

"London's leading couturier."

"Oh, no. There's no reason I would need to see her. Absolutely none at all."

"But there is."

"What?"

"If you don't, the dress she makes for you may not fit."

"She isn't making any dress for me. I don't need a dress. I already have more than enough dresses."

"I'll tell her she has to come here."

"No!"

"Good, I knew you'd see reason. I'll send in your maid. We're expected in an hour." He dropped a kiss on her nose, patted her behind with easy familiarity and strolled out the door. Morgana wasted one of her best glares on him before she realized he hadn't even noticed.

Damn the man! He was arrogant, insufferable, bewildering, magnificent...

There were two basins in the dressing room, one of warm water and the other of cold. She ignored the warm and splashed cold water on her face until she could hardly feel her cheeks. Madame Chanon indeed! She would undoubtedly be a haughty, imperious Frenchwoman used to dealing with the crème de la crème of London femininity and none too pleased to be saddled with a Welsh spinster.

Had Madame Chanon been privy to Morgana's thoughts at that moment, she would have agreed with them completely. Never could she remember making herself available at such an hour for any client. Well, there had been those ten years or so when she was scrabbling a living in Lyons making clothes for fat merchants' equally fat wives, but those didn't count. Since arriving in London and becoming Madame Nina Chanon instead of plain old Marie Blanc, she had acquired a reputation equal to none. Put simply, if you had any pretensions to being a woman of fashion, you absolutely had to deal with Madame Chanon. Provided, of course, that she would deal with you.

When the note from the Marquess of Montfort arrived the previous day informing her—not even asking, mind you, but informing—that he would be coming around the following morning with a young lady and naming the ungodly hour, she had been tempted to inform him that she would not be available. Then she remembered who he was. David Harrell, *the* David Harrell, richer than Croesus, a man who lived by his own rules, charted his own course and brooked no disagreement from anyone.

Certainly not from the likes of her. Her ample shoulders rose in a Gallic shrug. If his lordship chose to call on her at practically dawn, accompanied by a young lady, who was she to argue?

She sent a serving girl to open the shop door for them but bustled forward herself only a moment or two later. It was too much effort to contain her curiosity, and she didn't want to risk incurring his wrath.

First she concentrated on the marquess, noting that he was as fine a figure of a man as she had heard. But professional concerns took precedence, and she quickly turned her attention to the woman at his side. Hands on her corseted hips, magnificently garbed in black silk and Spanish lace, she raked her eyes over Morgana. And frowned.

What was this? No whore, certainly, for she lacked the stamp of coarseness no member of that sisterhood ever managed to escape, not the youngest or prettiest or most ingenuous. However much they tried, it always showed. Not that Madame Chanon minded. Some of her best customers were whores of one kind or another.

"*Monsieur,*" she said, inclining her head graciously. Morgana received another, if slightly lesser nod. "*Mademoiselle.*"

"Miss Penrhys requires a dress for evening," his lordship said.

"Of course," Madame Chanon replied. Never mind that Miss Penrhys looked as though she wanted nothing. Her wishes did not matter.

"For tomorrow evening," his lordship added.

Madame Chanon froze. He could not be serious. She permitted herself a small laugh as though appreciating the joke. More seriously, she said, "That is impossible, my lord."

He was not listening to her. All his attention was on the woman. As for Miss Penrhys, whoever she might be, she was looking around her with an expression of mingled amazement and awakening interest. And why not? Madame Chanon prided herself on having the finest collection of deluxe materials anywhere in London. You could not find better silk, more exquisite satin, more perfectly woven brocade. Well, you could, but you had to be willing to go to China, and most ladies of fashion were far too busy right here in Europe to consider that.

Madame Chanon smiled. The shop assistant could have told her visitors what an extremely rare occurrence this was, but she was too dumbstruck to say anything. First, by the man who was quite simply the most handsome and compelling male she had ever seen. Then by the woman who for all her lack of fashion was startlingly beautiful. And most of all by Madame Chanon herself, who bound her clients to her all the more tightly by making sure they understood how extremely fortunate they were that she noticed them at all, but who was suddenly extending herself to be polite, if not downright cordial. Truly it was a morning of wonders.

However, none of that solved the little matter of when his lordship expected the dress to be ready. He would have to be disabused of such a notion immediately. Madame Chanon fully intended doing that, but before she could utter a word he raised a hand and beckoned her closer.

She went, of course. Any female over the age of twelve would have done the same. A glance was sufficient to assure him that Morgana was distracted. She was looking around at the bolts of fabric like a child in a cavern of marvels.

The marquess quoted an amount. Madame Chanon put a hand to her breast. She swallowed her shock and smiled beguilingly. "Pounds?"

"Guineas."

Better and better. Her smile deepened and became quite genuine. "It is so nice to meet a serious man, your lordship."

Silently, she thanked whatever gods there were that the redhead—such remarkable hair—was beautiful. She would at least pay for the dressing. Actually, it was his lordship who would pay, and royally, but so far as Madame Chanon was concerned that was exactly how it should be.

"*Mademoiselle,*" she said, interrupting Morgana's dazed study of her surroundings. All business now, Madame Chanon gestured to her assistant. "So we begin."

"Drink your tea," David said. "You'll feel better."

Morgana shook her head. "No, I won't."

"You're being childish. It couldn't have been that bad."

"What do you know of it? You left. You actually walked out and left me with that...that torturer."

"I came back later and got you," he pointed out reasonably.

"Two hours later. I could have been dead by then." She shivered. "Pricked to death by all those horrible pins, thousands of them. Or smothered under all those patterns." Her eyes widened at the remembered horror. "Or crushed by bolts of fabric. She kept pulling them from the bottoms of piles and all the rest would begin to teeter and I'd think, this is it, here they come down on top of me. But somehow they never did."

"Terrible experience," David murmured, thinking how lovely she looked even with the lavender shadows under her eyes. She really was tired. He would have to restrain himself.

"Two hours for a single dress," Morgana said, shaking her head. With unmistakable satisfaction, she added, "And you won't even like it."

He raised an eyebrow. "No?"

"No."

"Why not?"

"It's too...too everything." She broke off and looked away from him.

"Too feminine?"

"Hmm."

"Too enticing?"

"Hmm."

"Too suggestive?"

"No," she admitted, "not that. It is quite lovely, actually. I just feel like a stranger in it."

He leaned back on the leather couch in the library and looked at her with that air of perfect assurance she was coming to know, if not tolerate. "You will become accustomed to it."

Oh, she would, would she? He was very sure of her, of everything, for that matter, while she was sure of nothing. Ever since he said ... suggested ... announced ... whatever it was he had done about his intentions, she had been certain only of a feeling of overwhelming confusion. He refused to discuss it any further, but they would have to, wouldn't they? Something like that couldn't be left lying.

"You need to rest," he said gently.

She shook her head. "I'm fine, really. Madame Chanon wasn't really that bad. I exaggerated."

"I know. You will become accustomed to her, too."

"I don't expect to ever see her again after tomorrow."

He let that pass, thinking there was no reason to explain to her that Madame Chanon would load her wares onto a wagon and personally drag them to Gynfelin for the price he was paying her. Instead, he rose and held out his hand. "Come."

Her eyes widened. It was barely noon. There were servants all over the house. He couldn't be serious.

"Chit," he murmured, bending closer. "I merely wish to see you to your room where," he admonished, "you will rest whether you think you need to or not."

Flustered, Morgana stood up quickly. "That isn't necessary, I will see myself."

He shrugged. "As you wish."

She hesitated. "I'm sorry, that was rude. It's only that..." What could she say? That this was all becoming too much for her? That she was beginning to be genuinely frightened? That with him she seemed to become a woman who was a stranger to her? She could say nothing of that. Instead, she murmured again, "I'm sorry."

He lifted her hand and touched it softly to his lips. "No apology is needed. Go and rest. When you are tired, everything looks more difficult than it really is."

She went up the curving steps and, looking back, saw him watching her. The imprint of his mouth remained against her skin. She touched her fingers to it lightly, wonderingly, and continued on her way.

It was done. David leaned back in his chair, struck a match and held it to the tip of a cheroot. Across from him, Lord Philip Westerley was sweating profusely. His plump, soft face was ashen. He stared at the cards on the table in front of him as though they were a nest of writhing serpents.

"How..." he murmured.

"A check will do," David said coolly.

Westerley looked up, bewildered. His eyes were small, almost colorless and dazed. "Check?"

"For the amount owed. You may have it delivered to my bank tomorrow."

"But... but I can't. That is... the amount..."

David frowned. "I don't understand."

Around them, in the airless confines of White's card room, a dozen or so men shifted uneasily. They had all observed the game, drawn by rumors of the vast amounts being wagered, and they all knew that the marquess had won fairly. Westerley's loss was too bad, but he knew the rules. For him to even suggest that he couldn't pay violated their code of behavior so profoundly that it was impossible for them to feel anything but disgust for him.

"Get a grip on yourself, old sod," one of them said. "He beat you fair and square."

"Yes, but..."

"No but about it," another said. "You knew what you were doing."

"But I won yesterday and the day before! I beat him easily. How was I to know that—" Westerley broke off, turning hunted eyes on the marquess, who continued to regard him without emotion. "Surely we can come to some accommodation," Westerley ventured.

David smiled. The gesture only bared his teeth and left his eyes untouched. Several of the men, the more knowledgeable among them, glanced at one another. They all knew of the marquess, of course, even if they couldn't say they knew him personally. It was quietly understood among them that they would welcome him at their back in any fight but would never want to go against him.

"I'm afraid not," David said. "Tomorrow at my bank, in full."

Westerley was breathing hard. Sweat shone along his upper lip, and on his brow where thinning hair clung damply. "I can't!"

"Really, old man."

"Disgraceful."

"Should never have sat down at the table."

"Won't be forgotten."

Backs were turned, men walked away, all without thought, for no thought was needed. Westerley had stepped outside the pale. They no longer knew him.

David set his cheroot down. He looked at the squirming, terrified man across from him. For a moment longer he let Westerley wait. Then he began to speak softly and without haste.

The gown was of apricot silk, a color that should not have gone well with her hair but did nonetheless. Looking at herself in the full-length mirror, Morgana had to admit that Madame Chanon had been right about that and a good deal else. Right, for instance, to keep the dress relatively simple without all the bows and beads others of her clientele favored. She said that Morgana's skin, the color and texture of alabaster, was enough and about that, too, she had been right. The neckline was modest as some went but still exposed more of the swell of her breasts than had ever been seen in public before. She had to resist the urge to tug at the delicate fringe of silk rising only slightly above her nipples. The sleeves were of tiered lace and began off the shoulders. The waist was narrow and elongated, the skirt full. She stood shaped and revealed to the hips, totally concealed below. There was something disturbingly erotic about that although she couldn't have said exactly what. But then she wasn't a man. Her opinion of the gown was secondary, to say the least.

David was waiting for her when she came down. He stood in the entry hall, a tall, powerful figure in evening dress. There was an air of distraction about him until he saw her.

The gaze that swept over her was relentless. She burned under it and had all she could do not to turn and flee. At length, he smiled faintly, as though at a joke on himself.

"Madame Chanon has outdone herself."

"So she informed me," Morgana said, taking refuge in tartness. "When she came today, I heard at great length what a magnificent job she had done under the most adverse circumstances. Apparently, it usually takes longer than a day to make a gown like this."

"Really?"

"I can't think why. It's not as though there was a great deal to it."

"It isn't intended as protection against a gale."

"Good thing," Morgana muttered. Any notion she might have had that he would be a wee bit jealous went straight out the window. Insufferable man.

"Madame Chanon brought something else for you, too," the marquess said. He lifted a hand. Fenwith appeared, rather magically, Morgana thought.

The butler inclined his head gravely. "Sir." He handed over what appeared to be a length of teal silk, the exact shade of Morgana's eyes in a certain light. Opened, it turned out to be a cloak. The marquess draped it around her shoulders, and while she was still savoring the liquid coolness of it on her skin, he fastened the closing beneath her throat. Enveloped in it, she felt slightly safer, an impression that was dispelled the instant she happened to glance into his eyes.

"Thank you," she murmured because it seemed the safest thing to say.

They went out into the night, into a carriage drawn by high-prancing black horses and through the gaslit streets of London to, wonder of wonders, the Royal Opera House. Morgana had heard of it, of course. She had seen engravings in the *Ladies' Quarterly*. But she had never in her wildest dreams imagined that she would be walking up the wide stone steps, through the embossed bronze doors and into a lobby crowded with the cream of London society. Most particularly she had not thought to do it on the arm of a man whose mere presence made him the immediate focus of attention.

Oh, not that anyone came rushing up to them. It was all more discreet than that. They merely stared, bejeweled ladies and bewhiskered men, tilting their heads together, murmuring and exchanging meaningful looks. Several did speak to David, but cautiously, as though they weren't sure how he would take their approaches and did not, under any circumstances, wish to rile him. A few were more natural and easy with him, but they were the exception and seemed somehow like him, big, hard men on whom the trappings of civilization hung but lightly.

Morgana sat on the edge of her tufted velvet chair, as close to the edge of the private box as she could get, and stared enraptured at the stage. The sound, the color, the movement all sent her whirling out of herself. She forgot where she was, indeed she almost forgot who she was, so caught up was she in the drama and ultimate tragedy playing out before her.

David sat back slightly and watched Morgana. She was far more entrancing than anything on the stage. Indeed, she transformed what would otherwise have been an ordinary evening into something far more.

When at last the curtain fell for the interlude, Morgana sat back with a sigh. "That was wonderful," she said.

The marquess smiled. Her eyes were glowing. Despite the sophisticated gown, she looked fresh, innocent and utterly unfeigned in her enjoyment. "The tenor is magnificent, don't you think? And the soprano, as well. But the staging. I would never have expected real animals on stage. It's all so real, so huge, so..." She broke off, suddenly aware of two things. The first was that David was gazing at her with a look of such tender enjoyment that her breath caught in her throat. The second was that they were once again the object of considerable attention. A wave of self-consciousness washed over her.

The second act provided some respite, but she was relieved when the opera ended and they were once again within the carriage. She felt no need to go out in London society ever again. Not even in Gynfelin would people be so rude. Well, perhaps the dragons Kennard and Armbruster would be, but they were only two, and here there were so many.

"You are very quiet," David said.

"I was just wondering why people here are so . . . so forward."

He smiled faintly. "So curious?"

"Yes, to the point of rudeness." More boldly, she said, "I may have grown up in a small Welsh town and lived these past few years in an even smaller village, but I do at least have manners. This is London, those people are supposed to be the aristocracy, and they . . . they behave no better than country bumpkins!"

David made no attempt to deny it. "They were merely surprised."

She frowned, puzzled. "Why?"

"Because you are remarkably beautiful, of course. They were wondering who you are."

"No one," Morgana said quickly. "So far as they are concerned, I am most certainly no one. And my looks are hardly so remarkable even in this extraordinary gown. You would think people would have something better to occupy their minds."

"You must tell my great-aunt that," he said. "She will agree with you."

"Your who?"

"Great-aunt," he repeated mildly, as though it was the most natural thing in the world. "Didn't I mention her? Lady Penelope Harrell Lambert."

Morgana shook her head. "No, you didn't."

"Careless of me. She is having a soiree this evening, and she would never forgive me if we didn't stop by."

His sudden concern for this great-aunt whose existence had been unknown to her a moment ago stunned

Morgana. Even more stunning was the notion that he would take her to meet a member of his family. Wasn't it enough that he had violated the conventions by taking her to the opera?

"By all means, you go," Morgana said. "I shall enjoy an early night."

"Nonsense, you had plenty of time to rest earlier today. Besides, I don't dare arrive without you."

She looked at him skeptically, this man who gave no sign of ever fearing anything. "Why not?"

"Because she will know I brought you to the opera, and once she hears that, she won't rest until she's met you."

"You did this on purpose," Morgana exclaimed. "But why? To what end?"

He shrugged. "You wanted to see London. My great-aunt is practically an institution. I'm sure you'll find her . . . interesting."

Interesting? The word had never sounded more ominous. She shut her eyes, summoning strength, and prayed most fervently that she would not disgrace herself.

Chapter Sixteen

Morgana wasn't sure what she expected when she came face to face with Lady Penelope—a more sophisticated and formidable version of Gynfelin's dragons perhaps. What she did not expect was a small woman with shining gray eyes and nut-brown hair sitting square in the center of a mob of guests all apparently vying for her attention. Her tiny form was enveloped in a gown that appeared to have been spun from gold. She sat perched on a tasseled cushion on a high-backed chair that fell just short of being thronelike. Her plump face was wreathed in smiles, and her laughter was positively ribald.

On David's arm, Morgana paused, gazing at this apparition. She looked at him, looked again at their hostess and shook her head in astonishment. "You should have warned me."

"You're right," he said, sounding not at all contrite, "I should have."

Just then Lady Penelope turned in their direction. For a moment, her smile vanished and a look that was positively speculative darted across her face. Morgana's initial impression was vividly confirmed.

"She bears a remarkable resemblance to Her Majesty."

Indeed, Lady Penelope Harrell Lambert looked like an older but vastly more lighthearted version of the sovereign. Victoria had been a pretty girl with a shy smile and a pleasing seriousness that came as a relief to a country worn out by its wastrel monarchs. But twenty years of being queen, wife and mother had transformed her into a living icon of propriety. The weight of majesty hung heavily on her and left few signs of the girl she had been. By contrast, this woman appeared weighted down by nothing whatsoever.

Lady Penelope gave free rein to her appetite for diversion, any kind of diversion even if it had to include all these boring people, the same faces that seemed to crop up everywhere. But not that face, well known and well loved but too rarely glimpsed. And who was that beside him, that girl with the extraordinary hair looking like something plucked from a fantasy garden? Oh, the evening held promise after all.

"Dear boy," she said and held out her hand. David bent over it gallantly, a genuine smile lightening his eyes.

"You look splendid, Penelope," he said for he had always called her that, just Penelope, never aunt or heaven forbid, great-aunt. Indeed, it was difficult for him to remember that she was old enough to be his grandmother. She had never been a steady presence in his life, only Sebastian had been that, but she had been there far more than any other blood relative. She'd flitted in and out, bringing him little things when he seemed most to need them and filling his imagination with the tantalizing thought that life could actually be fun.

She shot him a look that said she knew he was flattering her but didn't care because he did it so well, and besides, it was her due.

"Where *have* you been? Going off to Wales like that and not even saying goodbye. The dear Baron and Baroness of Wilhamshire were crushed. They thought you were coming to their cotillion."

"I can't imagine why they would have thought that," David said smoothly, "since I specifically told you I would not."

Lady Penelope sniffed. Her eyes had settled on Morgana, who was receiving a very thorough going over. The chit held up on close inspection, that was for sure. Trust dear David to arrive with a thoroughbred. "Perhaps I misunderstood, but enough of that. Who is this darling thing?"

David did the introductions. Morgana managed a small curtsy despite the way her knees were trembling. She braced herself for what she was sure must be coming.

Lady Penelope frowned slightly. "Penrhys, Penrhys... I don't know the name. Are you new to London, my dear?"

"Very," Morgana murmured. Silently, she damned David for doing this to her. How dare he bring her right into the midst of his family and risk exposing her to such censure as must surely follow? What happened between them in private, in this time out of time, was entirely their own business. Exposed in public, it would become very unpleasant very quickly.

Lady Penelope looked at the overly large eyes, the pale lips and the sudden pulse beating in the slender throat and sighed. It was just like David to do something outrageous, but to bring this lovely creature into her house without proper introduction or chaperonage was going a bit far. Still, he must have his reasons.

"Go and get us some champagne, dear boy," she said. She patted the chair beside her. "Sit down, Miss Penrhys. What a lovely gown you're wearing. Madame Chanon, is it?"

Morgana nodded. She sat because it was easier than standing and because there seemed no other option for her. David hesitated a moment, glancing at them both, but then he went off, seemingly satisfied that all was well.

Fool! She had walked straight into the dragon's den, and now she was going to pay the price.

"How did you find La Grande Chanon?" Lady Penelope inquired. "She can be quite difficult."

"I found her...bewildering," Morgana admitted. Did dragons have horns, or was that only bulls? Whatever, better to meet this particular dragon head-on and hope for the best. With dignity, she said, "I'm not used to such things. David was kind enough to pay for this dress, and it is beautiful, but it also seemed like a great deal of unnecessary fuss."

Lady Penelope had dark, slanting brows, which she disdained to pluck because they were one of her major means of expression. At that moment, for instance, they were wiggling up near her hairline.

"Kind, was he? Yes, he can be that, although truth be told, we haven't seen too much of it in recent years. He's had a hard time, and I'm afraid it's made him hard in turn."

This was not what Morgana had expected. The reference to David paying for the dress had been deliberate, a means of getting things out in the open so that they could be finished with. But Lady Penelope had refused the bait. Instead, she said what she did about David and took the conversation in an entirely different direction. The marquess was not the only Harrell full of surprises.

"He has been very kind to others, as well," Morgana said. "He saved a child in Wales who would have been doomed to a terrible life without his help, and he has gone beyond that to try to right some very fundamental wrongs."

"Indeed? And how do you know of all this, dear?"

Morgana took a deep breath. Her position was precarious. Discretion should be her watchword. And yet there was something about this plump old woman in gold, a current of genuine concern when she spoke of David, that was impossible to ignore.

"I come from Wales," she said finally. "That is where the marquess and I met."

"Ah, I see..." From Wales, perfectly beautiful and with no family of any import. Her great-nephew really was being naughty, wasn't he? "What do you do in Wales, dear, or is it indiscreet of me to ask?"

"I teach," Morgana said quietly, "at the school in Gynfelin." Quickly, she added, "I'm sorry if that shocks you but I really have been a good teacher. In fact, it's been my life up until recently." Almost to herself, she said, "Now everything's topsy-turvy."

"I should think so," Lady Penelope said. Her mouth tightened. Really, that boy! He might have washed his hands of convention, but there were others who couldn't afford to do the same. The girl obviously cared about her work—and just as obviously she cared for David. Poor thing, caught between two so seemingly irreconcilable worlds.

David noted his great-aunt's frosty glare as he returned with the champagne. He handed a fluted glass to her and another to Morgana. Inwardly, he smiled. Penelope had always been a great one for championing the underdog. That was exactly why he had brought Morgana to her.

"Miss Penrhys was telling me about the school," she said sternly. "Teaching is such a noble profession. Such sacrifice in the service of the next generation sets an example for us all. But it would be wrong to take advantage of so giving a nature, don't you agree, David?"

"Absolutely," he said, smiling at Morgana, whose gaze was locked firmly on her folded hands, the champagne having been set aside untasted. "Miss Penrhys teaches her students to appreciate the world as it is while still working to change it. She is a reformer, even something of a visionary, who isn't afraid to violate convention."

"So I gather," Lady Penelope murmured dryly.

"Please," Morgana broke in, Being spoken of as though she were no longer present was bad enough, but to have David refer even indirectly to her delicate situation was intolerable.

"There, there, dear," Lady Penelope said, patting her hand. "Don't take him too seriously. Actually, I'm glad David brought you here this evening. He may be no closer to following the rules than he ever was but at least his taste has improved."

"Taste?" Morgana asked.

"In women. Oh, don't look so shocked. In my day we spoke a good deal more honestly of such things. This middle-class morality we suffer from at the moment is most tedious. It's all that Albert, of course, and his stiff-lipped Germanness, but never mind. My point is that I have always been on David's side. I never believed he should settle for one of those dreadful little chits ambitious mamas keep throwing in his path. For a while, I thought that business in the Crimea might discourage them, but no, it only made it worse. He stood up to those horrible old fools, you see, just as everyone back here was wondering who in God's name had put them in charge to start with. So he came home quite the hero with a dash of the disreputable to add to his gloss."

She broke off to take a reviving sip of the champagne. Actually, she swallowed half of it and smacked her lips appreciatively before continuing. "Speaking of which, I hope your ducking is still up to snuff, dear boy. You're in at least a dozen sights that I can make out, and there are bound to be more."

"I count on your protection," David said. He appeared not at all disturbed by his great-aunt's revelations. On the contrary, he was smiling as he held out his hand to Morgana. "Would you care to dance?"

Of course she would. There was nothing she wanted more than to get up in front of all these people and make a spectacle of herself.

"No."

Lady Penelope chuckled. She reached over and tapped Morgana lightly on the wrist with her fan. "Go ahead, dear. I'll take care of things here."

Morgana went. What choice did she have without appearing insufferably rude? After all, Lady Penelope had been very kind to her. She really was a dear woman, sitting there in her oversized chair, with the steady stream of people descending on her. From the dance floor, Morgana glimpsed her, nut-brown head bobbing, eyes twinkling. David danced superbly. In his arms, she felt lighter than air, unbound by earthy restrictions.

Lady Penelope glanced in her direction. She raised a hand, waving genially. The people clustered around her chair stared until their hostess began speaking again. Then all their attention was on her.

"I wonder what she's saying," Morgana murmured. "They all look so intent."

"Gossip," David replied. "My great-aunt is one of the great practitioners of it. I observed that as a child, and it is truer now than ever. She knows exactly what to say and what not. The subtle suggestion, the hint, the indirection, she does them all brilliantly."

He smiled at her, silver eyes alight with amusement. "Right now she will be telling everyone what a lovely young woman you are, and from such a good family. 'The Penrhyses, of course you know them? A bit on the bluestocking side, generations of scholars, you know. The girl's rather shy, hasn't been out in society much. David's doing a good turn showing her around. Shouldn't wonder, though ... Ah, well, best not to say. Such a dear boy.'" He mimicked Lady Penelope's galloping intonation so perfectly that Morgana burst out laughing. Dear boy, indeed!

"You can't know that she's saying anything of the sort."

"No," he admitted, "I can't for sure but I can make an educated guess. This is simply far too good an opportunity for her to pass up."

Morgana laughed again and shook her head. The apricot gown swirled around her as they danced. The music played on, the spring night aged, and she let go of worry. It would come again, it always did, but for the moment she let the time of enchantment weave its spell around her. In his arms, at his side, safe within his gaze, she forgot all else. Never mind the stares and murmurs, they could not touch her now. Protected by his strength and Lady Penelope's kindness, she blossomed.

Stranger that she was to London society, she did not notice that no other man attempted to dance with her. Many thought of it, drawn by her incandescent beauty, but all thought better.

The marquess was not a man to cross. Look what had happened to Westerley. Whoever the girl was, she was his. Damn shame, that, for she was magnificent, but life went on.

"Such a lovely girl," Lady Penelope murmured, sipping her champagne. "Dear David." For just a moment she let herself remember the boy he had been, the child she should have done more to help but who loved her all the same. She remembered the long-ago touch of a small hand in hers and felt the bittersweet pain of missed opportunities.

Perhaps some day, if it wasn't too late, if God was as merciful as He sometimes seemed disposed to be, there might yet be a second chance. Morgana laughed suddenly, drawing Lady Penelope's eyes. No sense brooding over what was gone. So much better to think on what was yet to be.

She called for a footman to refill her glass and raised it to those two lovely young people whirling past. The future was theirs if only they had the sense and the luck to seize it.

"Courage," she murmured. It sounded almost like a prayer.

Chapter Seventeen

The following afternoon a stack of invitations arrived at David's residence. They were sent over by Lady Penelope. Somehow people had gotten the impression, she offered no explanation of how, that Morgana was staying with her. The invitations were for teas, soirees, cotillions and a ball or two, which the dear girl—Penrhys family, you know, very old stock, quite respected—might enjoy attending.

"I would rather be slowly roasted over a spit," Morgana said when she learned of them. For good measure, she added, "With my fingernails torn out."

David was relieved. He found the London social round unbearably dull. Looking up from his perusal of a letter from his bankers, he said, "It's a beautiful day. Let's drive out to Epping and have a picnic."

The former royal hunting preserve and sanctuary for city dwellers in time of plague had long since become a stretch of public land, some of it rented out to smallholders, where people could refresh themselves far from the city's noise and congestion.

The most popular stopping place was an inn on the Epping Road where visitors could sit at outdoor tables to enjoy the sun while sipping beer or, for the ladies, wine. Morgana and David avoided it, preferring instead to strike out on their own. They left the phaeton in the capable hands of a stable boy and wandered down a narrow lane that led eventually to a small lake.

David spread the blanket they had brought along while Morgana unpacked the picnic basket. They lunched on cold poached chicken, sliced hothouse tomatoes and crisp-crusted rolls. He tied a length of rope to a bottle of wine and let it cool a few minutes in the lake before pouring for them both. Morgana drank a small amount but no more, for the day was making her giddy enough. Everywhere was sparkling sunshine, cloudless sky, birdsong and the sense of the world awakening to new life.

She sat with her back to an oak tree in soft green bud and looked over the lake. On the other side, a few cows moved slowly, heads down, foraging. Closer in, a small brown hare peered from cover before making a dash for the safety of the trees. Across the water, a blue crane rose, turned majestically in the sky and sought its nest.

David lay with his head in her lap. His eyes were closed, his black hair disheveled by the breeze wafting off the water. He looked so peaceful that she wondered if he might be asleep. His features were more relaxed than she could recall ever having seen them. He looked younger, more approachable, even vulnerable.

The thought startled her, for it brought with it a sudden surging wave of tenderness. She allowed a hand to feather lightly to his brow, and before she could stop herself, followed it with the touch of her lips.

He stirred against her, his eyes opening slowly. In that half-awake state between dream and consciousness he had felt...what? Not passion, entirely, although that was part of it, but something else, deeper, far less familiar. The brush of her lips against his skin, the scent of lavender, the warmth and peace....

He looked up into the sea where currents ran through buried caverns and life stirred in the darkness. The sea captured within her eyes, illumined by her soul.

"Morgana," he murmured and reached for her, his hand cradling the back of her head, drawing her down, down, deep into the whirling throes of passion where sky touched sea and lightning flared.

Later, they finished the wine in the slow drifting afternoon. The cows moved on, clouds scuttered across the sun. Finally growing coolness drove them back to the phaeton. They drove the distance into town as day gave way to the gentle light of dusk. Morgana's dress was stained with grass, and a splattering of newly hatched freckles danced across her nose. David's frock coat was tossed over his shoulder, his stock undone, and his boots were spattered with honest English mud since he had ventured into marshy ground to pluck the pink flowering rush twined in Morgana's hair.

Fenwith opened the door for them. He showed admirable restraint in giving them one quick, all encompassing glance before looking properly away. "Sir," he murmured, "a pleasant day, I hope?"

"Very," David assured him. "But baths are called for, I think, and we'll be dining here."

"Very good, sir. Your factor sent some papers over for your signature, my lord. They are in the library."

David nodded. "I'll look at them now."

Morgana took that as her cue. She gave him a quick smile and made for the stairs. Her step was light, for the pleasure of the day still surrounded her. A golden day, lost to splendor, that she would remember forever. Lying in the tub, washing away the scent of grass and sun and love, she clung to the moment and did not let herself think beyond.

It was coming, that time after the time out of time, rushing toward her with the force of one of the great steam-powered locomotives that were crisscrossing Britain with increasing speed these days. She shut her eyes for a moment and thought she heard the terrible, thunderous sound drowning out all else. But it was only the rush of her heart, the blood singing in her ears, reminding her of her own life hastening on no matter how desperately she might wish to cling to this one moment.

She dressed slowly and went down the stairs. David was in the library. He had also bathed and changed into dark trousers, a white shirt and a dark frock coat. He looked elegantly masculine but far less approachable than the lover who had lain in her lap.

He turned as she entered and she saw his features once again guarded, the eyes watchful. For a moment, she wanted to go back, away from him, away from what must surely be coming. But she was a Penrhys, and Penrhyses did not run, not ever.

"Morgana," he said and came toward her. No preamble then but instead his eyes on hers and his beloved voice, suddenly so serious, for he, too, had been deep within his thoughts. "We need to—"

To talk? To love? To decide? Whatever he had been about to say, and it could have been all that or more, she would not know. What she heard instead, and he as well, was the knocking at the door, brass hammering on oak, and the rush of footsteps, Fenwith gliding past, grumbling and hurrying to answer.

The sense was already growing in that split second of eternity that something had fractured, fallen out of place, and whatever was about to be said, it would not be good or loving or of life.

And in fact, it was not.

They went by sea on a schooner called the *Lady Mary* that belonged to a friend of David's who had served with him in the Crimea and apparently saw nothing odd about lending his yacht on a moment's notice and the strength of a hastily scribbled note dispatched by a wide-eyed footman. They went swiftly, in the clothes they wore, with only a few others thrown into valises. Morgana remembered little of the first hour or two after the word came, only the flurry of activity, servants racing back and forth, and David in the midst of it all, the calm but remorseless eyes of the storm.

Fifteen were dead, the messenger had said, and unknown more dying. He wept as he spoke, silvered tears dripping from his exhausted, red-rimmed eyes. He was a small, dark man like the old people of long-ago Cymru and of Ireland, who had gone into the hills when the tall, Fair Ones came. The hills and what lay under them were still their world. They cherished it even as they saw it torn asunder. Dead, dying, the hills screamed out their rage.

The explosion had ripped through the mine an hour after the day shift went down. The few who managed to stagger out could not say what had caused it. Yes, the atmosphere below had been fetid with coal dust. Yes, there had been fear that something of the sort might happen. But it was always fetid and always fearsome. Why now? Why here? Why these men, these families?

Unknowable questions shouted silently at an unanswering sky. The night was quiet. At midnight, as the watchmen called near Southwark's piers, the tide changed. The *Lady Mary,* her crew hastily assembled, turned her prow downriver and slipped quietly away.

The sea was calm, the sky clear. A waxing moon spilled silver over the placid water. Morgana stood by the railing. The loveliness of the night struck her to the quick. Nature, the world, God Himself seemed so immune to the suffering of mere humans. The unfairness jabbed at her like a thousand prickling needles until she could bear it no longer.

She went below and found her way to the cabin where her own and David's valises had been left. The intimacy of this arrangement did not trouble her; indeed, she hardly noticed it. It seemed only natural for them to be together in whatever way they could for however long they could.

He was standing with his back to her, looking out the porthole at the city vanishing into darkness. The rigid set of his shoulders sent her to his side.

"David..."

"My people," he said quietly. "Those are my people dead and dying."

She stopped, hand frozen in midair to comfort him. "What do you mean?"

He laughed, a hollow sound holding nothing of mirth. "I won the mines from Westerley. Those papers in the library when we got back were the deeds."

"You won them..." The thought staggered her. If he had said *bought*, she could have understood, for property was bought and sold all the time, and all too often the lives of men and women with it. But won? On a chance wager, a hand of cards, a whim of fate? There was something almost obscene about that.

"It was the only way," he said, sounding very weary. "Westerley would never have sold."

That was true, Morgana realized. The Englishman had depended too much on the mines to finance his gambling extravagances. There was a certain justice in that it was his gambling that had finally forced him to give them up.

She put her hand on his arm gently. "There was no time for you to change anything."

"I know," he said, but the knowing did not help. They were his now, as the men in the Crimea had been, and he felt the weight of that as heavily as though the earth itself were pressing down on him.

"Lie down and rest," he told Morgana.

"You, too."

He managed a slight smile. "In a bit."

She did as he said and lay down on one of the narrow bunks. Sleep seemed impossible, but the gentle motion of the boat overcame her and she slipped into dreams. When she awoke some uncounted time later, the cabin was empty. She fumbled in the darkness for her shoes, put them on and went up on deck hastily.

He was standing near the prow, staring into the night. A ray of moonlight, emerging from behind the clouds, struck his profile with the sharpness of newly minted steel. Morgana stopped, staring at him. He looked as always—big, hard, indomitable. Yet there was a difference, a sense of him being not there on the graceful yacht cleaving through the sea but elsewhere, in the tear-soaked hills where his people wailed and raised their faces to the darkening sky, crying for relief.

My people, he had said, not my mines or my property. My people. In the old days, warrior chieftains had pledged themselves in the same way, understanding that with privilege came responsibility. The chieftain ruled in good times and bad, but in the bad a sacrifice might be called for to save the people, and then it was the chieftain's blood that ran to propitiate angry gods.

A chill shot through Morgana. She was letting her imagination run away with her. This was, after all, the nineteenth century. Progress and modernity were the watchwords. Sacrifice, old gods, the keening earth were all the stuff of superstition.

The night pulled at her. She rested a hand on the deck rail to steady herself and felt the powerful currents running through the *Lady Mary* as the ship plunged forward. The wind was at their backs; the canvas snapped. They raced under full sail through the night into day until at last the fair green hills of Cymru rose out of the mist, beckoning them home.

"Twenty-two dead," Sebastian reported. "When we mustered this morning, fifty-seven remained missing. I can only conclude that they remain below, sir. Although whether any remain alive is impossible to say."

David nodded slowly. He stood in the mine office, a ramshackle wooden building near the entrance to the shafts. It was late in the day. Already gas lamps had been lit against the gathering gloom. Outside, where the crowds were gathered, pitch-soaked torches sent curls of black smoke into the sky.

"Is there anything further on what caused the explosion?" David asked.

"It is presumed to have been the coal dust, sir. Ventilation was inadequate. That is one of the issues Mr. Dawkins and the others were fighting to change."

"Any sign of him?"

Sebastian shook his head. His eyes were red-rimmed, his face streaked with grime. He had come as soon as word reached Gynfelin of the disaster, and he had remained ever since, trying as best he could to organize a rescue effort in the face of overwhelming unconcern by mine officials. His relief at his master's arrival was overshadowed only by fear that not even the marquess would be able to make much of a difference.

"I'm afraid not, sir," he said. "Mr. Dawkins is one of those thought to be trapped below."

Morgana made a low sound deep in her throat. "I must find his sister."

"Go with her," David told Sebastian. He turned to Morgana. "Find Mrs. Fergus and as many other women as you think may be useful. Organize them to preparing food for the people here. Requisition whatever is needed from the merchants. Tell them they'll be paid in full. Along with food, I want medical supplies, every shovel you can lay your hands on, ten cords of lumber and five thousand feet of rope. Charles Whitcomb can help find the lumber. Tell him we're going into the shafts and I need men willing to work shoring them up."

Sebastian paled. He stared at his master for a long moment before nodding abruptly. "As you say, sir."

Morgana took a quick step forward. "David . . ."

"Go on," he said gently. "There's work to be done."

Still, she held her ground. What he was contemplating was incredibly dangerous. Noble, yes, but also filled with risk. Someone had to say what everyone would be thinking. It fell to her to do so.

"They may all be dead. It may be too late."

His expression did not change. Matter-of-factly, he said, "Then I will bring out their bodies. But they are my people, and they will not be abandoned. That much at least I can promise their families."

A short time later, standing in the back of a wagon in the glare of the pitch torches, he said the same words again. There was no cheering, people were far too worried and filled with dread for that. But a stir did go through the crowd when he explained that he owned the mine now, not Westerley. And when he called for every able-bodied man to muster off to one side to begin digging, the response was swift.

They went, old and young, for every man apparently considered himself able-bodied under these circumstances. If he was still breathing, he was better off than those poor sods below, and he'd be smart to show providence he appreciated it. What shovels were on hand were passed out quickly. David had one in his own hand and was heading toward the main shaft when a man suddenly stepped in front of him. He was a big man, not quite as tall as the marquess but close to it with a roll of fat around his middle to give him added heft. His head seemed too small for so large a body. He had a tight, mean mouth that parted to reveal blackened teeth.

After a moment, David realized the man was smiling and that he had no apparent intention of moving. On the contrary, his hands were balled into beefy fists, and the way he bounced forward on his feet suggested his intentions were less than peaceful.

David sighed. He was worn out, more worried than he had been since the Crimea, and struggling with all his might to organize a rescue effort that should have already been under way. Now here was this fellow, a dyed-in-the-wool bully from the look of it, daring to stand in his path. Vaguely, he heard the indrawing of breath around him, saw the fearful glances of his people and concluded that this blustering oaf was someone.

Farr. Of course, it had to be. The mine manager—former manager—who broke the strike as readily as he broke the spirits of the men unfortunate enough to be in his employ.

The marquess could have gone around him, but how much more satisfying the alternative. He smiled as he put down the shovel, smiled still as he straightened, bare-handed, and smiled all the more as he drove that hand into Farr's spongy middle. Later people would talk about that smile, how it appeared perfectly genuine, as though his lordship had a flash of high good humor. He was a man who enjoyed his work, they would say, when his work was taking the likes of Jack Farr apart.

Farr reeled, stunned by the blow, and struggled to regroup. He was accustomed to instilling fear, to men flailing at him with no great success, crushed by his brute stubbornness and willingness to take punishment as well as inflict it. This was different. This was lethal strength unleashed with remorseless skill. This was what set men apart and set some above others, making them rulers—and protectors.

The good Welsh ground came up to meet Farr. It took him roughly and without grace. He lay, eyes opened in bewilderment as the people surged past him.

They had been willing before, but now they were eager, for before them went a man they would gladly follow into the darkness and the terror, into death itself.

Chapter Eighteen

Morgana ladled another serving of stew into a
wooden bowl and smiled gently at the child who received it. She waited until he hurried off, clutching his
bounty, before she rubbed the small of her back. It
would be dawn soon. An hour or so before, a light
rain had begun to fall. It was little noticed by hundreds of men, women and children who remained
gathered in front of the mine shaft.

From time to time, rumors floated upward. They
were into the main part of the tunnel, the shoring held,
there was more destruction then they had expected, no
sign had yet been found of the missing men. Morgana
stood at the cooking pot, stirring stew and listening.
The rain fell, and she tried to pray but no words would
come. In frustration, she chopped another onion,
tossed it in, and went to work whacking at a pile of
potatoes. Whatever came, several hundred people had
to be fed.

Beside her, Wynne Fergus threw another log on the
fire and glanced at the lowering sky. "Beastly
weather."

"It could be worse."

"Aye, and it could be a hell of a lot better." Wynne wiped her hands, pushed her hair out of her eyes and looked at Morgana. "Don't see how hard you can be pushing yourself what with still being recovering and all."

"Recovering?"

"From the riot. Folks said you were staying at the manor till you got your strength back."

"What folks?" Morgana asked. The steam from the kettle stung her cheeks. Surely nothing else accounted for their sudden redness.

"The butler fellow and Mrs. Gareth, they let it be known you were there. Lady Kendall is in a fair snit, let me tell you, saying you ought to be let go, but she didn't get far with that. People are getting mighty tired of her high-and-mighty ladyship."

Sebastian and Elizabeth Gareth had lied for her, so that her reputation might be preserved while she went off to London with a man not her husband. The shame of it was galling. Truly, honor was a rocky path strewn with pitfalls even for the wary.

"I was in London," she said, "with David . . . with his lordship."

Wynne's mouth dropped open. She stared at her friend, the schoolteacher, and burst out laughing. "Lord love you, lass. You've the touch, that's for sure."

"What touch?" Morgana asked. Her mind was still reeling from her own bluntness.

"'Tis an old thing, hardly spoken of now, but there used to be stories of people who could change dross to gold with the barest touch. You're one of them, lass, for sure, for haven't you changed our children's lives beyond our wildest hopes and brought a spirit to this place that hasn't been before?''

''You credit me with too much,'' Morgana murmured.

Wynne snorted under her breath and went back to work. The night passed slowly. Hope flared, died and flared again.

Toward dawn Morgana gave up her place at the kettle and sought shelter under a canvas overhang that had been set up to provide some protection from the worsening rain. She was sitting there, sipping a mug of tea, when a shout went up. Morgana jumped to her feet, the tea forgotten, and ran along with everyone else toward the mine shaft. Charles Whitcomb was there, begrimed and exhausted like everyone else, but his face alight with relief.

''They're alive,'' he said. ''We reached far enough down the tunnel to hear them.''

''How many?'' someone in the crowd shouted.

''Fifty-seven, Mr. Dawkins said, the same number that's missing. Some are injured, and they can't say how long the air will hold up, but at least now we've got a chance to get them out.''

A chance, nothing more. The survivors were trapped several hundred feet underground in a small chamber they'd been lucky enough to find after the explosion. For the moment it was their sanctuary but it could just as easily become their tomb. The air was worsening fast. Another explosion could bring the remaining tunnels down, blocking all escape.

The tension in the crowd, already high, reached a fever pitch. Only so many men could fit into the shaft to dig, only so many to shore with the long planks of lumber brought up in wagons. The rest had to remain above. Women stood, white-faced, clutching their children to them as they waited to learn if they were to become widows and orphans. Elderly people clung together, praying for word that their sons would come back to them.

Among them moved a small man with rounded shoulders, a pale face and an air of simple comfort. The Reverend Armbruster had come like everyone else when he heard the news. For a time he stood on the sidelines, fumbling to comprehend the dimensions of the disaster. His wife was with him, having declared her intentions to "take the poor benighted souls in hand." But by the time they arrived, there seemed little need for their services. Food was being provided along with the all-essential tea, blankets had been distributed, and a full-fledged rescue effort was under way. Goodwife Armbruster expressed her surprise, followed hard by dismay when she caught sight of the young woman standing at the kettle.

"I might have known," she exclaimed. "That hussy would be in the middle of this." She glared in Morgana's direction.

The reverend flinched. He had been wrestling with his conscience of late and hadn't liked what he'd found. "Really, Winnifred, must you use that word?"

"I see no reason to shirk the truth. They were seen together! Lady Kennard made it quite clear that—"

"Lady Kennard has made a great deal quite clear," the reverend broke in. His boldness surprised him, but he went on all the same. "If you ask me, she has far too much to say for herself and far too little of it reflects well on a woman of Christian charity." He looked again at the slender figure pausing to smile at a child and said sternly, "We are simple folk sent here to be of service. Remember Martha, who through her hard work and industriousness became the handmaiden of our Lord."

Winnifred opened her mouth to speak but no sound came out. That was a most satisfactory response so far as her husband was concerned. He gave her a firm little nod and wandered off to see what he might be able to do.

The first thing he did was haul water, a great deal of it, in wooden buckets that were lowered into the shaft to keep the men who were working from becoming dehydrated and also to sprinkle on the tunnel floor and walls to keep down the dust. Laboring over ancient church records did not prepare a man for such work, but he persevered all the same. It seemed a small enough thing to do when others were risking so much.

He glanced up at one point to see the boy, Owen, working nearby. There were more familiar faces from Gynfelin and the other nearby villages, as well as many he did not know from Glamorgan, all of them striving together, largely in silence as the long night waned and a new day began. More lumber arrived and was passed down the shaft, more water was called for, more food was prepared, more sweat and strain expended, more hope and dread endured while the sun rose higher and higher.

The Reverend Armbruster straightened up. His vision was slightly blurred from fatigue, and he could hear a faint ringing in his ears. He dabbed at his forehead with a handkerchief.

"I'm too old for this," he murmured as a wave of dizziness slipped over him. The ground seemed to rock beneath his feet. He reached out a hand to steady himself and saw off to the side an old woman in a long white apron, head thrown back, screaming.

The sound hit Morgana before she was aware of any motion. It came up out of the ground, blasting through the opening of the mine shaft and ripping through the surrounding air. She half fell, pulled herself upright and ran.

Smoke and dust rose from the mine shaft where the men were working. Terror gripped her. She pushed and shoved her way through the crowd until she reached the entrance.

"David!" she screamed, her voice choking.

Others were also screaming the names of those they loved, forcing their way toward the entrance, seeking desperately to do something, anything. In the midst of them, a voice shouted, drawing their attention.

"Look!" the Reverend Armbruster cried. Arm thrust out against the painfully blue sky, he pointed to the great column of smoke rising from a secondary shaft some distance away. "It was there, not in the main shaft." He pushed his way through the milling crowd until he found Morgana. "What are we to do? The explosion must have rocked the main tunnel. The rescuers themselves may be trapped now. We must do something.''

Morgana hesitated a scant moment, looking over the sea of faces that were suddenly all turned in her direction. Off to the side, she was aware of Charles Whitcomb, the young builder, begrimed and sweat-streaked, his eyes dark with dread. So were all the others, men, women and children alike. The beloved earth had suddenly become their enemy. They were cast adrift without moorings, fearing the worst and not knowing how to confront it.

But she knew, and in that moment a hundred generations of women who had seen their men robbed of liberty, their children condemned to servitude, seen a people trampled down but still struggling to arise, all that poured forth in the cry of defiance she hurtled to the sky.

''We dig, by God! We dig until they're out, every last one of them. The mine will not have them!''

A roar went up, like the roar of the earth but this from human throats. The crowd surged forward. They scrambled into the mine entrance, choking on the swirling dust. Morgana was in the front with the good reverend beside her. They got only a few yards before the results of the explosion became evident. A wall of earth had fallen, blocking the entrance and trapping all within.

But earth could be moved if only by hands scratching at it, fingers clawing, backs straining, inch by inch. A human chain formed, men, women and children working frantically. The dirt was moved in buckets, in aprons, in anything that would hold it.

Morgana shoveled yet another load into a bucket and grabbed for the next one. Pray God they would be in time, pray God they were still alive, pray . . . pray . . . David. . . .

She thrust her arm into the mound of earth, grabbing for another handful and felt . . . nothing.

They were through! Bending down, she pressed her face to the blackness and cried, "David!"

Nothing, no sound, no movement, no hope. *"David!"* Oh, God, please don't let this be. She loved him, she always would. She would make any bargain, promise anything if only he lived. Please . . . please . . .

A pinpoint of light penetrated the darkness. Deep within it, dazed and only half-conscious, David stirred. He was aware of something pulling at him, drawing him toward a vast openness to which a part of him wanted to go. There was light there, too, radiant, glowing light that filled him with longing. He turned toward it, almost . . . not quite . . .

The pinpoint grew, a tiny distraction from the far greater light and yet . . .

"David."

The voice wrapped around him, enveloping him, holding him. The glory remained, just there beyond his sight but within reach. All he had to do was let go, but the voice held him, and beyond it something more, something powerful, eternal, like the great light, born of it but apart.

Morgana.

The thought moved through his mind, filling him. He drew breath, choked and breathed again. His eyes strained toward the tiny dot of light. "Morgana."

* * *

The mine entrance was reopened by late in the afternoon and the main rescue effort resumed. Shortly before dark, the chamber where the men had sheltered was reached. Four had died, fifty-three remained alive. Of the dead, one was Thomas Trelawney. The Reverend Armbruster stood with Owen as the boy looked down at his father, his young face sorrowful but accepting.

The rest came to the surface one by one as the sun burned out in glory. Faces turned toward the sky they had never thought to see again. Arms embraced them, families claiming them back.

Hugh Dawkins was among the survivors. He was also among the men who carried Gynfelin's lord home. They went by horse-drawn wagon over the hills and down the long road. David lay on a mattress covered with blankets. His face was ashen, his breathing harsh. He was half-conscious when they set off, but the first jolt of the wagon on the rutted road caused him such pain that he slipped away down the well of oblivion. Crouched beside him, her hands clasped around his, Morgana gave thanks for small mercies. At least he did not know the torment his bruised and battered body endured on that seemingly endless journey.

It was fully dark by the time they passed the village and turned onto the rising road toward Montfort. They did not go alone, for in addition to the men bringing the marquess, many others—men, women and children—lined their route. Beneath the star-specked sky, torches flared. Voices were low, gazes somber. Men bared their heads as the wagon rumbled past, women clasped their hands to their breasts and murmured prayers while the children stood straight and somber watching the passing of the man it was already said was a true lord in the old way, even the ancient way, one who would give his own blood for the safety of his people.

They came at last up the gravel drive to Montfort itself. The main doors of the house stood open; light poured forth from them. All the servants were there but it was Sebastian who had ridden beside the wagon all the way, who took charge. With Hugh and several of the others helping, he guided the litter up the curving marble stairs and finally to the marquess's chamber. David was laid carefully in the great bed. He did not stir, but a low sound escaped him before he slipped away again into darkness.

Morgana bit back a sob. She still clung to his hand, having refused to relinquish it and there being no one to try to persuade her. His touch was all the assurance she had that he yet lived. It was her lifeline and her only hope.

A doctor in Glamorgan had bandaged David's ribs, listened to his chest and shook his head gravely. "One of the lungs has collapsed," he said, "and there may be other internal injuries. His condition is grave, but unfortunately there is little to be done. He needs rest and quiet. The rest is up to God."

It was just as well David hadn't heard that, Morgana thought as she knelt beside the bed. She remembered his distrust of doctors and his own skill at healing. If only that skill could be turned to his service now. How ironic that a man who had learned to save others could do nothing to save himself.

"We must do something," she whispered brokenly.

Sebastian put a gentle hand on her shoulder. "There is nothing we can do but make him comfortable and wait."

She raised her head and looked at him. Sebastian was a brave man, but when he saw the terrible pain in her eyes, he flinched.

"How can you accept it so calmly?" she demanded. "He may die while we do nothing. I cannot bear that." Her voice gave way. Her head fell, as though her slender neck could not bear its weight. She buried her face in the covers beside David and wept as though her heart would break.

Sebastian gazed at her with an expression of mingled pain and compassion. He wished there was something he could do to comfort her but knew there was not. And yet perhaps it was for the best. His master's life hung by a thread stretching between this life and eternity. The fire-haired woman might be all that kept it from snapping. He felt the great strength in her and knew she would hold on at all cost.

He left the room but returned a short time later, bringing fresh water, clean clothes and a cup of Mrs. Mulroon's excellent broth. Seeing all that, Morgana dried her eyes and managed a wan smile. She was well aware that Sebastian could easily have delegated such a task to one of the servants. Lenore, for instance, or Mrs. Gareth. That he saw to it himself spoke volumes for his sensitivity. He was fully aware of how raw and exposed she was feeling and how needful of privacy.

She left David's side long enough to wash the worst of the coal grime from her and slip into the clean clothes. The broth she left untouched. Her stomach was simply too unsettled even for that.

Throughout the long night, she remained close beside him. It was Morgana who gently sponged the dirt from his face, who soothed the disheveled hair and who soothed him when he grew restless. Her voice in the darkness, through the haze of pain, washed over him like cool, clear water, banishing fear. He quieted, holding fast to her hand, and drifted into a more restful sleep.

In this, he was alone among all those gathered beneath the roof of the great house. The men of Glamorgan returned there reluctantly to see to the other injured and comfort the bereaved. But many from Gynfelin remained, sitting without in the courtyard, eyes turned toward the high windows beyond which the master of their land lay. They stayed because they felt the better for being close to him, and because they took it as their right. This was the bond between ruler and ruled, the pledge that knit the two together. Generations had passed since any in Gynfelin had experienced the truth of that bond, but it resonated within them all the same, echoing to ancient chords of memory.

In the house, the servants moved silently or sat, bleak-eyed, and merely stared. They had all passed beyond weariness. Their thoughts, too, were locked on the upper chamber and the man who lay between life and death. To most of them, he had until recently been a stranger, but no more. Like the people outside, they, too, recognized him for what he was. Beneath the silvered moon, wrapped in night, Gynfelin remained awake and alert lest death descend unaware upon her and steal her lord.

But death, unpredictable thing that it was, seemed elsewhere occupied that night. Morgana looked for it in the shadows of the room, all her senses painfully alert for the least little sign of its coming, but there was none. Night passed, the horizon turned to rose as the sun crept up over it, and a freshening breeze blew from the west. Morgana stirred beside the bed. Her fingers were cramped and her knees ached, but she felt none of that. Indeed, she felt nothing but the first, tremulous stirrings of joy. For raising her head, she found David gazing at her with such tenderness that the breath caught in her throat.

He was still very pale beneath the night's rough growth of beard, and his face had the taut, strained look of one who has come a great distance. But his voice was steady as he murmured her name and reached out gently to brush the tears from her cheeks.

Chapter Nineteen

Once David's recovery began, it proceeded swiftly, although not as swiftly as he would have liked. Predictably enough, Gynfelin's master proved himself to be a poor patient. Barely had he regained the ability to sit up in bed, much less venture from it, than he became vexed and impatient, liable to terrify even his most loyal and adoring servant.

Not Sebastian, of course, for he quickly hit upon the simple expedient of avoiding the sickroom and its occupant. Without a twinge of conscience, he left Morgana to deal with the ill-tempered marquess and did it in the perfect confidence that his master was in excellent hands.

Perhaps so, but they were not quite as sweet and gentle as David would have liked. Once she realized he wasn't going to die, Morgana stiffened her spine and declined to take much in the way of guff.

"Stop that," she said firmly, when he rattled the tray on his lap in a manner that suggested he was considering upending its contents. "We've had quite enough of that. Mrs. Mulroon has prepared you a perfectly nice meal. You have no excuse not to eat it.''

''I don't want it,'' he said and glared at her.

Morgana ignored any and all such attempts at intimidation. She had gotten to the point where she knew perfectly well that his bark was far worse than his bite, at least where she was concerned. Never mind that she was infinitely grateful for his continued life or that simply being near him made her heart turn over, that was no excuse for tolerating bad manners.

''I'm surprised at you,'' she said. ''I should think you'd be so glad to be alive that you wouldn't have any time for ill humor.''

''I am glad,'' he said with a snarl. ''But I am damn tired of being stuck in this bed.'' Deliberately, he added, ''I wouldn't mind if you'd climb in with me, but you seem to have decided I'm some kind of invalid.'' His eyes narrowed, raking over her. ''I assure you, madame, your present cockiness is ill placed.''

''Cockiness, me?'' Despite herself, she grinned. He looked so devastatingly handsome with a lock of ebony hair falling over his forehead and his eyes all agleam with pent-up emotions of various sorts. He was bare-chested save for the bandages swathed round his middle. With each passing day, his breathing was less labored, his features less taut with pain. Whenever she touched him—to give some small service, accidently or simply for reassurance when he slept—she felt the strength returning to him. Soon, he truly would be well.

Soon, there would be no need for her to remain.

That thought made her throat thicken. She looked away for a moment, fighting for control. When she looked back, he was staring at her.

"What's wrong?" he demanded.

"Nothing. I am merely tired."

Immediately, his expression changed. Where there had been haughty, ill temper there was suddenly concern and regret.

"I'm sorry, Morgana," he said. "I've been thinking only of myself. You've been here night and day, and little thanks have I given you for it. Yet without you, I believe I would have—"

"Don't say it," she entreated, reaching out quickly to seal his lips with the gentle touch of her finger. "Perhaps you are right. A change of scene might do us both good. Would you like to try getting up and sitting by the window?"

"No," he said firmly. "I would like to go for a walk with you in the garden. And," he added before she could interrupt, "I think I am being supremely cooperative by suggesting so gentle a pursuit. You would be wise to accept it."

Oh, she would, would she? He was past bearing. If God had set out to make the epitome of masculine arrogance and stubbornness when he made David Harrell, he had succeeded admirably.

Abruptly, she made up her mind. What was the point of arguing with him when giving in would prove her point far more effectively?

"All right," she said, "the garden it is. But don't blame me if this proves to be harder than you think."

He suffered her to help him dress. In fact, she thought he made it rather more difficult than it needed to be. Surely putting on breeches couldn't be that hard? By the time they were done, her face was flaming, and she had little patience for his obvious amusement.

"I'll call Sebastian for help," she said. "You will need assistance walking."

"Nonsense," David said briskly. "I'll manage perfectly. Only let me lean on you a little."

A little? The man felt like granite bearing down on her. She staggered slightly and squirmed under the arm weighing across her shoulders. He must be weaker even than she realized to have to hold on to her so tightly. At that thought, compassion overwhelmed any other consideration.

They went slowly, step by step, until they reached the gardens. Morgana had not been outside in almost a week, since bringing David home. She had almost forgotten the glory of the late Welsh spring. Beneath a brilliant sky, yew and oak trees burst forth in leaf, birds sang, irises and tulips raised their heads to the sun. The garden was crossed by gravel paths lined with lilies of every hue. They nodded gently in the breeze as though in acknowledgment of the human presence come among them.

Near to the house, beside a small, gurgling fountain, was a white stone bench. Morgana fell upon it gratefully.

"Let's sit down," she said, struggling for breath.

David looked surprised. "Already? Oh, well, if we must. Are you quite all right? You look a bit pale."

"I'm fine," she assured him as she struggled for breath. He, by contrast, looked positively robust. The color had returned to his cheeks, his eyes gleamed in a most disconcerting fashion, and he was smiling.

"A beautiful day," he said, "don't you think?"

"Beautiful," Morgana agreed. How nice that they could sit here side by side on the bench and make polite conversation as though they were at a London garden party. All the dark fire and passion of their private hours together, and all the wrenching horror of the mine, seemed a lifetime away.

Sitting there with him in the sun filled her with gentle melancholy. She cherished every moment with him and yet each one drove home to her the impossibility of her position. She had chosen her path and she did not regret it, but neither had she fully anticipated where it would lead her.

"Look," David said quietly and touched her hand.

She followed the direction of his gaze to where a small brown hare stood poised on the edge of the path. It remained frozen, its nose twitching, until suddenly it darted out of sight.

She smiled, thinking how contradictory he was, this strong, indomitable man who found pleasure in such small, tender things. He would make a wonderful father.

Her breath stopped. Pain twisted through her so keenly that for a terrible moment she thought she would cry out. Only by an act of the greatest will was she able to subdue it, and even then not entirely. The pain remained, throbbing and insistent, reminding her of all that could not be.

Her skin was suddenly clammy. Despite herself, she shivered.

"Cold?" David asked. He looked concerned. It had been all well and good to tease her with his supposed disability, if only to have an excuse to hold her close, but this was different. For a moment, she really did look ill.

Without waiting for an answer, he began to strip off his jacket to put it around her. The action was not recommended for a man whose ribs had so lately undergone such a pounding. He winced slightly but did not stop.

"Don't," Morgana said urgently. "You will injure yourself."

"Then we should return to the house."

She shook her head and mustered a smile to reassure him. "The day is too lovely for that, and I truly am not cold. Let us stay awhile longer."

David was more than willing to do so, but he felt a need to walk more. After a week of lying in bed, his body fairly cried out for exercise, among other things.

"Come," he said with that unconscious imperiousness that was bred into him. He rose and held out a hand to Morgana.

She looked up at him, eyes narrowed. "You move more easily of a sudden."

He smiled. "I must have just needed to get the kinks out."

"Hmm." Still suspicious, she rose and went with him for, after all, what else was she going to do? With every moment precious, there was no time for wasted emotions.

They strolled arm in arm along the gravel path, following where it wound beside a sylvan lake. Swans swam by regally, and here and there a duck fluttered. All the rest of the world seemed to rush away from them, dwindling into nothingness. It was Epping again only more so, for this, above all, was home.

She shut her eyes tightly, as though against the sun, but in fact it was to blink back the hot tears that threatened. His home, not hers. A well of longing opened within her. Fool! She had known all along that theirs was a time out of time, a world of their own making that could exist only briefly. To wish otherwise now was to go yearning after the moon.

His arm was strong around her waist. She did not resist when he turned her to him. Passion leaped between them as it always did, perhaps it always would if only in memory. She lifted her head, eyes still closed against the burning light, and blindly found the hard warmth of his mouth. The kiss he began became hers as she slipped past the boundaries of restraint and for one last, glorious moment flew high and free.

They walked silently to the house. David was puzzled by her unnatural quiet and by the tumult of emotions he sensed within her. After an initial burst of strength, fatigue had crashed down on him with little warning. Like it or not, he was still some distance from full recovery.

By the time he was once again in bed, his eyes were closing. He drifted to sleep listening to the birds singing outside his window and feeling the cool touch of Morgana's hand on his brow.

She was gone when he awoke late the following morning. There was a stillness to the house that felt ominous. He could not explain it, but he knew immediately that something was wrong.

"Where is Miss Penrhys?" he demanded when Sebastian brought in a tray.

"She has returned to her cottage, sir."

"Why?"

"She didn't say, sir."

It was marvelous, really, when you thought about it, how much Sebastian could convey in the single, lip-curling use of the word "sir." Men of the cloth had declaimed from pulpits for hours on end without conveying so much.

"I take it," David said, "that I am somehow to blame for her departure?"

"No, sir," Sebastian said, looking down the side of his nose, "at least not directly. However, you are to blame for her having been here in the first instance, so a case could be made that you also bear some responsibility for her leaving."

"I see . . . I think. The cottage, you say?"

"So she said, sir, but I rather suspect she will be at the school. The Reverend Armbruster has revealed an unexpected gift for teaching, but I still rather think he will be relieved by her return." He paused, cleared his throat and let go with both barrels. "However temporary it may be."

David scowled. "What is that supposed to mean?"

"Only what it says, sir, but I have no objection to elaborating." Indeed, try to stop him. Sebastian had already decided to have his say, but the sentiment be-

lowstairs made it imperative. Although the marquess
remained blissfully unaware of it, he faced outright
mutiny, so deeply did the feeling run for the fey
schoolteacher.

"Miss Penrhys," he said, slowly and distinctly, "is
a young woman of unusual intellect and refinement
who finds herself in, shall we say, an irregular situation. It is only reasonable that she will draw her own
conclusions."

David wanted to deny it. She had no bloody right to
be drawing any conclusions—her own or otherwise—
when she belonged to him. But much as he hated to
admit it, he suspected Sebastian might be right. She
was a bluestocking, after all, however adorably so, and
she had that streak of reformer zeal that led her to
seize the bull by the horns, so to speak. A woman who
was capable of facing down a drunken bully, clawing
her way into a ruined mine and coping with an ill-
tempered marquess was capable of doing anything.

He shot Sebastian a baleful look. "She wouldn't
just . . . go, would she?"

"If you say so, sir."

"By God, she would." The fiery-tempered witch
would go off and leave him without a word. She would
vanish from his life as suddenly as she had appeared.

To the marquess's credit, he restrained himself long
enough to hand the tray back to Sebastian without
spilling a drop. That was the last evidence to be seen
of any check on his will.

Leaving his bed, his hand grazed the bandages
around his chest. "Get me out of these," he de-

manded even as he reached for his breeches. "Where are my boots?"

"Right here, sir," Sebastian said and held them out. "I will fetch a pair of scissors."

"While you're at it, get my horse saddled."

"Horse, sir? Wouldn't a carriage be better—"

"Horse, Sebastian, and snap to it. I've wasted far too much time as it is."

The butler smiled gently. "I wouldn't say that, sir. There was the small matter of your near demise. However, now that you are—"

"Later, Sebastian, much later."

"As you say, sir."

As he said. As he chose. As he ordered. Always, his wishes had been respected and his word obeyed. Even Sebastian, for all the liberties long service provided, knew very well where to draw the line.

Morgana was another matter entirely. She had no notion of obedience at all. She continually challenged and provoked him. He ought to be infuriated by her. Instead, all he could think of was the terrifying possibility that she might somehow be lost to him.

In the mine, he had been driven by the need to save the lives of others. Now it was his own life and all so lately dear to it that compelled him. The great black stallion was waiting in the courtyard when he came down. A groom hurried to help him mount. David brushed him away and vaulted into the saddle. His ribs twinged, but not even they dared to slow him. He murmured a word of urging to the horse. Nothing more was needed. Hooves pounded down the drive, flashing in the sun.

Sebastian watched him go. He summoned a last memory of the loveless boy who had grown to be a hard and solitary man. Then he let the memory go without regret and walked into the great house.

Chapter Twenty

It was very quiet in the schoolhouse. The half day of lessons was over and the children departed along with the good reverend. The only sounds were the ticking of the clock and the soft tread of Morgana's step as she moved around the small room. She straightened a row of books, her fingers lingering on them as she scanned the titles. Most were new and as yet hardly touched. She thought of the children delving into them, discovering the wonders they held, and smiled faintly.

There was writing on the slate. She fetched a bucket of water from the old well outside and wiped it clean. Next, she took the broom and began sweeping around the neat rows of benches. She would leave the place tidy.

The thought tore at her. She shut her eyes for a moment, fighting tears, and told herself not to be a ninny. What had she expected, after all? To involve herself with a man like David Harrell and think to survive unscathed was the height of idiocy. She had known the moment she walked into his world that her life would never be the same.

She had to go. The pain she had felt when she realized he was entombed within the mine still threatened to overwhelm her. At that moment, she would have given her very soul to save him. A merciful God had not demanded it, but neither was she allowed to hide any longer from the full cost of her folly.

A cruel word, that, for surely loving was never folly, but pay she must all the same, pay now or pay when the inevitable parting came. She wiped her cheeks quickly with the back of her hand and went on sweeping. She had always tried to teach her students not to fear, and now she must do the same. But the world loomed inhospitable and empty. Memories alone would not fill it but they would have to do. They, at least, could not be taken from her.

She would leave the schoolhouse clean, go to the cottage and pack her most necessary belongings. She could stay with her married sister in Abergavenny for a while and get her bearings before deciding what to do next. Perhaps she would apply for work in the colonies. India was a possibility; so was Australia. Thousands of miles would do nothing to still her longing but at least they could give her the illusion of a fresh start. There was nothing wrong with illusions. Sometimes they were all people had.

She put the broom away when there was nothing left to sweep. Her desk was clear, the shelves were tidy, everything was in order. Beyond the windows standing open to the spring breeze she could see the site where the new school would be built. It would serve generations of Gynfelin's children far better than she had ever dreamed. She had to be content with that.

She turned to go and noticed a book peering out from the bottom of a pile. Somehow it had missed her attention. She pulled it free and glanced at the title. *The Poems of Milton.* A classic, to be sure, and good for the children to know, but she had never liked Milton much, finding him too steeped in melancholy for its own sake. She was about to return it to the shelf when a sound stopped her. The schoolhouse door opened. A rush of wind followed, fragrant with the robust scent of spring. Outside the sky was growing stormy. Inside was no more serene.

"I thought I saw you in here," Lady Kennard said, her tone reeking with disapproval. She lifted her skirt several inches higher as though to avoid any taint of contamination and pursed her small mouth. "Does this mean you have finally remembered your duties or did you expect the good reverend to assume them indefinitely?"

"I expected nothing," Morgana said quietly. She had not seen her ladyship since the evening of the spring fete and could have done very well without seeing her now. But her sudden appearance held no surprise. On the contrary, it seemed somehow fitting.

"The reverend has been very kind," she went on with dignity. "As you know, this has been a difficult time."

Lady Kennard sniffed and looked down her rather long nose. "What I know is my own affair, miss. You may think you've pulled the wool over everyone's eyes, getting them all to sing your praises, but it isn't true. There are those of us who aren't fooled in the least."

Morgana repressed a sigh. She supposed she should be angry but she couldn't muster the necessary energy. After what she had been through of late, the Lady Kennards of the world seemed singularly unimportant.

"I'm sorry if you're displeased in some way," she said, "but now if you will excuse me—" She moved toward the door.

Her ladyship's plump cheeks reddened. "How dare you! I have not dismissed you, Miss High-and-mighty Penrhys. You may think that warming a noble bed puts you ahead of the rest of us, but I assure you the privileges you gain are as fleeting as the marquess's interest undoubtedly will be. Once his ardor cools— and believe me it will—you will be nothing! Do you hear me? Nothing!"

Morgana swallowed against the sudden tightness of her throat. Much as she would have liked to dismiss the other woman's vitriol, she could not. It held too much truth, however unpalatable.

"Excuse me," she said, very low and took a step toward the door. A gasp broke from her as Lady Kennard's hand lashed out, closing on her arm. This was more than she had bargained for. Words hurled in anger, mean-spirited innuendo and vicious gossip were the common currency of people like her ladyship. But physical contact was another matter altogether. Those with pretensions to the nobility shunned such contact with the lower orders as though by it some fateful stain might rub off on them.

But any such consideration seemed beyond Lady Kennard's capacity. Her eyes burned furiously as she tightened her grip.

"Whore," she said. "Hypocritical, two-faced strumpet! Prattle about the squire not spending enough money on the school, will you? Bring down Montfort's anger on us? I'll see you in hell for that. You'll be run out of here in disgrace. There won't be a school anywhere that will hire you. You'll end up exactly where you belong, walking the streets like any common doxy!"

"That's enough!" Morgana shot back. Her weariness was evaporating. There were limits, even in her present state, to what she would accept. She wrenched her arm free and leveled a look at Lady Kennard that would have withered a more sensitive individual.

"You and your fine husband robbed the children of this village of the education that should have been theirs all these years. You did it out of greed and selfishness. If either of us ends up in hell, it isn't going to be me!"

She had the satisfaction of seeing Lady Kennard's high color fade to a sickly gray. The older woman grasped her amble breast and reeled back. It was one thing to dish out insults and quite another to take them, particularly when they struck so close to home. However, Lady Kennard wasn't done yet. She had plenty of fight left in her, as she quickly proved.

"Viper! Despoiler of the young! To think that all this time we have nurtured such as you in our midst. Have you no sense of decency at all? No shame?"

"I would not stoop to discuss decency with you," Morgana said coldly, "for there would be no point. As for shame, no, I feel none for I have done nothing shameful." Caution flung to the winds, she added, "There is no shame in caring for a decent, good, honorable man such as I have done, no matter what you or any of your kind seek to make me believe. You will never succeed!"

In their preoccupation, neither Morgana nor her ladyship had noted the large black steed come prancing up in front of the school, blowing steam and snorting from its hard gallop. Similarly, they failed to note the black-garbed man who swung from the saddle and walked determinedly up the path to the schoolhouse door.

However, he noticed them. Indeed, the marquess stood transfixed as he listened to the last part of their conversation. Had he come scant minutes earlier, anger would have overwhelmed him and he would have intervened at once. But this business about Morgana not having done anything to shame herself, not to mention what she said about caring for a good, decent man, all that was too tantalizing to pass up.

Still, it was clear the discussion was not a happy one, and he saw no reason to let it run on. He put an end to it by the simple expedient of stepping forward.

Lady Kennard gasped. It was getting to be a habit with her. Morgana turned fiery red. Her cheeks almost matched her hair as she stared at him in disbelief.

"You," she exclaimed. "What are you doing here?"

He smiled tenderly, thinking how lovely she looked all riled up. With deceptive mildness, he said, "Something of mine became misplaced. I felt called upon to go looking for it."

Morgana's blush deepened even further, defying all limits. She had the terrible sense that events were spinning beyond all control. Had he heard what she said about caring about him? Oh, yes, most definitely he had. The light in his eyes left no doubt about that.

A tremor ran through her. She had never felt so exposed and vulnerable in her life. Damn him!

And damn her insufferable ladyship, too! Wheeling on her, Morgana said, "This is still my school, and I have some say about who comes into it and who doesn't. You will kindly leave now!"

"I will—"

"You would be wise to do as she says," David said. He spoke softly but with unmistakable resolve.

Lady Kennard stared at him in mute dismay. She wanted to stand her ground, but every ounce of sense she possessed told her she would regret it. The marquess was bad enough, but the schoolteacher was worse. There was something about her, something ancient and awesome, that Lady Kennard was quite incapable of recognizing yet that filled her with the most primitive sense of danger. She backed away, shaking her head, and stumbled down the steps from the schoolhouse. The last Morgana saw of her, she was bolting for her carriage.

"Infuriating woman," she murmured as she turned her back and began straightening books again. Perhaps he, too, would take the hint and go.

Perhaps the stars would cease to shine.

What he did instead was take gentle hold of her shoulders and turn her to him. "You are a great deal of trouble," he said. He spoke matter-of-factly. Morgana stared at him. His dark, powerful presence filled the room. "Why did you leave Montfort without telling me?" he demanded.

Never let it be said that Morgana was burdened by an excess of caution. Indeed, at that moment she appeared to possess none at all. She lifted her chin and said, "I am not accountable to you."

His eyes darkened. They swept over her in a single, all-encompassing glance. She was painfully aware of her disheveled state. Her clothes were dusty, her hair in its usual disarray and her face begrimed.

"You must excuse me," she said stiffly. "I was just going."

He dropped his hand but otherwise did not move. Tall and indomitable, he stood before her, the dark lord of the hills returned from the earth. In his eyes was the memory of how closely the wings of death had brushed him. But in them also was the memory of life embodied in this one woman and of the passion that had called him back to her.

She was suddenly very pale.

So much so that David did not hesitate but gathered her to him. "Are you all right?" he demanded.

"I'm fine," she said hastily. He looked so fierce, the eyes like shards of steel cutting through any defense she might offer. Only honesty remained. Unable to do otherwise, she blurted the single unassailable fact that had haunted her all these days. ''I ... I was so afraid you would die.''

A moment longer he stared at her and then he did something she would never have expected. He blinked once, twice. Yes, she was not mistaken. There was a sudden sheen of moisture in those steel eyes.

He cleared his throat and smiled. ''So was I, but I didn't. You see, I happen to have an excellent reason for living.''

''Oh,'' Morgana said, staring into his beloved face. She could not possibly be seeing there what she seemed to be, and yet ...

She raised a hand and lightly with the tips of her fingers brushed the mouth that had so deliciously tormented her. His lips parted slightly, catching her, sharp white teeth nipping.

''Oh.''

He laughed, the sound masculine and confident. It found its answer within her, in the strong, secret place that had welcomed him not as stranger or conqueror but almost as an old friend come back to where he had never been but always belonged. The laughter resonated, bringing joy. Her head tilted, fire-born hair spilling over the burnished hand that had slipped to the back of her neck. Her eyes were very bright. Like the sea, he thought, running deep and silent, the cradle of life.

She had tasted slightly of the sea when he touched her most intimately. The memory made him harden with need so sudden and remorseless that he felt the force of it in his very soul.

"Morgana," he said again, very seriously, laughter gone now for this was the moment, come at last after so much evasion in a hectic and often difficult life. Come now to this instant, this woman, this reality. "We need to talk."

Talk? Right now? "What about?" she managed to ask and was pleased with herself for sounding just a wee bit breathless, nothing at all as much as she felt.

His smile deepened as though to say he knew exactly what was in her mind no matter how she might try to conceal it. Worse yet, she suspected he was right. "Remember my honorable intentions?" he asked.

"What?"

"Did you imagine they simply went away?"

"I...I didn't imagine anything at all." What *was* he talking about? Whatever she'd expected him to say, it wasn't this.

"I'm afraid not," he said, looking pleased with himself but also with a tiny shadow of uncertainty she wasn't supposed to notice but did.

"Afraid?"

"It's just an expression. I'm not exactly afraid, not at all."

Which told her that he was. Which meant perhaps she ought to be, too.

"David...what is this?" When he didn't answer at once, she went on, prompting. "What talk do we need? What troubles you?"

"You thought I was lying," he said clearly, no mistake about it. No way of getting around it, either.

"Not lying exactly," she said, still trying to understand. What was the point of this?

"Saying whatever I had to in order to seduce you?" He was angry now, although he tried to conceal it. But he did not frighten her. With a start, she realized that she could never again be frightened of this man. For him, yes, but never of him.

Her head lifted. She met his gaze unflinchingly. "Yes, that is what I thought."

His eyes narrowed. "A fine thing, believing the worst of me."

"If I'd believed the worst," she pointed out reasonably, "I wouldn't have gone to London with you."

."Hmm, but you didn't believe I meant what I said?"

"I didn't know what you meant. What are honorable intentions? You said you would do nothing to hurt me and you haven't." That was true enough, for he wasn't responsible for her unruly heart.

His face gentled slightly. She expected so little, this woman who by rights should expect everything. Life had taught her that, and she did not resent it at all. She simply went on, charting her own course, making the best of whatever she encountered. She was, he thought suddenly, very independent. The first faint sense of doubt stirred within him. What if she said no? Ridiculous, absurd even. Of course, she wouldn't. It didn't bear thinking about.

"I also said lovemaking has consequences," he reminded her, a shade sternly. "Have you thought of that?"

Not really, there hadn't been time, but there was now. The possibilities flooded through her, chief among them the chance that she might conceive. The thought of a child—his child—should have filled her unmarried spinster self with horror. Instead, she was uplifted on a wave of joy so intense that it was impossible to conceal. He saw it in the sea-storm eyes, in the sudden warmth of her cheeks, in the instinctive sway of her body toward him.

"Sweet," he murmured. The back of his hand brushed lightly along the curve of her jaw, down the slender line of her throat to pause near the swelling fullness of her breasts. Sweet and real, this woman. His woman.

"Honorable intentions," he said, as though he was the teacher and she the pupil, "are generally taken to mean matrimony."

Her eyes darkened. Abruptly, she pushed both her hands against his broad chest. "Let go."

Startled, he did not think twice but held her all the more firmly. He was, after all, a Montfort. "What are you talking about? What's wrong?"

She pressed back as far as he would let her and glared at him. "Mayhap this is a joke to you but not to me. Now let me go!" For added emphasis, she rammed her foot down on his instep and at the same time ducked to squirm under his arm.

It almost worked and would have if he hadn't been a trained warrior with lightning-quick reflexes. He ignored the pain, which was inconsequential, and stopped her attempted escape by the simple expediency of lifting her feet off the ground. Holding her firmly against him, he walked out of the school-house.

"What are you doing?" Morgana demanded. "Put me down. You can't do this. You can't..."

"Be quiet," the marquess said. "You'll disturb the neighbors.

The neighbors? She was hollering loudly enough to be heard all the way in Glamorgan. If he thought he could just... She balled her hand into a fist, pulled it back and let fly. David ducked. The blow went by ineffectually. He shot her a chiding look and kept going. "Behave yourself. I gave you plenty of warning. You can't pretend to be surprised."

"Surprised by what? That you'd be so cruel? Yes, I'm surprised. I thought—"

He sighed, the habitual sound of the long-suffering male. Slowly and with exaggerated patience, he said, "It is not cruel and it is not a joke. I intend to marry you. I would never have taken you to my bed were that not the case. And," he added for good measure, "I wouldn't be taking you there now if you didn't appear to need more convincing."

He had the satisfaction of seeing her fall silent, a state that continued until they reached her cottage. When the door was closed behind them, he set her cautiously on her feet and released her. She stood unmoving, looking at him. The anger had gone out of her. She appeared merely bewildered.

"Why are you doing this?"

From another woman, the question might have suggested a lack of self-confidence or esteem. From Morgana Penrhys, it did nothing of the sort. It was merely a realistic assessment of the way of the world. Cats didn't dance with kings, lions didn't lie down with lambs, and marquesses most certainly did not marry schoolteachers.

David was busy stripping off his shirt. He spied the big tin tub sitting upended near the stove. They both needed to bathe, and it looked big enough for two. Besides, his ribs could use a bit of pampering, the last they'd get for a bit if he had his way. Now all he had to do was persuade her to get into hot water with him. He laughed at the thought and laughed again when she glared.

"You will admit we deal tolerably well together," he said.

Morgana moistened her lips, which were suddenly very dry. He was so big, standing there, and so unapologetically male. Illusions were all very well, but this was real. There was no escaping that, if only because he wouldn't let her.

Sweet heaven, what had she done?

"David," she said softly as she took a step back, her eyes never leaving him, "you can't want to marry me, not really."

He stopped, his hand at the waistband of his trousers. "I can't?"

"No, of course not. We're too different. We come from entirely different backgrounds and we have such different expectations. You want a woman who can fit into your life, be a hostess, be...ornamental. All I would be is trouble."

Silence reigned. It stretched out long enough for Morgana to finally dare a peek at him. What she saw was hardly reassuring. David was staring at her in dumbfounded amazement.

"You are an idiot," he said. "A sweet, beautiful, wonderful idiot with a head full of book learning and absolutely no knowledge of men at all. You really believe what you said? Even after what happened between us, you actually think I would hesitate to bind you to me by every means I can?"

He shook his head in wonder. "I grant you're right, you are trouble. But I've developed a strange fondness for having my life turned upside down. You can't possibly expect me to go back to having it all neatly ordered. What would I do without Owen Trelawneys to be rescued, injustices to be righted, social dragons to be defeated? In short, sweetling, what would I do without you?"

She opened her mouth to respond but he raised a hand, forestalling her. "Enough talk," he said. "Between us it only sows confusion. There are better ways." He reached out, his hand running lightly over the curve of her breast to her waist and beyond. The tremor that followed his touch could not be hidden.

For the first time since sailing off the cliff in London, Morgana began to think she might actually be able to fly.

David smiled. "Forget all else. Say only this, do you love me?"

Insufferable man, leaving her nothing. Giving her everything.

"You called me fey," she said. "But which one of us is truly the spell weaver?"

"Perhaps we both are, sweetling. Do you love me?"

"Yes," she said on a long sigh. "Heaven help me, I do."

He took both her hands in his and looked down into her sea-storm eyes. "Morgana Penrhys, proud daughter of Wales, love of my life, marry me."

Give the man credit, he had a way with words. She took a deep breath, whispered a silent prayer and flew.

"Ah, well, let it not be said I refused Gynfelin's lord."

He laughed and lifted her, high, higher, soaring into his arms, into the future, into eternity. Cymru's fire-haired lady, and for all time, his own.

* * * * * *

Historical Romance™

Coming next month

THE KNIGHT, THE KNAVE AND THE LADY
Juliet Landon

NORTH YORKSHIRE, 1350s

Marietta Wardle *never* wanted to get married—but her stance proved no hindrance to the desires of Lord Alain of Thorsgeld! He wanted her and had no scruples about compromising her into marriage. Their nights were ecstatic, and Thorsgeld Castle provided her with plenty of work. Marietta began to love her role, and her husband, until she realised that she was playing second best to his dead wife—a position that would lead her into danger…

A HIGHLY IRREGULAR FOOTMAN
Sarah Westleigh

KENT/LONDON 1803

Jack Hamilton was the new footman at Stonar Hall, and housekeeper Thalia Marsh could sense that he was trouble! He was so charming, smooth and friendly, spoke a little too well and liked to take charge—even though she was his superior! He was surely no footman and Thalia was determined to discover his true identity even if this risked the exposure of *her* darkest secrets. But Thalia soon succumbed to his charms—and fell in love! But *who* had Thalia fallen in love with—the footman
…or someone else?